Next
to
Heaven

ALSO BY JAMES FREY

A Million Little Pieces

My Friend Leonard

Bright Shiny Morning

The Final Testament of the Holy Bible

Katerina

Next
to
Heaven

———

JAMES FREY

AUTHORS EQUITY

Authors Equity
1123 Broadway, Suite 1008
New York, New York 10010

Cover design by Rodrigo Corral Studio
Book design by Scribe Inc.

This is a work of fiction. Names, characters, places and incidents either are products of the author's imagination or are used fictitiously.

ISBN 9798893310269

Printed in the United States of America

Next
to
Heaven

Behind every great fortune lies a great crime.

—HONORÉ DE BALZAC

The Beautiful and the Rich

Devon often dreamed of punching her husband in the face. She didn't necessarily want to hurt him. And he often didn't do anything to deserve it. She was just tired of him. Of his voice, of his smell, the way he breathed, how he chewed, the way he sniffed, the way it sounded when he swallowed, that he picked his fingernails and sometimes dropped them on the bathroom floor instead of the trash can, that he both snored and farted while he slept. None of it was done to deliberately annoy her, and he didn't know that any of it did. It didn't matter. She wanted to punch him. Right in his rotten fucking face.

Like so many marriages among the one percent, and even more so among the one percent of the one percent, their marriage was one of convenience, a business relationship. They met when she was twenty-eight and he was thirty. At an art opening in Chelsea, New York City. The show was of highly sexual, abstract expressionist paintings made by a beautiful young French woman. It was called Nympho, and the paintings were believed, though the painter neither confirmed nor denied it, to be portraits of her and a series of wealthy older men with whom she had had affairs, one of whom was the richest man in Paris, another whose brother had been the President of France.

Devon had been working at the gallery for six years. It was the largest and most prestigious art gallery in the world, with three spaces in New York, and outposts in Los Angeles, London, Paris, Rome, Dubai, Hong Kong, and Tokyo. Each of them had three or four directors, essentially high-paid salespeople with fancy titles. At twenty-five, Devon had become its youngest director. Yes, she had an art history degree from Princeton, and yes she had grown up around art and the art world, and yes she was smart and capable and knew her shit, but none of those things really mattered. What mattered was that she was young and beautiful, and she had young and beautiful friends who would come to the shows, and she could sell extraordinarily expensive art to rich men who wanted to sleep with her. And occasionally she did sleep with one of them. Never to close a deal, but for the fun of it, the thrill, the feeling of power and agency it gave her, so she had a good story the next time she went out with her girlfriends. And she always made the stories better, made them what she wished had happened, instead of what usually did, which was five minutes of foreplay (if she was lucky), two minutes of sex (if she was lucky), thirty seconds of cuddling (far too long after the aforementioned performance metrics), and a quick exit.

As happened before every opening, Devon and the other directors studied the guest list. As with every guest list, it was heavy with bankers, hedge fund managers, private equity partners, their wives and girlfriends, the art advisors who helped them build their collections and make them feel important, other artists, friends and family of the artist. The directors only cared about The Money, as they called the various men who worked in finance. The Money bought paintings from them, and they only got paid when they sold paintings. All fourteen of the paintings in Nympho had already been sold. The waiting list for future paintings by the artist had 220 names on it. So in many ways the list for this particular show was irrelevant, but you could always sell The Money something else, and it was always interesting to see if any new names had become rich enough to be added to the list.

And there was a new name, Billy McCallister. Though she did not know Billy, his reputation preceded him. He was the son of a plumber from New Hyde Park, Long Island. He had gone to Exeter on a full ride and graduated at sixteen. From there he went to the Wharton joint undergrad/MBA program on a full ride and graduated at twenty. He immediately went to work at Goldman, who had started recruiting him when he was seventeen, and became the second-youngest partner in the bank's history at twenty-four. At twenty-five, he was making twenty million dollars a year. He left Goldman at twenty-eight and started his own hedge fund. It was a spectacular success and his twenty million a year jumped to fifty million a year. And though he had not made any major art purchases yet, it was known that he was looking, and every gallery in the world wanted to land him as a client. He was thick, gruff, unpolished, rude, arrogant, aggressive, ruthless, and brilliant. His father, a physically imposing man known all over Long Island for his short temper, meaty hands, and wrench skills, never understood him. Until he died, when Billy was twelve, after mistaking a bottle of rat poison for Gatorade while he was drunk, he called Billy Little Mister Softie, and he routinely told Billy that math was for pussies, that real men did real work, with their hands, and with their wrenches.

Billy didn't mourn his father. He didn't cry when he heard the news, and he has never visited his grave, but the torment never left him. And he was determined to prove his father wrong. Billy understood that math was the governing language of the universe. That whatever you wanted in life could be provided by math, and that whatever you wanted to understand could be explained by math. And he vowed he would never be a pussy, as his father so lovingly branded him. He would be an AFL, an Asskicker for Life. A Great White Shark. A Silverback. An Alpha among Alphas. Nobody would ever fuck with him or demean him again, and if they did, he would respond in ways he never could with his father. He would use mathematics and his gifts in understanding and manipulating it, to build an empire, to become a King, or as close to a King as you could in America, which is a Billionaire.

He was well on his way when he and Devon met. The hours leading up to an opening can be frantic and stressful, so she had forgotten about him when the gallery doors opened. There was a huge crowd, a line that wrapped down 24th Street and on to 11th Avenue. The exhibition space, a huge open white room with thirty-foot ceilings, was teeming with people, all either rich or cool, and almost never both. Despite their advantages, rich people were rarely ever cool, though they spent huge amounts of money trying to achieve it. And cool people were rarely rich because they were lazy, and part of being cool is not giving a fuck. But rich people and cool people often interact because each has what the other wants. Whatever they were, rich or cool, very few of them were looking at the paintings. If you want to actually look or contemplate art, you don't go see the paintings on opening night. Openings are some combination of cocktail party, fashion show, and peacock's parade. Everyone's currency, whether it is cash or cache, is on full display, and most people spend their time at openings checking each other out, judging each other, and gossiping about each other. And that was the case at the Nympho show. Except for one man, standing motionless in front of a painting, staring intently at a swirl of pink and orange and beige and brown bodies, all of them engaged in sinful activities with each other, a painting called *A Night at the Office*, believed to be the depiction of an orgy the artist attended with one of the Princes of Monaco. Devon saw him, and she was curious, and she made her way through the crowd, and stood next to him, staring at the painting without speaking. She knew if she stayed silent, at some point he would speak. So she did, she stood silently next to him and stared as the crowd drifted around them, and so he did, after two or three minutes, in a deep voice that sounded like a mixture of gravel, dirt, and menace.

I want it.

It's already sold.

I don't care. I want it.

I can't help you.

Yes, you can.

I can't.

Go tell your boss I'll pay him five times more than whatever he sold it for.

It's not about the money.

Yes, it is.

We try to place paintings in collections where they will be loved and protected and kept off the secondary market.

It's about the money. Everything is about money. You of all people should know that, Miss FancyPants. Now please go deliver my message.

Neither looked away from the painting during the conversation. And unwilling to leave after his order, Devon stood and stared at the painting until he walked away, moving on to the next one. Part of her was enraged. Part of her was intrigued. Part of her was turned on. Nobody had ever called her anything like Miss FancyPants before. If people knew about her background, and she assumed most did, they never brought it up. It was an unspoken rule. One of manners, of discretion. He clearly didn't give a fuck. And she kind of liked it.

And indeed it would be fair to call Devon Lodge Kensington a Miss FancyPants. She had grown up in Greenwich on an estate called Willowvale, with a very large ivy-covered stone house that was laughingly called a cottage on a very large piece of perfectly manicured land in the Greenwich Back Country, where homes stood behind gates and hedges and on lawns large enough for polo fields, which were not uncommon. Devon's ancestors had come to America on the Mayflower. They founded a bank in New York, built a railroad empire, opened copper, silver, and gold mines. If there were such a thing as royalty in America, her family was royal. Not Kings or Queens, but close enough, similar to powerful Dukes or Duchesses. They didn't run the country, but when a member of her family expressed an opinion to the people who did, which was rare, the opinion was heard. She had gone to Greenwich Academy, one of the best girls' schools in the country, for nursery, elementary, and middle school. After GA, she went to boarding school at Miss Porter's, whose notable alumnae include Laura Rockefeller, Jacqueline Kennedy Onassis, Lilly Pulitzer, Gloria Vanderbilt, and Agnes Gund. After Porter's, she went to Princeton and was a member of The Ivy, its most prestigious dining club. She graduated with an honors degree in art history and job offers from eight galleries and three auction houses. She took the job that paid her the most and offered the most opportunity for her to make money. Although no one but her, her parents, and their bankers knew she needed it.

6 | James Frey

For as with most great and wealthy families, after a few generations, its descendants had grown lazy. Though highly and very expensively educated, her parents had never worked. They played tennis and golf. They read books and tanned by the pool. They went to parties and got drunk and took recreational drugs, most often cocaine. They traveled. They bought art and cars and expensive clothing. They had affairs. And gradually their part of the family fortune dwindled away. By the time Devon was finishing college, most of it was gone. There were assets, the house, some paintings, a smaller house in Rhode Island, but nobody wanted to suffer the humiliation of having to sell them. So right before she graduated, her parents took her out to dinner and apprized her of their situation. When she recovered from the shock, they told her they expected her to help them, to support them, to save them. She either needed to make a fortune, or marry one. It was the least she could do, considering how much they loved her, and how much money they had spent on her childhood.

And it was entirely possible for Devon. Aside from carrying a famous family name, she was legitimately and stunningly gorgeous, the latest in a line of classic, elegant Kensington beauties. She was tall, thin, she had deep blue eyes like a warm calm sea, naturally streaked dirty blonde hair to the middle of her back, sometimes loose, sometimes braided. Clothing hung on her body as if it were made for her. Her skin glowed, a tone of the lightest olive, as if there were a distant descendant that might not have been white or Christian, though that was certainly never acknowledged or discussed. Her beauty was such that men rarely hit on her, or even spoke to her, so dumbstruck and intimidated were they by simply being near her. When the shock of the revelation faded, she agreed to do what she could, which meant doing what her parents had asked and what they expected, which meant saving face, saving the family name, saving them.

She dated a movie star. The son of a billionaire. A tech founder. She dated the scion of another famous family, though they quickly discovered they were in exactly the same situation and amicably parted ways. She dated a famous writer a few years older, and though he was funny and weird and cool and great in bed, he was broke, and that just wouldn't do. She often appeared on Page Six, in *Women's Wear Daily*, in the society pages of the *New York Times*. She was alternately called an *It Girl*, and the most eligible single woman in New York. There was no shortage of suitors for Devon, though none was ever both rich enough and interesting enough for her to stay, much less marry. When she had agreed to the arrangement with her parents, she had promised to be married by the time she was thirty, which was around the time they would be out of money. When she met Billy, she knew her time, and their time, was running short.

At the dinner and party after the opening, where the already exclusive guest list was trimmed by 80 percent, she ignored him. She could feel him watching her, staring at her, trying to get close to her, and every time he did, she moved away. She could feel his lust and desire for her filling the room like cigarette smoke, drifting everywhere, filling everyone's lungs, including her own, she could taste it and smell it, it was aggressive and passionate and primal, and she didn't mind it, she breathed it in and held it, she breathed it in and let it fill her. She knew she could have him if she so chose. And she knew that avoiding him and ignoring him would make him want her more. When she left before the party was over, he tried to follow her outside. She had called a car and it was waiting for her. She watched him watch her drive away. He waved to try to get her attention and she looked away. And as the car took her back to her apartment in Nolita, as she stared out the window and watched the lights of Lower Manhattan pass, some part of her knew. Now it was just details. How it would happen and how long it would take. She knew.

She spoke to her boss, the great man, the King of the Art World, the slickest motherfucker to ever hawk art in the history of the world, the next day. She told him about Billy's offer. He was fucking thrilled. As happy as she had ever seen him. It took enormous amounts of capital to keep an operation as large as his running, and he knew Billy had enormous amounts of capital. Though the painting had been committed to longtime friends of his, loyal patrons of his gallery, he was willing to take the painting away and sell it to someone else, if it benefited him. They were rich, but not as rich as Billy, and nowhere near as rich as Billy would someday be if he stayed on his current trajectory. He told Devon to close the deal immediately, sell Billy the painting, get the cash as soon as possible, let him know when the wire cleared. He was trying to buy a thirty-million-dollar painting in LA that he knew he could flip to a Russian for three times what he was going to pay for it, and he needed Billy's cash to close the deal. Devon smiled and nodded, but she had other plans. She was going to make Billy wait. She was going to make him sweat. She knew everyone in his life jumped whenever he said he needed something done, and she wasn't going to do it. Especially given what she was feeling and what she believed was in their future. She was going to make him understand that she was not his, even though, like the painting, he was buying her with his fast-expanding riches.

He called the gallery twice that day, twice more the next, three times the day after. He sent her multiple emails. She didn't return the calls or respond to the emails. He got her cell and left two messages. She did not respond. Her boss was calling her every hour to check on the money, and she stopped picking up the phone when she saw it was him. Midway through day four, after she decided exactly how she was going to handle the call, and what she was going to try to learn, which was how much she was worth to him, she called him. He picked up after the first ring.

Why'd it take so long for you to get back to me?

Both the gallery and I were doing some checking.

Checking? Checking on what?

To see if you have the money you are soon going to owe us.

Seriously?

I don't know you, Mr. McCallister.

Call me Billy.

I don't know you, Mr. McCallister, and the gallery doesn't know you, and we do our due diligence with new clients before we do deals with them.

I think you, and everyone at your gallery, and your boss, all know I have the fucking money.

We shall soon see.

That mean we have a deal?

There are some additional terms.

You want me to pay more than fiveX what the painting is worth?

We want you to make a commitment.

What kind of commitment?

To purchase ten million dollars more of art from us. Art to be chosen for you by me. We want *A Night at the Office* to be surrounded by other works of art that are worthy of it. Art with which it can converse.

Ten million more.

Yes.

Why don't we make it twenty. So that it's a really good fucking conversation.

She laughed.

Twenty million it is, Mr. McCallister.

Call me Mr. McCallister again and the deal is off. My name is Billy.

I'm sure we will be able to inspire some exceptional conversation with twenty million, Billy.

Any more new terms?

The initial ten million for *A Night at the Office* needs to be wired by the end of the day.

Cool. Any more?

No, that's all.

Now I have one.

I can't promise you we'll accept it.

You're not going to blow a thirty-million-dollar deal.

We'll see.

I want you to have dinner with me.

She pauses, makes him wait.

And wait.

And wait.

Until he says

Still there?

She takes a deep breath so he knows she's still there.

Makes him wait longer.

Until she says

I don't fuck men that buy art from me.

He chuckles.

You mean you haven't yet fucked a man that buys art from you.

She smiles.

I mean don't expect anything from me, except lively conservation and a polite thank you at the end of the evening.

I wouldn't expect anything more, Miss Kensington.

Call me Devon.

I wouldn't expect anything more, Devon.

I'll send the invoice over now. Check your email. We'll expect funds by the end of the day. Let me know when you want to have dinner.

I'll pick you up at six tonight, when the gallery closes.

You move fast, Billy.

Yes, Devon, I do. See you in a few hours.

He hung up and Devon sent the invoice and the money arrived five minutes later. Devon went to tell her boss, and also told him about the additional twenty million, and he stood up and cheered and asked if he could give her a hug, and she said no, and she left. It was already three and she didn't think she'd have time to go home and change, so she waited. She called a couple friends. She looked at online auction catalogs for the upcoming contemporary art sales. She read some book reviews. She bought a new handbag and pair of heels, rewarding herself for the giant commission she just earned from the deal with Billy. At 6:15 she left the gallery and stepped outside. Billy was waiting for her, standing next to a vintage red Ferrari from the late '60s, a dozen roses in his hand. He smiled, and despite trying not to, Devon smiled.

Hi, Devon.

Hi, Billy.

You ready to go for a ride?

I'm not sure I have a choice.

You always have a choice, you just have to be willing to deal with the consequences if you make the wrong one.

She motioned toward the flowers.

Those for me?

Yes.

He handed them to her.

Thank you.

May I get the door for you?

That would be nice, thank you.

She walked to the passenger door. He opened it. She got into the car. The leather was soft, supple, worn, but worn in a way that made it more comfortable, more luxurious, so that it wrapped itself around her like an old blanket. He closed the door and walked to the driver's door and got behind the wheel and started the engine and the engine growled, low and strong, with the promise of pleasure and power if pushed properly. He turned and smiled at her.

Ready to go?

You going to tell me where we're going?

I think you already know.

Yeah?

Yeah.

Tell me.

We're going all the way, Devon. You and me. All the way.

The Beautiful and the Rich, Part 2

They did indeed go all the way.

And rather quickly.

She moved into his Tribeca penthouse after three months.

They were engaged after six.

The wedding was a year later, at Christ Church in Greenwich.

They honeymooned for a month.

Lamu for a week, the Seychelles for a week, Florence for a week, Paris for a week.

She was pregnant three months later.

They sold the penthouse in Tribeca and bought a townhouse in the West Village.

She furnished it, decorated it, filled it with beautiful paintings.

She gave birth to their daughter, Charlotte Kensington McCallister.

He doted on Charlotte, loved to give her the bottle, changed her diapers, sang her nursery rhymes when she couldn't sleep.

His fund grew to three billion four billion six eight ten fourteen.

Their fortune grew five hundred million one point five billion three.

They were great friends.

They respected each other.

They fucked wildly and often, with great passion and enthusiasm.

They were happy.

She had saved her family and had fallen truly and deeply in love.

He had married into a famous family and made his name and his fortune and had fallen truly and deeply in love.

She trusted him and believed in him and supported him, and she let herself be vulnerable with him, showed him what lived beneath her looks and her name and her upbringing, a strong smart woman who was scared of the future, even though she had no reason, and was often insecure about herself, even though she always exuded what appeared to be unshakable poise, grace, and confidence.

He trusted her in a way that he never trusted anyone and was vulnerable in ways that he never was with anyone else. As brutal and gruff and demanding and harsh as he could be at work and in the world, at home he was kind and generous and helpful and supportive.

Her days were spent raising their daughter and looking at art and seeing old friends and running their home.

His days were spent accumulating information and making trades and tracking returns and demanding more, more, more.

They spent some weekends in Connecticut with her parents, some weekends in Cold Spring Harbor, where he had bought his mother a house, some weekends at their place in Sagaponack, some weekends they stayed home.

They traveled often and always on their own plane, Capri and Beaulieu, London and Paris, Barcelona and Marrakesh, St. Barts, Turks, Angra dos Reis.

She got pregnant again when Charlotte was two.

As easy as her first pregnancy, the second was as difficult. She gained three times the weight, she was depressed, rashes came and went, she had abdominal pains, migraines, there were days she couldn't get out of bed, it all compounded, each issue made the other worse, she was scared, so scared, she was so so very scared.

After a long run of sustained success, his fund was struggling. The markets were volatile, he was overleveraged, time at home had taken away from time at the office, he lost his focus and he lost his edge, returns were down if there were any at all and investors were withdrawing, he was depressed, angry, and despite having accumulated vast wealth, he was scared it would all go away, he was scared, so scared, so so very scared.

He spent more time at the office ten twelve sixteen hours a day when she needed him most at home, needed his love, needed his strength, needed his support.

Her depression became worse she became quiet and withdrawn when he needed her most, needed her love, needed her strength, needed her support.

She gave birth to their son, Nicholas Kensington McCallister.

Nicholas was born on a Thursday, Billy was back in the office on Monday, there were signs of a recession, he stayed there until Wednesday.

He needed his focus, he needed his edge.

She needed him.

There were night nurses and nannies, a chef and a driver, a trainer and a yoga instructor, none of it mattered her depression got worse.

They drifted.

Into their own minds, their own hearts, their own fear, their own pain.

They drifted.

Apart.

Something had to change but they were both too lost to find each other, something had to change they couldn't keep going as it was, they both knew.

He couldn't leave her because if he did the prenup was invalidated.

She couldn't leave him because of the prenup.

Staring out the window at the concrete street, at the trash lining it, at the rats in the trash, at the cars moving past, at the people quickly walking, at the other buildings one on top of the other on top of the other, at the streetlights and storefronts, at piles of dogshit on the sidewalk, her heart spoke to her, her heart said go.

Go.

Go.

Go to the trees and grass and birds, to an open sky, the stars at night, room to wander and room to dream, space for their children to run wild and free, maybe a horse, maybe horses, a long driveway lined with flowers, a happy dog always there when they got home, neighbors they knew, a country club, their own garage, somewhere she could breathe again, somewhere that offered peace, somewhere that offered them a new life, and a new chance.

She wanted to go home.

For the first time in months they sat and had a long dinner together, they were open and vulnerable again, spoke of their fears and their sadness, and it felt like they had a chance at rekindling the old, and finding something new.

They agreed it was time.

They went.

A Kind of Holy Land

The town was founded in 1690 by a man named Amos Mudge. Amos was a farmer who needed somewhere to sell his carrots and potatoes, his apples and corn. So he started a small market that grew into a larger market that grew into a small village that grew into a town. The town needed a name. Amos loved Jesus, and he prayed to Jesus every night and every morning and before every meal. He believed Jesus would soon return to Earth to save humanity, and he wanted the new town to be the kind of place where Jesus might choose to live and preach and do his Godly work. He wanted the town to be, next to Heaven, the most beautiful place in existence, the most peaceful, the most moral, the most Christian. He called the town New Bethlehem.

The land around the town was soon bought up by other farmers, attracted by the local market. As they plowed the land, they discovered it was filled with stones, some small, some large, all bad for farming. Needing a place to put the stones, they built low stone walls along the roads and their property lines, both of which were winding and irregular. Two rivers ran through the town, and the farmers started creating small ponds around the rivers and all over the town in order to irrigate their crops. Jesus didn't come, but the town prospered, and the farmers built lovely saltbox, cape, and colonial homes along the roads. The more successful the farmer, the larger the house, and many of the farmers were quite successful. In 1715, the Legislature of Colonial Connecticut officially recognized New Bethlehem as a Colonial Parish and Village.

When the American Revolutionary War started in 1775, the farmers were almost unanimously on the side of the rebels. They could help feed and shelter the soldiers, but many wanted to learn a new trade and expand beyond farming. Several sons of prominent farmers learned the skill of cobbling, making shoes and boots, and opened shops in the town in order to provide the new American soldiers with shoes and boots that would keep their feet warm in winter.

As the war dragged on and eventually ended in the birth of a new nation, the cobblers' success drew in more cobblers, and soon the town was one of the cobbling centers of the new United States. It remained so for almost one hundred years and also supplied the boots for many of the Union soldiers during the Civil War.

The railroad arrived after the Civil War, and because everyone needed shoes, a special spur was built off the New Haven line, which runs from New York City to New Haven, Connecticut. New Bethlehem was the only town with its own spur off the main line, and the smallest town with its own station. The train brought new merchants, and the expanding upper-middle class of lawyers, bankers, and doctors, who wanted to get out of the dirty, smoggy, and dangerous New York of the Industrial Revolution, and provide better and quieter lives for their families. The two streets of the town, Main Street and Maple Street, which were lined with one and two-story buildings that housed cobblers and small shoe factories, expanded and new buildings were built. The new merchants opened dry goods stores, general stores, butcher shops, doctor's offices, lawyer's offices, groceries, tailor shops, confectioneries, apothecaries, bookstores, and a host of taverns and saloons. Many of the cobblers sold their buildings and moved away. The population grew from one thousand to four thousand in a decade.

Around this new class of New Bethlehemians grew the institutions to serve them, a town government, a fire department, a police force, public and private schools, and churches. On one intersection just outside of the main area of town, churches were built on three of the four corners, all facing each other, and the intersection became known as God's Corner. Within half a mile of town was a Catholic church, a Presbyterian church, Episcopal, Lutheran, Methodist, Congregational, and Baptist churches. New Bethlehem became known as a safe and prosperous town, one where a man could earn a good wage and raise a family. And with that reputation came more visitors, members of New York's upper class, America's first wave of Robber Barons and Industrial Titans, and their closest associates. Many of them owned summer homes in places like Newport, Saratoga

Springs, Bar Harbor, Cape Cod, and Lake George. None of those places was, at the time, particularly quick or easy to get to, so they began looking for areas where they could purchase large plots of land to build country estates. The farmers were happy to oblige, and from the late 1880s until the Stock Market Crash of 1929, almost all of the farms in New Bethlehem were purchased and converted into large homes on big plots of land, or estates, the largest of which had eight hundred acres and a thirty-five-thousand-square-foot Tudor mansion modeled after Montacute House, Somerset, England. The estates started getting broken up during the Great Depression by formerly wealthy estate owners who needed cash. To prevent over-crowding, the town government instituted zoning laws requiring ownership of certain amounts of land in order to build a house. Directly in and around town was designated the Half Zone, requir-ing a half acre of land. In a tight ring around the town was Zone One, requiring one acre. In a tight ring around Zone One was Zone Two, requiring two acres. The remaining 80 percent of land within the town's borders was designated Zone Four, requiring a minimum of four acres of land to build a house. These laws remain in place today, though a plot within the Half Zone can be reduced to a quarter acre with the approval of the Town Zoning Authority, which rarely happens.

After World War II, the town boomed, as did the rest of the coun-try. The wealth lost during the Great Depression was rebuilt, often by the same families who lost it, and by many new families, though almost all of them were white. As the suburbs expanded and more people could afford to leave cities, particularly New York City, the richest and most successful of them moved to Connecticut, which at the time did not make its residents pay income tax. Towns like Greenwich, Darien, Westport, and New Bethlehem became the wealthiest towns in the country. Each of them had their own char-acteristics and types of residents. Greenwich was where you moved if you were wealthy and wanted people to know it and is both the largest and the closest to New York. Westport was primarily Jew-ish, and most of the town was on Long Island Sound, its coast lined with beaches and parks and homes on the water, and is the farthest from the city. Darien was the new money, the loud money, half of the town on Long Island Sound, and half of the town more rural. New Bethlehem was where you moved if you were rich, but never wanted to discuss money, and is the smallest of the towns, the most discreet, the most rural, and the most artistic. All four towns were almost entirely white and continue to be, though they have all become slightly more diverse.

In the '50s and '60s New Bethlehem also underwent an architectural revolution. Architect Philip Johnson and his partner David Whitney bought a forty-nine-acre parcel of land on Ponus Ridge Road and built a complex of mid-century modern buildings on it, the most famous of which is the Glass House, the most famous mid-century building in the world. Johnson's presence brought in a number of other architects, including John Johansen, Marcel Breuer, Landis Gores, and Eliot Noyes, who became known as the Harvard Five, and who built over two hundred houses in the town, making it the most architecturally significant small town in the world, and the global center of mid-century modern architecture.

Today, New Bethlehem remains what it has long been, and will likely remain for as long as it exists, a place where wealthy people, who value privacy and discretion, and who make achievement, both educational and athletic, a priority, live quietly and raise their families. Until the tech boom in Silicon Valley, the town had long reigned as the wealthiest town in the United States. It has one of the best public school systems in the country, three elite private prep schools. Its athletic programs are among the best in the country, with the best facilities and the best coaches money can buy, and it currently has players competing in every major professional sports league in the United States, on the pro golf and tennis tours, and had eleven athletes representing the United States in the last Olympics. The houses are large and the lawns are beautiful, and much of the town is still wild, heavily wooded, filled with wildlife. The town protects the land and limits what can be done with it and on it, and bobcats, bears, packs of coyotes and coywolves, herds of deer, wild turkeys, hawks eagles ducks geese and owls are regularly seen going about their business. As they mostly do with each other, the residents of the town leave them alone, and let them go about their business in peace.

And the residents, there are seventeen thousand of them, which has been the approximate population for the last fifty years. They are 95 percent white, 1 percent black, 3 percent Asian, 1 percent other. They are 84 percent Christian, 12 percent Jewish, 3 percent other. Like most of the wealthiest towns in the country, New Bethlehem is not a diverse place, though it is vastly more diverse than it was fifty years ago, thirty years ago, fifteen years ago. Almost all of its residents, regardless of their ethnicity or religion, are rich. Some of them are beautiful. Many of them are famous, a few are infamous. There are movie stars, rock stars, athletes, the hosts of all three major network news shows, famous comedians and famous artists, a notorious writer, a beloved writer, too many CEOs to count, being a partner at a private equity firm or hedge bank or bank in New Bethlehem is like being a teacher or an accountant or a corporate middle manager in more middle-class towns. The residents generally leave each other alone and protect each other. The rich and the famous are never bothered. They can go to the local coffee shop or grocery store or their kid's soccer game without being hassled or being treated any differently than anyone else. In New Bethlehem the cool kids are the ones who get grades, play sports, and are good people. They are expected to go to excellent colleges and universities, and they are expected to have long lucrative careers when they reach adulthood, and almost all of them do. Achievement and success and security is the goal for everyone. Being great and not having to advertise it is the common goal. The town has a fifty-million-dollar library. A sixty-million-dollar YMCA that costs ninety-nine dollars a month to use. On its two main streets, and in the entire town, there are no fast-food restaurants of any kind or chain stores of any kind. It has twelve public parks spread over two thousand acres of land with public pools, tennis courts, a dog park, a public theater, spaces for art exhibitions, hiking trails, paddle tennis courts, an outdoor ice rink. It has a nature center with walking trails and a large bird rescue. It has a ten-acre field specifically planted with flowers that attract fireflies that light up on summer nights like a sky filled with a billion dancing stars. It has one of the most heavily funded per-capita police forces in the country and one of the lowest crime rates. It has its own living facility for its elderly residents, with its own medical facilities. It has one of the oldest and most respected addiction and mental health hospitals in the world. It's housed in several century-old mansions that were purchased over twenty years and sit on fifteen acres of land. Though it's not specifically for the town's residents, plenty of them end up spending time there.

New Bethlehem is as beautiful and safe and perfect a town as exists in the United States, as beautiful and safe and perfect a town as exists anywhere in the world. But no beauty exists without flaws, however hidden. Absolute safety is but an illusion. No matter what we think or see or believe or feel, perfection isn't real. And beneath the beauty and safety and perfection of New Bethlehem, there are secrets and there are lies, and there is sadness and there is rage, there is failure and there is desperation, betrayal and heartbreak, hate and violence.

And once or twice a century, there is murder.

The Perfect Wife

She didn't like to admit it, because in today's world women were supposed to be ambitious and want careers, to be feminists, and to want to be strong and independent, but all she ever wanted, her life's great dream, was to be a wife and to be a mother.

To be a great wife.

To be a great mother.

To live a long and beautiful life with a man she loved in a safe, quiet town where they could raise at least two children, but hopefully four, and if she was really lucky, at least one boy and one girl.

Her dream came true.

Kind of.

Grace Hunter grew up in Chicago, on the North Side of the city in Lincoln Park. Her dad, Peter, was a Political Science Professor at DePaul, and her mother, Jen, was a nurse. She was an only child. Her parents had wanted more children, but complications during her birth prevented her mother from bearing any more children. They didn't mourn the loss. They dedicated themselves to being the best parents they could be for Grace. As her father said—you can't mourn losing something you never had, and you should always be happy with whatever God decides to give you.

Her father was not a religious man. But he did believe in God. He believed very deeply in a God of his own choosing. A kind God. A loving God. A God that wanted the best for him, and for his family, and for the world, but also sometimes had other plans. Her father found his God when he quit drinking. He had just finished his master's degree and had just started dating Grace's mother, Jen, his future wife. He had grown up in Cleveland in a family of hard-drinking men, almost all of them steelworkers, or unemployed steelworkers. Though he had chosen a different occupational path, he carried on the family tradition of getting drunk. He was not a daily drinker, but when he did drink, he got fucking drunk. And when he got fucking drunk, he liked to fight. On their fourth date, after a lovely and very promising first three, they went to a Christmas Party for his political science department. One of his colleagues was dressed up as Santa. He asked Jen if she wanted to sit on his lap. She politely declined. He asked again, and reached for her in an attempt to pull her on to his lap. Peter, who had had nine whiskey sours, and was almost done with number ten, saw what was happening and rushed across the room, dove through the air, knocked Santa off his chair and on his ass, and pummeled him, his fake beard turning the same red as the suit from a broken nose and a split lip. While Jen appreciated the chivalry involved, she was embarrassed and scared. She immediately got him out of the party and safely home to bed, but the next morning, she called him and told him if anything like it ever happened again, she would leave him. He knew if he kept drinking, it would happen again, so he quit. And while he didn't need a full recovery program, he looked into them, and he liked AA's approach to God, and each person believing in a God of their choosing. And his God was good to him, even if his God didn't grant him all of his wishes. He had a sweet beautiful daughter. Grace would be their only child. He and Jen would be absolutely the best parents they could be to her, and for her.

They lived in a small townhouse. They bought it in the '70s when most people were leaving cities for the suburbs and prices were low. It was on a street of other townhouses, some large, some small, none of which they could dream of affording today. Grace went to local public schools, Abraham Lincoln Elementary and Lincoln Park Middle and High Schools. She loved and was exceptionally good at playing tennis, practicing on rotating days with each of her parents. She was tall and athletic, brownish/reddish/auburnish hair and bright hazel eyes, freckles that came out in the sun, which if you loved playing tennis, meant most of the time. She wasn't good enough to go pro, but she was good enough for tennis to pay for her college. Tired of the long brutal Chicago winters, she went south to Vanderbilt, where she played #2 singles for all four years of her time there. After school, which she loved with all her heart, she moved to New York and worked in fashion PR, managing guest lists and press releases and seating charts for big designers at Fashion Week. She lived on the Upper East Side with two friends from Vanderbilt, spent summer weekends in the Hamptons, Bay Head, and Central Park.

She met her husband, Alex Hunter, on a steaming-hot late-August afternoon at Sunset Beach on Nantucket. She had been day drinking, a great American tradition practiced often and with great enthusiasm on Nantucket, and she was a bit tipsy. She was leaping and skipping and frolicking in the waves, freckles on full display, when she frolicked herself right into the chest of a tall, buff, black-haired blue-eyed steaming hunk of Connecticut Beefcake. She hit him mid-skip and ended up flat on her ass in the water, and as she looked up to see what had happened, and saw the aforementioned Beefcake, she got hit by a wave, filling her eyes, nose, and mouth with water, causing her to cough, and spit, and snort like the snortiest snortface the world had ever seen. Beefcake, and everyone else who saw and heard it, laughed, but because he could sometimes be a gentleman, he offered her his hand, and helped her up, and made sure she was okay. And when she had regained her composure, which she tried to do and was successful in doing very quickly (she did, after all, make her living dealing with fashion designers, fashion magazine editors, and fashionistas), he offered his hand for a formal shake and said

I'm Alex Hunter.

She smiled and took his hand.

I'm Grace.

He was beautiful, and she was entranced.

Cool to meet you, Grace.

And he felt the same, she was beautiful, and he was entranced.

You as well, Alex Hunter.

You have a last name, Grace?

All you need to know is that someday it's going to be Hunter.

He smiled, and what a Beefcake kinda smile he had, and she smiled back, a classic Midwestern girl next door.

You drink beer, Grace Someday Hunter?

Fuck yeah I do.

You wanna have a beer with me?

How about we have a few?

That sounds great.

Let's go.

And they went. Back to where he had a large towel on the sand, and a cooler full of beer next to it, and they sat on his towel, and drank his beer, and after a few beers, lay down on the towel and started making out, and they made out for the rest of the afternoon, in front of and in full view of everyone on the beach, until each of the friend groups they had come with were ready to leave. On the drive back to the house where they were staying, Grace's friends rather excitedly told her about her day-drunk make-out partner and future husband, Alex Hunter.

Alexander Hunter was from New Bethlehem, the youngest of three brothers, son of a JPMorgan investment banker. An athletic prodigy from a young age, he had been All-State in football, hockey, and lacrosse for three years in high school, and in his senior year, won state titles in all three, the first and only time anyone had achieved such a feat, which led to his local nickname, Alexander the Great. He went to Notre Dame and played football, started at QB for two years, was in the NFL for three years. Though he was good enough to make it, he knew he would never be a star, or even a starter, and believed he could use his athletic success to achieve financial success in banking, so he had recently quit and moved to Manhattan to work at Citibank. He lived in a loft in Union Square, he had been going to Nantucket all of his life and his family had a house there, half the girls on the East Coast wanted to date him, and the half that didn't only didn't because they had never seen him or heard of him, and if they had it would have been every girl on the East Coast.

Grace was smitten. She loved his eyes and his hands and his voice and the taste of his lips and taste of his tongue and the way he smelled and the way his skin felt when it was pressed against her own. She thought the sports stuff was cool, but it was really only a bonus for her. She would have been into him if he had been working in the shoe department at Walmart, or stocking shelves at Trader Joe's.

They met later at the Sandbar. They spent the night at his parents' house. And the next night. And the next. When they got back to NY, they spent every spare minute they had together, almost always at his place, where they could be alone, and make all the noise they wanted, and they made noise, for as late they wanted to make it. He went to Chicago for Thanksgiving, and she went to New Bethlehem for Christmas, and both sets of parents came to New York for Easter. Everyone got along and everyone approved and a year to the day that they met, on the beach where they met, Alex got down on one knee and fulfilled Grace's prophecy by asking for her hand in marriage.

They stayed in New York for five years, young and happy and beautiful, loving each other and succeeding at their jobs and living a great life. They got more invitations than they could handle, and spent most weekends away, either in the Hamptons or Nantucket, skiing in Vermont, going to Bermuda or the Caribbean when they wanted sun. They knew they wouldn't be in New York forever, so they took advantage of it, ate at great restaurants, saw art, went to Broadway shows, Alex could get free tickets to almost any sporting event, they went to Knicks, Rangers, Yankees, and Giants games, sat courtside at the US Open. People often recognized him, occasionally asked for autographs or photos, his minor kind of fame opened doors and generally wasn't a hassle. He got promoted she got promoted he got promoted again they started trying to have a child together. They were still very physically attracted to each other, and were both in great shape, so they tried often and with great gusto. It didn't take long.

They moved to New Bethlehem when Grace got pregnant, bought an old colonial on two acres just outside of town, got a Golden Retriever, a Jeep, and a Mercedes station wagon. Many of Alex's childhood friends had also gotten married and come back, so they had an immediate group of friends. The men were all former athletes, many of whom went to Ivy League schools for lacrosse or football, and they were all either lawyers or worked in finance. Their wives, like Grace, were already either stay-at-home moms, or pregnant and preparing to be, or trying to get pregnant. They joined the New Bethlehem Country Club, which waived its normal rule of having to have owned a house in the town for five years before being able to apply for membership, because every club within twenty miles, and there were a fairly large number of them, wanted Alexander the Great as a member. In the city, his past as an athlete meant something, but amidst the ocean of other highly successful men across the sports world, all of the various arts and entertainment worlds, and finance, it wasn't that big a deal. In New Bethlehem, a town that prided itself on athletics, in particular the sports Alex had played, he was a big big big deal, still a legend, likely always a legend. He was asked to get involved with various town sports programs, to coach, to headline fundraisers, and he almost always said yes. Grace was often tired, and often stayed home. On nights she did, he often stayed out late, came home smelling like booze, occasionally weed, and very occasion- ally perfume, which he always said was from giving hugs to women he had known all his life. As they fully settled into their new life together, very familiar to him and very comfortable for her, Grace gave birth to their son, Preston Hunter. He was the spitting image of his father, and from the moment he was born, great things were expected of him. Nine months later Grace was pregnant again, and gave birth to a daughter, Madeline, who was the spitting image of Grace, same brownish/reddish/auburnish hair and bright hazel eyes, same freckles. Not as much was expected of Madeline, though there was an occasional joke about Madeline pulling off the same athletic feat as her father, winning state titles in three sports, though field hockey replaced football. Grace laughed it all off. Marry an athlete, it comes with the territory.

Grace threw herself into motherhood. Though they had a nanny to help her during the day, so she could try to catch up on sleep,

Grace did everything. She breast and bottle fed her babies, she changed their diapers, she scheduled cuddling and bonding times for each of them, she put them down for their naps and the nights, she read to them, gave them baby massages, she bathed them, took them to their doctor's appointments, she scheduled separate tummy time for each of them, she took them to playdates with other mom friends, though when they're babies they don't really do anything at playdates. She showered them with love, and told them how much she loved them dozens of times a day, separately and together. Alex helped when he was around, but his office was still in the city, and he commuted to Tribeca every day. He took the train into the city early every morning, and because he was in equity sales, he had drinks and dinners with clients most weekday evenings, and he usually got home when she and the kids were asleep. On weekends, when she would have wanted a break, he either slept in or played golf or had some local sports commitment. He was great with her and the kids when he was around, he just wasn't around that often. Occasionally they'd have date night, or go to a party, or an event at the club. Very very occasionally they'd have sex, but most of their free time together was spent lying on the couch trying to decide what to watch on the television. Many of her girlfriends lived the same kind of life, so it didn't really bother her. It was how it was with a successful husband and young children. This was her dream. Sometimes dreams aren't what people expect them to be.

She heard the first rumor when the kids were four and two. A friend of a friend of a friend saw Alex having dinner with an attractive young woman at a restaurant in Greenwich. He said the woman represented a family office he worked with, and it was nothing. The next one was six months later. What appeared to be a romantic evening with a woman in the city, he said she was a client and that was her favorite restaurant. The next came a year later, and it was more than a rumor. Another woman's husband called her at home and asked to please keep her husband away from his wife. Alex worked with the woman, and he told Grace the husband was psycho and nothing was going on. Every time it happened, there was an explanation, and the explanations always made sense. He was a famous man. A local legend. People were going to talk and spread rumors, whether they were true or not. And Grace wanted to believe him. She wanted to believe he was a loyal and loving husband just doing his job, earning a fine living, a living that provided her and the kids with a great life.

To ease her anxiety, she threw herself even deeper into motherhood and the New Bethlehem community. As soon as Preston started kindergarten, she joined the Parents Association, and volunteered for everything, bake sale, book drive, library committee, playground duty. She took cooking classes and cooked the kids a healthy dinner every night. She did yoga and dance and cycling and was the captain of the country club tennis team. She was in three book clubs. She had a strong group of mom friends and they had girls' night twice a month. She had an occasional glass of wine, often earlier in the day than she probably should have, usually with a friend or two, but sometimes alone. The kids played soccer and lacrosse and hockey and field hockey and football and tennis and were on the club swim team, and she went to every practice, and every game. She had a full busy rewarding life. Alex worked and golfed and coached and watched sports with his buddies at a local sports bar called the White Rhino. They went on spring break to a different island in the Caribbean every year, Grace and the kids went to Nantucket with Alex's parents every summer and he came up on the weekends, they went to Chicago every year for Thanksgiving and Easter. They had sex once a month or once every couple months. When she heard rumors she ignored them. There was nothing concrete. Just vague gossip. She dismissed it. She missed the early days of their love and their life, but also believed that this was what happened, this was how people raised families and got older. Days moved slowly and years moved quickly. And she woke up one day and she was in her forties. Time doesn't fly, it vanishes, like mist in the morning, summer flowers, dreams.

When the invitation came, she wasn't sure how to react or what to do or if to go. They were definitely at a low point. Alex was distant and stressed and spending more time away than normal. She was tired and lonely and often felt lost and desperate. Both put on a good public show, and nobody who knew them thought anything was wrong, the kids didn't seem to notice or care, but it was definitely the most difficult time that they had ever had together. Something had to change. Maybe it would be a spark for them, reignite their passion. Maybe it would be a fun night that they would laugh about when they were older. Maybe it would be weird and creepy and a good story to tell her friends. Maybe it was just a joke. She wasn't sure how to react or what to do or if to go. She certainly never thought it would go where it went, or end how it ended. Like her father, and despite, at Alex's insistence, taking her kids to church every Sunday, Grace had her own God. And like her father, Grace believed that her God was good and kind and wanted the best for her, and her family, and her children. When the invitation came she told herself that sometimes you just have to go where God takes you, and trust that everything will be okay.

And so she went with her God.

Coach

Charlie Dunlap truly and deeply loved three things in life.

Charlie truly and deeply loved playing hockey.

Charlie truly and deeply loved smoking marijuana.

Charlie truly and deeply loved eating pussy.

Charlie also loved fast cars and warm swimming pools and cold beer and heated socks and baseball caps and the Grateful Dead, sweatpants cheeseburgers outdoor summer parties soft-serve ice cream his mom and dad the United States of America and sometimes actually most of the time his girlfriend, but the three things Charlie loved most, the things most dear to his big ridiculous heart were hockey, wacky tobaccy, and making a woman quiver with the tips of his fingers, his lips, and his extralong tongue.

Charlie also loved having affairs with married women, but he believed in absolute discretion, so he never admitted that to anyone but himself and he certainly never included it on his Favorite Things List, which he updated once a week.

Charlie grew up in Las Vegas. His dad was a blackjack dealer, and his mom was a bartender at a strip joint. His earliest memories are of casinos and strip clubs, gamblers and strippers. He rarely went to school. Every kid he knew said school was lame so he thought he was lucky he never had to go. He liked gamblers and strippers. He thought they were funny. He didn't like teachers and principals at all.

Charlie discovered his first love when he was eight, and saw a hockey game on a ten-foot-tall and twenty-foot-wide TV at the casino sportsbook. He was spellbound. *What is this magic*, he asked himself. Men flying around on razor sharp steel blades swinging sticks at each other and fighting? Fuck yeah, he said to himself, even though he knew he wasn't supposed to say fuck.

Fuck Yeah!!!

He started hassling both of his parents to sign him up for hockey lessons, and spent all his time at the casino and the strip club and the various places they each lived watching hockey games. Because he couldn't skate, he couldn't play hockey, so they put him in a skating program at the only ice rink in Las Vegas. He was a natural. And he started spending all of his time at the rink. After a month he was ready for hockey. And again, he was a natural. In his first year, he led the Las Vegas Squirt League in goals, assists, penalty minutes, and ejections, and got banned from the league for fighting. His mom had a sister in Buffalo who also worked in a strip joint. The sister agreed to take Charlie in exchange for having her rent paid by Charlie's mother and father.

Off he went.

To Buffalo.

He tried out for and made the best youth team in the city, the Junior Sabres. But in order to play, he had to go to school. So he went to school and hated it and played hockey every day after school and loved it. And he was a sensation, leading the team, and the league, in goals, assists, and penalty minutes in his first season. He did it again in his second season. And again in his third season. And he managed to stay in school, getting straight Ds. He knew his future was in hockey. And that he would never ever ever use grammar, geometry, or anything he learned in social studies.

At sixteen, he left Buffalo and moved to Toronto to play Junior A, which is the most common route to the NHL. He was no longer a sensation, but he was very very good, and at eighteen, after three years in Canada, there was a chance he would be drafted by an NHL team. As he had always been, Charlie was an aggressive player. He liked to score goals and he liked to fight. Both of those things tended to bother other teams, and he often got the wrong type of attention from them, which means everyone in the league wanted to kick his ass. During the middle of his final season, he got hit headfirst into the boards, and he got knocked out, and he woke up two weeks later, and the doctors told him his career as a player was over, that he had suffered a traumatic brain injury, and if he ever hurt his head again, he would die.

But Charlie couldn't quit hockey.

He'd sooner cut off all his toes and eat them.

He could absolutely not ever ever ever quit hockey.

That would be like Santa quitting Claus.

He became a coach.

He took an online class and got certified.

He went to an on-ice coaching clinic and another and another.

He started applying for jobs.

Any job, any age, anywhere.

Nobody wanted to hire an eighteen-year-old who didn't finish high school to coach their children. And he could be a little much, a little, it might be called, aggressive.

So he got a job driving a Zamboni.

And nobody did it faster or better.

But sometimes he went too fast, and he lost the job when he didn't give himself enough room to stop, and he drove the Zamboni through the wall of the rink and hit two cars in the parking lot.

After the crash, he started having headaches. Or rather, a perpetual headache. He went to his doctor, and his doctor suggested he try medicinal marijuana. He went to the dispensary and bought as many different types of marijuana as he was legally allowed to buy. He went home, and he started experimenting, and he discovered his second great love. Not only did the weed evaporate his headache, it made him feel wonderful, tingly and sweet, like a swirl of cotton candy, like a bright-pink helium balloon. It fundamentally changed him in ways that made him able to exist peacefully in the world. It brought out the best of him and made the worst of him take a nap.

And the next time he got an interview, to coach a team of eight-year-old girls in a mite program, he was wonderful, charming, and enthusiastic, deeply knowledgeable on hockey training and strategy for someone so young, and ready to go to work. He got the job. And he was great at it. His team had three rules: hockey is fun so let's have fun, teammates are our best friends on and off the ice, always do your best and play your hardest. The girls followed the rules and they won the State and Regional championships, and came in fourth in Nationals. His second year they won the Nationals. And suddenly he had options. Not NHL level, or college, or even high school, but plenty of youth programs were willing to pay a young, ruggedly handsome, enthusiastic, and proven young coach to come work with their teams.

He took some interviews, and considered jobs in Minnesota (couldn't handle the accents), Wisconsin (the focus on cheese was weird), Boston (couldn't handle the accents), and Connecticut, which are four of America's hockey hotspots. He discovered his third love, and his secret fourth love, while interviewing for the job in Connecticut. After the interview he went back to his hotel room, smoked a giant joint, and was trying to decide if he wanted Taco Bell or Burger King for dinner. There was a knock on the door. He looked through the keyhole. An extremely attractive woman in her mid-forties, a board member of the club where he had interviewed earlier, was standing outside his room. At the end of the interview, he had been noncommittal about the job. He had two more interviews, one in Providence, and one in Philadelphia. He opened the door, and the woman stepped inside, and before he could speak, she said

I love hockey, and my sons love hockey, and we'd love for you to come coach here. Our kids need some toughening up and you could certainly help them. I just wanted you to know that if you do decide to take the job, we can do what we are about to do, whenever you want.

She pressed him against the wall and started kissing him. And he, as high as the moon sits in the sky, kissed her back.

Charlie had never really cared about girls, or women. Hockey was his love. He thought about it when he woke up every morning, he thought about it all day, he thought about it before he fell asleep, he dreamed about it. And having essentially grown up in strip clubs, he was desensitized to naked women, and in many ways, to sex. He had tried it. As an athlete he had had plenty of women who had wanted to date him, but it had always been awkward for him, fast and messy and a little bit embarrassing, he didn't know if he was good at it and didn't know what he was doing. He did know, though, that he had been blessed with certain physical gifts, that if he ever focused on it and learned some basic skills and techniques, it would likely make him pretty good at it. This was the first time he had ever done it while he was high. And my oh my oh my oh my oh my oh my. My oh my. Everything slowed. He didn't think. He let whatever she wanted to happen to happen. He responded to her, and when she responded to him, he followed her lead. At one point she pushed his head down, and kept pushing it until he found his way, and as he explored, she spoke to him, and told him what she wanted him to do. And once he was inside of her, the weed allowed him to last much much longer, and what happened was infinitely more physically pleasurable than anything he had ever experienced in his life. When she left, he called and accepted the job. And smoked another joint. And went to Taco Bell and feasted. He moved to Connecticut two days later.

And as far as he was concerned, he was never going to leave. There was great hockey, great medical marijuana, beautiful and fun and discreet married women whose husbands weren't interested in them anymore. He never broke anyone's trust, or spoke of his adventures. That, however, doesn't mean they did the same. And within a reasonably short period of time, he developed a reputation. A quiet reputation, whispered at lunches, and tennis dates, and between small groups of women waiting for their kids at practice. He never approached anyone. He was always respectful and cool. He kept a separate phone so that no call or text messages could ever be traced back to him. And he lived a normal life. He coached teams in three different age groups in three different towns. He did private clinics. His teams won titles, the kids he coached went on to play at elite boarding schools and colleges. He had a girlfriend, a math teacher at New Bethlehem Middle School. He loved her, and neither of them were in any rush to get married or have children, she was as sexually adventurous as anyone he had ever known, and knew about and was okay with his extracurriculars. Sex, and cunnilingus in particular, were just like hockey, an awesome physical activity, one of life's great games, that was exciting and fun and made him feel great.

But like hockey, playing the hanky-panky horizontal refreshment game also had its dangers, the most dangerous of which was love. Love with a married woman was always going to be complicated. Love with a married woman was always going to be dangerous. And love with a married woman never ended well. And he had promised himself he would never fall in love with a married woman. But promises are like glass, and they break just as easily.

Besties

It was love at first sight.

Platonic love.

The Great Great Great Friend kind of love.

Besties for Fucking Ever love.

Conspiracy theorists often pontificate on a supposed Illuminati network that rules the world. Don't listen to them. It's bullshit and there is no such thing. There is, however, a network of rich people that does rule the world in a certain kind of way. They all know each other or of each other, they go to the same schools and live in the same towns and they vacation in the same places. They share information with each other and they share secrets. They own most of the world's most valuable property, assets, and art. They move markets and they influence governments. When they speak, people listen. And if they don't, they use their money and influence to make sure that they do. They are a tribe. Not bound by religion or race or geographical location, but by money and power. Like any tribe, they help each other, and watch out for each other, protect each other. Their tribe does not have a name, for it does not need a name, and to name it would be to diminish it. And like the members of any tribe, they recognize each other, wherever they are, and whatever they may be doing. When they see each other, they know. They are drawn to each other, they understand each other, and they trust each other.

And so it was with Devon Kensington McCallister, glamorous WASP of the East Coast, and Belle Hedges Moore, Texas oil heiress and Dallas debutante. It happened at a cocktail party hosted by the New Bethlehem Newcomers Club. The Newcomers Club welcomes all new families who move to town. They send a Welcome Guide. They send a Care Package with products from local stores. They have Ambassadors to help or offer advice with anything a new family might need, or might need to know. And of course, they host cocktail hours, because there is nothing rich people love more than cocktail hour.

Neither Devon nor Belle wanted to go to the party that evening. The organizers had told each that the other was invited, and the only reason either of them did go was to meet the other. The New Bethlehem Newcomers had hoped that because both were attending, they would each think the club was cool and want to get involved. But alas, things don't always work out the way people hope they will. Devon and Belle arrived within five minutes of each other. Met each other and got glasses of wine (rosé, of course). Went into a corner away from everyone and started talking, and after about half an hour, Devon left the party, and five minutes later, Belle exited, and they went to dinner together. And though there had been an immediate sense of familiarity and friendship, dinner sealed it.

Belle had grown up in Highland Park, the wealthiest part of Dallas. Her great-great-grandfather had to come to America from Liverpool, where he was a pickpocket and petty criminal. In 1871, he killed a man with a knife in a pub fight. At that time in England, the sentence for murder was death by public hanging. He didn't want to die by public hanging, so he stowed away in the engine room of a steamship and ate mice and paper for ten days until he arrived in New York. Wanting to be as far away as possible from anyone who might recognize him, however unlikely it was, he rode on the roof of a freight train to St. Louis. In St. Louis, he stowed away on another steamship and ate some more mice and some more paper, and some wood from the sole of his shoes, and made it to Louisiana. In Louisiana he stole a horse and rode West as fast as possible, staying ahead of a posse sent to capture him. The sentence for horse thievery in Louisiana at the time was public whipping followed by public hanging, and he didn't want to experience either of them. He got to Jefferson County, in southeastern Texas, and changed his name from Edward Kelly to Henry Taylor Hedges, choosing Henry Taylor Hedges because he thought it sounded like the name of a rich man. He forged a birth certificate and applied for a US land grant and was given 162 acres by the federal government. He forged fourteen birth certificates and applied for several more land grants and was given a total of twenty-four hundred acres, most of it contiguous. He created fake Bills of Sale from all of the fictitious landowners transferring their acreage to him, and he had a nice piece of land. He married and he and his wife had one son, Henry Taylor Hedges Jr. His wife vanished when little Henry was two, falling off a boat while the three of them were taking a Sunday afternoon cruise on Sabine Lake. Much of Henry's land consisted of dense pine forest, and he made his first fortune by clear-cutting it and selling it all for timber. In the early 1900s, oil was discovered on the land. Henry didn't tell anyone of the discovery. He used his fortune to buy up all of the land around his acreage until he had ten thousand acres. An enormous amount of oil was beneath it. And after giving himself the name of a rich man, he became one, a very very very rich one. Henry Jr. married and had one son, Henry III, and managed the family's money and land, buying up more of it, most of which also had oil beneath it. Henry III had one son, Henry IV, and took over the family business when Henry III retired. Henry IV had two sons, Henry V, known as Hank, William Henry Hedges, known as WillieBoy, and at last, after several generations, a daughter, Belle.

Belle grew up loved and protected and spoiled. She had a mane of thick black hair, rosy cheeks, big brown eyes like mudpies. Being the only girl in the family, she was a bit of a tomboy. She rode mustangs, fished, shot guns and hunted deer and wild pigs, went to Cowboys games and rodeos. And she talked shit with the best of them, with the sweet cute lyrical lint of old Texas. She was a lifer at the Hockaday School, and went to SMU, where she partied and went to sorority functions and broke the hearts of half the men at the school. She moved to LA after SMU and theoretically worked in the film business, but mostly went to lunches and drinks and shopping and the beach. She met her husband, Teddy Moore, at a party in Venice. He was tall and blond, green eyes and a great smile. He had a mellow, laid-back way about him, made friends quickly and easily, could charm the pants off just about anyone, and make them feel good about it. He worked in tech-focused private equity in San Francisco. He was visiting a friend for the weekend that he knew from Stanford, where he played water polo, and where his parents were both professors. He was an exceptional beer pong player, and Belle lost to him several times over the course of the afternoon and early evening. At sunset they went for a walk along the beach and had dinner at one of the tourist trap restaurants that line the Venice Boardwalk. The party was ending by the time they got back, but Belle and her roommate, who shared a cottage near the beach in Ocean Park, Santa Monica, decided to keep it going at their place. Later that evening, Teddy literally charmed Belle's pants off.

They did long-distance for a year, seeing each other twice a month at a minimum, taking turns flying to either LA or SF. After a year she moved to the Bay and they got a small house in Mill Valley, and a chocolate lab they named Pong. They got engaged a year later, he proposed at a Cowboys game after asking for and receiving her father's approval. They got married at the Dallas Country Club in front of eight hundred guests in what Texas magazine called the Wedding of the Decade. A former President of the United States from Texas officiated the ceremony, and they hired the Backstreet Boys to be the wedding band. She got pregnant right after their second anniversary, had another two years later, and another two years later again, three girls named Avery, Harper, and Tenley. Teddy got transferred to New York and they lived on Fifth Avenue in Greenwich Village until Avery was ready to start kindergarten, when they moved to New Bethlehem. The reason was simple. If they stayed in New York, the first time their daughters would see the inside of a nightclub would be as freshmen in high school. If they lived in the country, the first time their daughters would see the inside of a nightclub would be as freshmen in college. It was an easy decision.

Belle loved her life in New Bethlehem. She and Teddy and the girls, the Moore Girls as they became collectively known, all carbon copies of their mom, black hair and rosy cheeks and some wild in their souls—lived in a reclaimed farmhouse renovated and expanded by a famous architect, half glass and half 250-year-old timber, on eighteen acres. They had a new barn on the back of the land, with stables and four horses, a paddock, trails. There was a pool behind the house, a playground the girls used when they were young, a tennis court. Belle loved to entertain and they hosted a huge holiday party every December, and Texas-style BBQ every Fourth of July, invitations to which were highly coveted around town. They donated regularly and generously to their church, the town library, the YMCA, the New Bethlehem Country Day school, which their daughters attended, and each of those institutions had rooms or buildings named after the Hedges-Moore family. The property was, as Belle liked to say, *staffed the fuck up*, with nannies when the girls were young, two housekeepers, a full-time stablehand, who lived in an apartment on the second floor of the barn, and a full-time groundskeeper to care for the land. She still loved her husband, and after almost twenty years together, they were still close. They had date night once a week, they socialized often and were invited to more things than they could attend, they often traveled without their daughters, weekend in Turks, or to Aspen, or a few days in London or Paris, where Teddy often traveled for work. Though the passion and intimacy of their relationship had faded, and they occasionally slept in separate bedrooms, neither could imagine life, or wanted to live life without the other. With their oldest two daughters away at boarding school, both at Choate, and the youngest a year away from also likely going, they were starting to think about what might be next, where they might want to live, who they might want to be. Teddy had expressed a desire to go back to California, living in Carmel or Big Sur, one of the small beautiful towns on the coast south of San Francisco. Belle wanted Europe for at least part of the year, and loved Ibiza, Saint-Tropez, Positano, which while overrun in the summer, were all lovely and calm during the offseason. While a close couple both publicly and at home, they also gave each other space, and had lives separate from each other. Belle loved going on yoga trips. She often visited the girls at school, and had always taken them away for spring break, sometimes to the Caribbean, sometimes to Europe. She and Devon went to Las Vegas every fall for a weekend of drinking, shopping, gambling, nightclubs and sun.

Teddy loved shooting birds and fishing, and often went on shooting and fishing trips with his friends, to Argentina, England, fishing in Wyoming and Alaska. He went to the Masters every year, and Jazz Fest in New Orleans. Belle trusted him absolutely, and knew he never strayed, though she couldn't say the same thing about herself. Despite the normalcy and stability of her life, she had always loved gossip and secrets, drama and intrigue. Getting away with things was fun, and keeping them from ever getting out even more so, and Belle loved the feeling of getting away with things she knew she shouldn't have been doing, and knowing things no one else did.

Devon was the exception to that rule. They came from the same world. They lived in the same world. They were best friends. They did everything together. There was absolute trust between them. Absolute discretion. She never shared any of Devon's secrets, and she knew Devon had never shared any of hers. And both knew if either of them ever did, it would lead to the end of both of their marriages, the breakup of their families, it would end the lush comfortable privileged lives they lived within the safe, beautiful, manicured borders of New Bethlehem. If one broke the trust, floodgates would open, fires would start that couldn't be put out. And neither of them wanted to live through a flood or an inferno. But what they didn't consider before they had the party was that not everyone was like them. Their comfort and their privilege was their blind spot. Some people wanted to wash their lives away, some people like playing with fire, some went to the party hoping they would find a match so they could light the town on fire.

The Golden Boy

Alex Hunter had always handled the family finances. As long as Grace's credit card always worked, and it always did, and her checks cleared, and they always did, she didn't care. And she didn't ask. And she didn't check.

On the day it happened, Alex went to the office, as usual. Parked in the same spot in the New Bethlehem parking lot he had parked in for years. Sat on the same seat of the train with the same men he sat with every day. Took the subway to the same stop and walked the same streets to the same office. He took the same elevator and said hello to the same colleagues. It was just another Monday. Just another day at the grind. Another day of calling clients and following up with clients and taking clients out for drinks after the market closed. When his boss, who he considered a good friend, and who had been his boss for over a decade, asked him to come to his office, he didn't think twice about it. It could have been anything. An equal chance it was just a Monday morning bullshit session as it was something to do with work.

When he stepped inside, he knew there was trouble. His boss had a small designer sofa and two chairs in a small meeting area opposite his desk. A company attorney and a rep from Human Resources were sitting on the sofa. His boss was in one of the chairs. None of them were smiling.

It could have been any number of things. He did drugs with clients, he slept with clients, he flirted with young attractive female colleagues, he took his days off and played golf when he said he was doing sales calls, he cheated on his expenses. He was lucky when they told him that the downturn in the economy had required them to make some difficult decisions, and that the uptick in AI-directed algorithmic trading had made equity sales less important. They gave him two months of severance and offered to provide him with a positive reference to any future potential employers. He had been there for almost twenty years. His boss, his supposed close friend, shook his hand and thanked him for his service. A rep from security was waiting for him outside the door. They gave him an hour to clean his office and leave.

He had never failed before. Or at least not in a way that materially impacted his life. He had always excelled, always won, always been the best. As far back as he could remember, he had had the nickname Alexander the Great, and he had always lived up to it.

Though they were kind on the terms, and told him that his shit-canning was part of a larger culling of salespeople, he knew it was bullshit. He was tired, and he had gotten lazy. Yes, the world had changed, yes the economy was down, and yes AI was impacting markets and changing how people bought and sold equities, but the reality of his situation was that he had been cruising, resting on his laurels for the last three or four years, and was focused on other things. And while he would have liked to say those things were his wife or his children or his community, the reality was he had been getting drunk and doing drugs, chasing women, and gambling. He had busted his ass and he had been perfect for most of his life. He thought that his past, and his reputation, and his good looks and charm, and his nickname insulated him. While he sometimes vaguely contemplated something going horribly wrong, he didn't believe it would ever actually happen.

When it did, he called Grace from the street in front of what had been his office, and told her he had a dinner that night and was going to stay in the city. He called a dealer who often sold him cocaine, he went to a liquor store and bought a fifth of whiskey, he rented a hotel room. He called two women he knew who were something in-between hookers and sugar babies, and invited them over. They spent the next twelve hours engaging in a cocaine and bourbon-fueled fuckfest. The next morning, he went home. He told Grace he had closed a big deal the night before and had the rest of the day off.

He went for a run.

He took a long long long shower.

He shaved but avoided looking into his own eyes.

He played lacrosse toss and catch with Preston in the backyard.

He took Madeline to field hockey.

He took the family out to dinner at a local New Bethlehem Italian joint. After the drinks came, Grace raised a glass and offered congratulations to him for closing his deal. He smiled and said thank you, as he did whenever anyone praised him.

The next morning he followed his usual routine. Shower coffee drive park train to the city. Instead of going to what had been his office, he went to the New York Public Library. He spent the day looking at Instagram and in the periodicals section reading magazines he didn't know were still published. He took the train home from Grand Central at the end of the day, as he did most days.

He did the same thing the next day.

And the next.

And the next.

And so it went for six months.

He followed his routine. He didn't tell Grace he'd lost his job. He didn't tell Grace they were burning through their savings. That he was going to empty his retirement accounts next. That the kid's college funds would come last. He hated himself and felt a shame unlike anything he had ever known or experienced, a shame that weighed on him every minute of every day, that terrorized him every minute of every day, that paralyzed him every minute of every day. He had made some calls and sent some emails, and looked at online job listings. But no one was looking to hire a white suburban equity salesman in his mid-forties. And every rejection destroyed him. Pierced his heart. Brought on more shame. Shame and fear and guilt and embarrassment, anguish and regret and insecurity and loneliness, anger and sadness, disgust and despair, helplessness and hopelessness.

When he was tired of the magazines, he decided to try to read the Modern Library's 100 Best Novels. He thought reading would take his mind off his life, his impending doom, his shame. It didn't. He got through two books and gave up. Even though he couldn't afford it, he joined a gym near the library, and started working out for hours every day. It felt physically great, but didn't help his heart, or his mind, or his soul. He tried meditating, yoga, walking, Tai Chi, deep breathing, Pilates, Qigong, guided imagery, cold plunges. He found no escape, no relief. Every second of every day, two things ran through his mind.

You fucking loser.

What the fuck are you going to do.

He thought about Grace. It made him feel even worse. It made him want to die. She had always been so good to him, so caring and supportive, loving, faithful. She was the best person he had ever known. He was so deeply lucky to have her in his life. He had taken her for granted for years. Cheated on her more times than he could count. Lied to her. And he knew that she knew he was doing it. And he did it anyway. Told himself that marriage was hard and being a parent was hard and everyone did it. He lied to her and he lied to himself. Every time he tried to think about telling her about their situation, he froze. He had opportunities at home every day, and every time they were alone and he could do it, he froze. He knew she'd be what she had always been, loving and supportive, and he knew she would tell them he'd find a new job and they'd be fine. He knew she would be his ally and cheerleader, hold his hand and stand by his side, stay with him, love him, but he couldn't do it.

You fucking loser.

What the fuck are you going to do.

He was Alexander the Great. He was the greatest athlete New Bethlehem had ever seen. He had played quarterback at Notre Dame and in the NFL. He couldn't admit he was a failure. As an employee, as a husband, as a father, as a man. He knew it but couldn't say it, not to himself, to his wife, to his parents and children, to his friends, to the people of the town who loved him.

He started gambling, betting on sports, believing that maybe his background as an athlete would give him an edge, that if he could string together some wins he could make some money. He started with a nice streak and won a couple grand. He started betting more and the streak turned, from winning to losing. He doubled-down to make up for the losses and the bad streak continued, and continued, and continued. He stopped looking at his online bank statements. He threw away whatever mail he got that might have been related to his finances. He didn't know how much longer he would be able to pay his family's bills.

You fucking loser.

What the fuck are you going to do.

When the invitation came he had an idea. It would be complicated, hard, and very very risky, but if it worked, it would save him, and though he would no longer have an intact family, in a way it would save them.

And it would be better than any of the alternatives.

You fucking loser.

What the fuck are you going to do.

And he knew.

It was worth the risk.

It would be worth the fallout.

It was his only chance.

You fucking loser.

What the fuck are you going to do.

He knew.

Geometry

It had taken all four years of college, lessons with a private teacher and a voice coach, and hours and hours and hours and hours of practice, but Katy Boyle had done it.

Park was no longer *paahhk*.

Harbor no longer *haahbaah*.

Quarter no longer *kwataahh*.

Party no longer *paahty*, and water no longer *wattaah*.

It had taken all four years of college, lessons with a private teacher and a coach, and hours and hours and hours and hours of practice, but she had done it.

Erased all outward evidence of her childhood.

Erased all outward evidence of where she was from.

Her childhood had not been happy, fun, or easy. Her father was an abusive alcoholic dockworker. He drank and screamed and threw punches and occasionally worked. Her mother was an abusive alcoholic who had given birth to her when she was seventeen and blamed her for ruining her life. She drank and screamed and threw punches and occasionally disappeared, for a day or two, for a week or two, once she was gone for a month. The only reason Katy hoped she would come back was because then her father would have another target for his abuse. Her father tended not to hit her when her mother was hitting her. And her mother's punches hurt much less.

From an early age, for as long as she could remember, all Katy wanted to do was escape. Run. Get the fuck out. Because of the general state of neglect in which she and her parents lived, and the neglectful manner in which she was treated and raised (when her parents weren't screaming at her or hitting her, they almost entirely ignored her), most of what Katy learned about being successful in the world came from watching TV. And though money was extremely tight, because her father loved the Red Sox and the Bruins, and her mother loved Oprah, they always had cable, and the cable bill would get paid before everything else, which resulted in sometimes there being no heat, sometimes the oven didn't work, sometimes the car wouldn't move, sometimes she had to wear the same shoes or clothes despite there being holes in them, but the TV always worked. When her parents were gone, or out, or in their bedroom sleeping off the latest bender, Katy parked herself on their tattered, stained sofa and watched Nickelodeon or the Disney Channel. And in the shows, kids were happy, they had food and nice clothing, they played sports and went to nice schools and got good grades, and they had parents who loved and cared about them, and they had fun, cool adventures with their friends. Although she knew some version of what she was watching on TV existed in the real world, it seemed so far away, and so impossible, and so difficult to have if you didn't win the genetic lotto. But she decided she was going to try to find it. That if this other world was real, there must be some way for her to become part of it. It was all she wanted and thought about, how to escape, how to find another life.

And despite her parents' lives, Katy had been born with gifts. She was great at math, and she was great at sports, which she knew in some basic instinctual way, though she didn't know what to do about developing those gifts. In fourth grade, she got lucky, or maybe God intervened, or maybe life just works out sometimes. Her teacher, Miss Murphy, recognized her gifts, and knew a bit about Katy's home life, started helping her. She made sure she had food at lunch. She got her math textbooks that were being used in middle school. She bought her a lacrosse stick and played with her after school. At first Katy was suspicious. She didn't understand why Miss Murphy wanted to help her. Every adult she had ever known had hurt her—her walls were up. But as fourth grade moved along, the walls came down, and Miss Murphy, who'd grown up in a similar environment, became the most important person in her life, the first person Katy ever loved, and the first person who ever loved Katy. For the first couple months, Katy's parents didn't notice that her schedule and routines had changed, or they didn't care. When her father saw a bag of equipment in Katy's room, he asked why she had it and where she got it and asked her if she stole it. She was hesitant, but told him about Miss Murphy. And the next day, for the first time ever, he was at Katy's school, demanding to see Miss Murphy.

The meeting, with the principal and school security officer, was tense. Though Katy's father had showered and put on decent and mostly clean clothing, he still reeked of alcohol. Miss Murphy, expecting that something like this would happen, as it had with her own father, was very careful to follow all school rules and policies. She was charming and kind and told the truth, which was that she was helping a gifted child, and that Katy was excelling in both school and sports, and that she would like to continue helping her. Katy's father said no, that he was Katy's father, and he didn't want anyone helping her but him and her mother. The school, not wanting drama and seeing him as he was, agreed. And when Katy came home from school that afternoon, her father gave her a good beating, one she deserved for believing she was fancy and special.

Determined to continue, and knowing, even as a fourth grader, that she had found her best route both to escape and to some kind of happy and productive life, Katy studied on her own at home, and practiced throwing her lacrosse ball against the wall of the apartment building where she lived with her parents. Miss Murphy continued making sure she had food for lunch, and told her to keep working, and that if she ever needed help, to come to her and she would help her.

Eighteen months later, Katy's father died in a bar fight in South Boston. Katy's mother had been increasingly absent, and though she attended her husband's funeral, she didn't come home for a month after. After three weeks, when the electricity stopped working, Katy went to Miss Murphy. Miss Murphy went to Child Protective Services. Child Protective Services couldn't find Katy's mother, and Miss Murphy agreed to become her foster mother.

Katy thrived.

She got nearly perfect grades.

Joined a travel lacrosse team.

Had as much food as she needed or wanted.

Didn't worry about getting beaten when she came home.

And most importantly, she experienced how it felt and what it meant to be loved. For the first and only time in her life, she was loved, and she felt loved.

The next five years were like some kind of dream. She and Miss Murphy lived in a small two bedroom in the South End. Katy transferred to a much better school and was accepted into a magnet school for STEM students. She played lacrosse after school and was one of the best players on the best travel team in Boston. Miss Murphy came to all of her events and all of her games. She was Katy's caretaker, cheerleader, tutor, guardian, role model, coach, mentor, best friend, and when Katy's birth mother died of an overdose in her junior year of high school, she adopted her and became her mother. They were a beautiful pair. Mirror images of each other. Katy loved her deeply, and depended on her mightily, and would have done anything for her.

When it came time to apply to college, Katy had multiple scholarship offers for both academics and athletics. She wanted to be a teacher like Miss Murphy, and coach lacrosse. She also wanted to leave Boston, where she'd lived her entire life, and where she had plenty of great, but also plenty of awful memories. When she got an offer from Columbia, in New York, to attend its School of Education, she accepted. Life was so good. Her dreams were coming true. She thought she was the luckiest girl in the world.

But luck always runs out. And midway through her senior year, Miss Murphy was diagnosed with advanced ovarian cancer. And though there is always a chance, and miracles do sometimes happen, the diagnosis was terminal. She had surgery and started chemo, but it didn't work. She died three days after Katy graduated from high school. And though her doctors had advised against it, she attended the graduation ceremony, the last time she breathed free open air. She spoke her final words and held Katy's hand.

Go be great, and go make your dreams come true, and know that I loved you so much, and being your mother was the greatest experience of my life.

Katy was destroyed. Utterly and absolutely devastated. But she also knew she couldn't let her pain derail her future. Miss Murphy wouldn't have wanted that, and would not have allowed it. Katy spent three days crying in bed, and on the fourth day she got up. It was time to leave. All Boston held for her now was pain; she'd had enough pain in her short life. She was done. She wanted to erase Boston from her life. She sold all of their belongings. She moved to New York. She started school.

The city was jarring. It was crowded, loud, and stressful. While she had been a star in high school, everyone at Columbia had been a star in high school, and the pressure to perform was real. But she was well prepared. She studied, she got her grades, she practiced, and she performed on the field. And for the first time in years, she had free time, time to do with whatever she chose. And she chose to try to have a social life, to make friends, to date. She went to parties and drank, though given her family history, she was very careful with drinking. At one of the parties, she met a boy. He was rich and handsome and had grown up in New York and had gone to prep school. When she was in high school, she'd see boys like him at lacrosse games or tournaments, and always hoped she would meet one who liked her. They started dating. They had sex. It was a revelation. To experience such intense physical pleasure. To shake and moan. To quiver. To cum. And the first time she came, the first time she saw and felt the blinding white light of ecstasy, the first time the world fell away and disappeared and became irrelevant and all she knew was bliss and joy and frenzied elation, she knew she wanted more.

She slept with the handsome boy a few more times. And she encouraged him to explore her body, to play with it, to indulge his fantasies. But he wanted something exclusive and emotional, and she had no interest. She had been hurt so many times in her life that she wasn't going to make herself vulnerable or allow herself to get hurt. She left him and started seeking out physical relationships, sexual experiences. She dated young men, older men, white men, Black men, Asian men, Hispanic men. She went to strip joints and sex clubs. She had affairs with married men, married women, went to lesbian bars, dated a trans man, explored BDSM and group sex. Occasionally men would offer her money. To go on trips, to go to parties, to make videos with them, to sleep with their spouses. Occasionally she did it, and occasionally she took the money. In whatever free time she had she explored her sexuality, and she did so without guilt or shame. She was young and free. It was her body. It was her heart. She was a woman in the twenty-first century who believed she had the right to do with them as she pleased. And she often pleased.

While having her adventures, she continued to excel in school and on the field. She got perfect grades and was All-Ivy. On weekends she coached underprivileged lacrosse players in the Bronx and Harlem, tutored kids in New York City public schools, did summer internships with the Board of Ed. She never went back to Boston. It was too complicated, and she wanted to move on. Whenever she spoke, because of her thick South Boston accent, people knew where she was from, and wanted to talk about it, joke about it, mimic it. She wanted to leave it behind. And so as soon as she could afford it, she started working on getting rid of the accent, working toward a voice that kept people from asking her about her childhood. As graduation neared, she started looking for jobs. Ideally, she wanted work in a place that reminded her of the television shows she watched as a kid. A place where kids were happy, had food and nice clothing, played sports and went to nice schools and got good grades, and had parents who loved them and cared about them. A place that reminded her of those Nickelodeon, and Disney Channel shows, where fairy tales were real, or where she could convince herself they were at least possible.

She heard about the job at New Bethlehem Middle School at a lacrosse tournament. An under-twelve girls team she coached from Harlem beat New Bethlehem in the finals, in what was a huge upset.

After the game she started chatting with the New Bethlehem coach, who had seen her play at Columbia, and asked what she was doing after she finished school. Katy said she was figuring it out, and the coach told her they had an opening for a math teacher, and she could also coach in the town lacrosse program. Katy had played against New Bethlehem, and almost always lost, for years. She knew it was a wealthy town with great schools and great sports. She asked how she could apply. When she went out for the interview, she couldn't believe the place was real. The town was clean and beautiful, the houses were huge, the people were all good looking and well dressed, the kids she met were friendly and polite. It all seemed like something out of the movies, or those TV shows she'd loved as a child. When she was offered the job, she took it without hesitation. And after five years, she had no regrets.

New Bethlehem was indeed everything she first thought it was, and she had a lovely life. She taught advanced math to bright, motivated students with supportive parents. The school was the top-ranked middle school on the East Coast, heavily funded, the teachers given everything they needed to succeed, and help their students succeed. She liked her colleagues and her department head. The principal was available if she ever needed him, which was rare. The lacrosse program was one of the best in the country, hyper-competitive, and there were enough great players to field two or three teams every year. The lacrosse parents could be a bit much, but they knew complaining to coaches would only hurt their kids' chances at making the best teams, so they mostly fought with each other, and left the coaches alone to do their jobs. She lived in an apartment on the second floor of a small house right outside of town. She had a boyfriend, or a sort of boyfriend, a local hockey coach. He wasn't super smart, or ambitious in any way, but he was funny and fun and one of the happiest people she'd ever known. Neither was interested in marriage or even monogamy, so she could pursue her own erotic pleasures and delights without fear of upsetting him, and he could pursue his without fear of upsetting her. And they both did, though he played in and around the towns surrounding New Bethlehem, and she generally went to New York, not wanting to get involved with someone she might see in town. Her life was simple, routine and rewarding. Though she did hope to someday settle down and start a family, she was as happy as she believed she could be, and she wasn't interested in drama or complications, and thus far, she had avoided them.

But all that changed when she went to the party and met Billy McCallister.

Billy told her that he knew her deepest, darkest secret, something from her time in New York, something she thought was behind her.

And she became part of a murder investigation.

Ladies Who Lunch

Devon and Belle had lunch at least once a week.

Sometimes they went to the country club.

Sometimes they went to a quiet Italian spot on Maple Street.

Sometimes they went to the New Bethlehem Diner.

Sometimes they went to Greenwich and shopped on Greenwich Avenue before and after sitting down to have a glass of wine and push their salads around their respective plates. Most of the time it was just the two of them. Almost always on a Wednesday. A nice break in the middle of the week where they could gossip, complain, laugh, and vent, share their joys and frustrations, make plans, share their secrets, talk about other people's secrets.

Occasionally they invited another woman to join them, or two women, or three. They both liked the idea of a larger group, but it never felt right, and they never trusted anyone else to be completely open with them. The only time they had a great time with someone else was when they invited Charlie Dunlap. He spent the entire time asking them for tips on how to better eat pussy and they spent the entire time laughing and telling him to go light with the tongue and deep with the finger, which he said was already his go-to technique and surely they must have some super-lady-cum-secret that would take his game to a new level and they started making things up and laughing more. But given that Devon was already fucking him, and Belle wanted to fuck him, they decided not to do it again.

On the day that changed both of their lives, they were sitting outside, it was the end of summer, school was about to start, and they had both just returned from vacation. Devon had been in Amagansett and Belle on Ibiza. During the spring, summer, and fall, as early and as late as the weather allows, all of the restaurants on Maple Street put tables directly in front of their storefronts. On most days, except when it's raining, all the tables are full for both lunch and dinner, and there are people waiting for them as soon as they become free. Devon and Belle were both very generous with tips. They always tipped the maître d', the waiters, the busboys, the bartenders. They did it at each meal, and at the holidays, and they did it with discretion, without talking about it or making a show of it. But in exchange, they expected to always get a great table, and a table with some room around it so they could talk without fear of being overheard. When they made a reservation, as was the case on this day, a table was prepared for them. Each had a glass of rosé, and an untouched Caesar with salmon. Belle took a large sip, almost a gulp, of her wine, and spoke, in her sweet Texas drawl.

Am I bored already?

You've only been back for two days.

Ibiza was so damn great.

How was the house?

On the north side of the Island. On the sea. Far enough away from the clubs so I had peace and quiet, but close enough that I could go party or find a sweet, reckless, beautiful boy whenever I wanted.

Sounds perfect.

Perfect doesn't even begin to describe it. It was beyond. Yoga and the sand and the pool during the day, whatever I wanted at night. The girls were all away at camp. Teddy came for two weeks, but mostly it was just me. It was beyond beyond.

Devon laughed.

You're making me jealous.

I invited you. More than once.

I know. I should've come.

How was Amagansett?

Same as ever. Kids went to camp and the beach and hung out with their friends. Billy came out on weekends and played golf every day.

We went to the same parties we go to every summer with the same people we see every summer. It was fun enough.

Well, you got a great tan.

Thank you.

Any drama, gossip?

You see Page Six?

I'm staying away from the media these days. I just can't.

Devon smiles.

Langleys split up.

Belle fake gasps, smiles.

Tell me.

She caught him nude in the pool with one of his sugar babies and took a golf club to a couple of his Warhols and his Porsche. He had her arrested. It was insane.

She's insane.

Yes.

I never understood why he married her in the first place.

Love does crazy things to people.

Prenup?

Of course.

She's going to fight it.

Of course.

It's going to last forever.

Years and years and years.

If it's already in the papers, everything about it is going to be in the papers.

There have been almost daily updates.

I might have to start back with the media. Or at least Page Six.

It's all you really need.

Even with the prenup, she'll get a fortune.

Not a real fortune, but enough of one.

We need something fun and ridiculous to happen around here.

We moved here and live here to avoid the drama.

How about some location-appropriate drama.

Devon laughed.

I have no idea what that would be. Somebody doesn't get into Harvard? Cheating in the club golf championship?

I have an idea.

Lord help me.

It's a good one.

I'm not sure I want to know.

Yes, you do.

Devon smiled.

Yes, I do.

Guess what happened in Ibiza?

There are far too many possibilities for me to even consider taking a guess.

Belle smiles.

Teddy and I got invited to an orgy.

Devon laughs.

No way.

Belle smiles.

Way? Or sort of?

Devon laughs again.

How do you sort of get invited to an orgy?

We got invited to a swingers' party, but it was a big one, so the only thing it could have ended up being is an orgy.

How big?

They invited a hundred people.

That's an orgy.

Right?

Who invited you?

A Russian billionaire.

Of course.

But a good one. Anti-Putin. He lives on this huge guarded estate with a bunch of models. He has bulletproof windows on the house, ex-KGB guys with machine guns everywhere. Teddy knows him through work.

You get an email, a phone call, what?

We spent an afternoon at the estate, and he just asked us. There were, like, four models hanging out with us. They kept telling me how fun it was going to be and trying to convince me to come.

Were they wearing anything?

No, nothing. And their bodies were insane. Like, insane.

What did Teddy say?

He said if I wanted to go he was cool with it.

Was he going with you?

I've told you before, he can be a bad boy.

Devon laughed.

I guess so.

You know Key Parties were invented here.

I've seen the movie, I've read the book.

I think we should have one.

Devon laughed again.

It really was quite a summer for you, wasn't it.

Don't pretend you're some kind of prude.

I haven't said no.

We could keep it small, discreet.

Alex Hunter?

See if he lives up to the nickname?

I've heard he does.

Can I have Charlie?

I'm sure he'd love it.

Belle smiled.

I think we should do it.

Devon smiled.

So do I.

The War Room

At its core, it is a simple game.

Buy low.

Sell high.

But with tens of millions of people around the world trying to play this simple game, in order to win, you need an edge.

And that edge is information.

Billy always kept his staff as small as possible.

Loose lips sink ships.

More than making trades or analyzing balance sheets or verifying the validity of projections, the most effective way to buy low and sell high is to have information that no one else has or knows.

Billy kept the office cold. Everyone sat at a desk, in a comfortable chair, but not too comfortable.

Everyone's office had a door that could be closed so that conversations could be kept private. Sometimes getting information requires discretion, among other things, and Billy didn't want to know how his teams got their information, just how it affected whether he was buying or selling. Billy didn't care about office hours or dress codes, he didn't care where people are from or where they went to college or if they did at all, he didn't care what they do when they are not working for him, Billy cared about returns.

How low was the buy, and how high was the sell. That's all that mattered.

If your returns weren't high enough, Billy would scream at you, throw things at you, insult you and demean you. And nobody's returns were ever high enough. In exchange for tolerating him, and generating returns, Billy paid his employees extraordinarily well. If they complained about his behavior, or did not generate returns, he fired them. If they kept their mouths shut and stayed loyal and got information no one else had and generated returns, Billy rewarded them. Once, at the start of his career, an employee filed a lawsuit against him for his behavior. He hired some former CIA agents to comb through the employee's life until they found something that could hurt the employee. Once he had the information, Billy hurt him. A second time, just after he moved from New York to Connecticut, another employee filed a lawsuit against him for his behavior. Billy's former CIA agents combed through his life, but they didn't find anything, so Billy had them comb through the lives of the employee's wife, and parents, and his wife's parents, and they found information that could hurt them, and Billy did what Billy always did when people threatened him, he hurt them.

When Billy opened his first office he called it the War Room, and asked his employees to call him the General. He approached what he did as if it was war. Not a war for land, or to enlarge borders, or because someone believed in a specific political philosophy, but a war for the only thing that matters in life, a war for the one thing that can get anything that exists in the world, a war for the one thing that supersedes power, a war for money.

Billy would do anything for money. Though he was well aware of various laws of the United States of America and the states of New York and Connecticut related to the trading of stocks and the movement of money, he didn't care about any of them. He thought laws were made for people who weren't smart enough to figure out how to break them. In the pursuit of money, Billy was willing to do anything. In the pursuit of whatever it was Billy wanted, be it money, or a house, or a painting, or a wife, Billy was willing to do anything. It was war, and if you lost a war, you lost everything.

Billy went to the office every morning at 5:00. He spent an hour on his treadmill, in front of which he had four screens, two with financial television shows on them, and two that flashed up-to-date information of his positions in the European and Asian markets. He showered after, went to his desk, where there were four trading screens and two large TVs above them. He spent much of his day on the phone. He had two telephones. One he called *Peace*. It was a normal iPhone. He used it for most of his calls, both his work and personal emails flowed into it, he texted with business associates, friends, his children, and Devon on it. He kept his social media accounts on it. He read the news on it. He checked sports scores on it. He kept his photos on it, and his calendar on it. It was a normal smartphone, and he used it like most people in the world use their smartphones.

He called the other phone *War*, and it was a secure, encrypted satellite phone that used a secure, encrypted, and extremely expensive private network that only hosted one thousand other phones. It was untraceable, unhackable, and unbreakable. It was the most secure phone that money could buy. Billy used *War* to broker the purchase of information that would generate returns, he used it for emails and texts that he didn't want anyone, especially government and banking authorities, to ever be able to see, he used it to move money from accounts in countries with extremely private banking laws to accounts in other countries with extremely private banking laws, he used it to communicate with his attorneys, with the ex-CIA agents he still and always kept on retainer, and he used it to arrange dates with women, almost always young women, many of whom had worked in porn and with whom he had sexual relationships. Very few people, including people who worked for him, knew that *War* existed. Of those who knew it existed, none knew what was on it or what exactly he used it for, though all of them had their ideas.

Throughout the day, at his desk, on his phones and his screens and his computers, he sought out information that would help him generate returns. In the best-case scenario, which is what he preferred and what he spent his time and money seeking, the information would guarantee returns. If he got hold of a quarterly earnings report before it became public. If he learned of a sale or acquisition of a business before it was announced. If he learned of a product that was being made or a drug that was going to receive FDA approval before anyone else knew it. If he could learn what financial positions his competitors were taking or the moves they were making without them knowing that he knew. Whatever it was, he didn't care if it was legal to have it or not, he wanted it, and in most cases, he got it.

Most days he stayed at the office until the early evening. Some days he stayed later. Some nights he stayed. He had a small apartment built off his office, a bedroom, a small sitting room, a bathroom. When the other employees left, he often had young women come visit him in the apartment, or he'd tell Devon he had dinner in the city and would rent a hotel room. Devon knew, vaguely, what he was doing, but she didn't care. They had long stopped loving each other. He did what he wanted, and she did what she wanted, the rules unspoken but mutually understood: never make it public, never embarrass the family. Both of them knew divorce wasn't possible. They were tied to each other for life, whether they wanted to be or not. They were friends, in a way, or at least friendly. They put on a good show in public, the socialite and the hedge fund titan, the perfect couple, with their beautiful homes and their beautiful art and their beautiful children. Most of the time they enjoyed each other's company, though neither of them sought the other. He had his life. She had her life. They lived in the same house, and sometimes slept in the same bedroom. Their social lives were tied to each other, and they both loved their children.

And Billy was involved with his kids. He read books with them, taught them about money and how it was made and how it could be deployed, he showed up for most of their games and matches and recitals and parties. Though he wasn't around as much as they would have liked, his children loved him, or loved the version of him that they knew.

He was surprised when Devon brought up the idea of the party. She loved to entertain, and he generally went along with what she wanted to do. If he didn't feel like being part of whatever she was doing, he would stay at the office or go into the city with one of his girlfriends. The party was an interesting idea, and in his view, a positive development. Maybe something that would rekindle some of their love. Or, if it went well, something they could continue to do on their own or do together. At the very least it would relieve him of worrying about her and how she felt about what he was doing. If she wanted to have a swing party at their house, he could do whatever the fuck he wanted to do, and she couldn't say a word.

And that's exactly what he did.

The Closer

He had it all.

And he had always had it all.

Anything and everything anyone could reasonably ask for in life.

Loving parents.

An idyllic childhood on one of the most beautiful, prestigious college campuses in the world. A free four-year education on said campus, where he excelled in the pool and in the classroom.

A long career in one of the most lucrative business sectors in the world.

A wealthy, kind, beautiful wife.

A beautiful home in one of the safest, most picturesque communities in the country.

Three beautiful daughters, all great students, great athletes, great people.

Friends around the world who admired and respected him.

And yet, there were many many many days where Teddy Moore just wanted to die.

It started ten years ago. A feeling that something was wrong. A creeping sense of dread. A black cloud in his soul that got larger and darker, larger and darker, larger and darker. He told no one. He didn't feel like he could tell anyone. And he didn't have anyone to tell even if he had been willing, or open. He had a perfect life. What was he going to say? What did he have to complain about? What right did he have to feel like shit?

He was a partner in a large private equity business. They bought companies, they helped them become more profitable, they sold the companies. If it worked, and you were good at it, it was incredibly lucrative. It was entirely possible to spend ten or twenty or thirty million dollars and turn it into a billion or two or three. Teddy and his partners were very good at it.

Teddy's job was to close deals. Often companies were identified that were not for sale, or had owners or founders that didn't want to sell them. Teddy would meet with them, take them to dinner, play golf with them, go fishing or shooting, ski with them. He would charm them, he would seduce them. Rare was the deal that Teddy could not, or did not, consummate. He was the Closer, and he closed again and again and again, reliably and dutifully, with style and panache.

Yet that was the problem.

At home, or anywhere else, he couldn't close.

He had always loved sex. Had a very positive relationship with sex. His parents had a loving faithful marriage. Maybe the only one he'd ever truly believed was loving and faithful. They were great role models. He knew if he found the kind of love that they'd found in each other, it would be enough. And when he met Belle, he believed he'd found it, and in many ways, in almost every way but one, he still believed he had found it.

It came on slowly. When they would start to fool around, it would take him longer to get aroused, for his dick to get hard. He noticed it, but didn't think much about it. He figured it was age. He knew he couldn't run the way he ran when he was younger, or hit a golf ball as far, or ski black diamonds as quickly or easily. The years catch up to you, no matter how hard you work to slow them down.

But it gradually got worse. He didn't tell Belle. And without her knowing why they engaged in foreplay for two, three, four times as long; she loved it. Wanted even more of it. The condition expanded, from taking longer to get hard, to taking longer to cum, to not being able to cum at all and having to fake it. He went to his doctor and the doctor could find nothing wrong. He went to a specialist and the specialist could find nothing wrong. Both suggest he take drugs that might cure his condition, and gave prescriptions for them. When he took them, nothing changed. So he took more of them, and nothing changed. He took more, nothing.

He saw a therapist, a psychiatrist, a performance therapist, a coach. He heard the words *performance anxiety* over and over and over again.

He tried deep breathing and meditation, he tried visualization, pro-gressive muscle relaxation, positive self-talk, exposure therapy, beta-blockers. Nothing worked. He drew the line at group therapy, or a support group. He couldn't risk anyone finding out. He was, after all, the Closer.

It got to the point where he had to discuss it with Belle. She was, as always, kind, supportive, and understanding. She was also willing and excited to expand their sexual playbook in order to find some-thing that would turn him on enough to achieve both an erection and a coconut cream explosion. They tried sexy lingerie, role-play (one time she was a Cowboys Cheerleader and he played Coach), tantra, they messed around with BDSM, *Kama Sutra*, they bought toys and outfits, they watched porn of almost every type (many of which they regretted immediately), they tried dirty talk, they tried dirty dirty talk, they tried filthy talk, they tried age play, anal play, she sucked his toes and he sucked her toes, they got dressed up as a unicorn and a bunny rabbit. And while they had fun, and laughed more than they had in years, there was no well-cooked tube steak and no coconut cream explosion.

While Teddy laughed with Belle, inside he died. His failure, his impotence, and his humiliation were complete, and part of him died. Outwardly he was the same man he always was, but inside his soul had been crushed, destroyed, his confidence was gone, the soft swagger with which he had always walked through life just an act. He stopped seeing his therapist, stopped looking for a cure, stopped trying to fix himself. The idea that he would never be hard again, that he would never have sex with his wife again, that he would never feel like a man again, made him want to die. When he saw his friends, he wondered if they knew, when he met new people he wondered if they could sense it, when he was at work he wondered what his colleagues would think of him if they somehow learned. Every time he saw Belle he wondered if she was going to leave him, to find an actual man, to find someone who could be more than her friend. He expected it. He almost hoped for it, because he loved her and wanted her to have a complete life, and a complete husband, though if it happened, he wasn't sure if he would survive it. She was his best friend, the only person who knew what lay beneath his polished, handsome, charming veneer, the only woman he had ever loved, the woman he had committed to for life. He wasn't sure if he would survive it.

They were at dinner, alone, on a date, the kind that in brighter days would have ended with a hot, fun, intimate, loving fuckfest in their bedroom, their appetizers having just been cleared, when he told her she was free to pursue sexual pleasure with other men. He wanted her to be free to indulge herself, her body, that part of her life, he wanted her to be a woman in every way it meant to be a woman. He asked that she consider a few requests if she decided to do so. They were

Don't bring it home.

Don't say I love you.

If you're going to leave me, give me fair warning.

She was silent. And they stared at each other across the table. In a way that they hadn't for many many years. They stared into each other's eyes, into each other's hearts, into each other's souls, into whatever it is inside of us that we don't have words to properly describe, that deep, deep part of us, that part of us that we think no one will ever know, and they knew. They stared with love and longing, with love and pain, with love and forgiveness. And she forgave him for whatever happened, and he forgave her for whatever was going to happen. And after staring, and staring, and staring, she stood and stepped to him and she leaned over and softly kissed his lips, and whispered

I will always love you, Teddy Moore.

And somehow the burden was lifted. Not entirely, it was still always with him, but at least in a way that made him able to keep going, even if that burden sometimes got real heavy. So that when she brought up the party, he was surprised, and hesitant. He didn't want to share his shame with anyone else, and he didn't want to be expected to perform, when he knew he couldn't. She asked that he keep an open mind, that if nothing else it would be a great story, and they planned on inviting some people they didn't believe would participate, and one woman in particular, one woman she would make sure he was with if and when it came time for everyone to find private spaces.

He wondered about the woman.

He wondered what they would do or talk about while their spouses were in the same house fucking other people, or maybe each other.

He wondered how much heavier the weight would be the day after.

His failure, his impotence, his humiliation.

How much heavier the weight.

So heavy.

So very heavy.

So very heavy.

The Culling

They had each made a list.

Devon's had nine couples.

Eighteen people.

Belle's had twelve.

Twenty-four.

There were four overlaps.

Both lists were too large.

Both knew it.

They sat outside, on Devon's back patio. On comfortable, absurdly expensive modern furniture resting on a Carrara marble floor, a Carrara marble pool a tasteful distance away, gardens mimicking Giverny just beyond, in the distance a pond, with water lilies, swans. They each had a glass of rosé, an unsmoked joint on the table before them, bowls of edamame, pistachios, olives. Devon took a sip of her wine, spots of the sun dappling across her golden hair, her olive skin.

They need to be discreet.

Belle, in the shade wearing a Cowboys hat, her rosy cheeks having had more than enough summer sun, nodded.

Obviously.

They need to be beautiful.

Duh.

They need to be down.

Double duh.

They both laughed. Devon looked at her list.

The Fairchilds?

Definitely not.

Why?

He drinks too much and has terrible breath, she's as tight as a nun.

Devon laughed, looked back at the list.

Chaunceys?

I've seen her naked in the club locker room. Trust me, no.

Laughed again.

Carrintons?

She doesn't shave her pussy. I don't know about your husband, but that's a hard no for mine.

Hard no.

Hunters?

Alexander the Great?

Yes.

Obviously.

Do you think she's down?

Grace will come to make him happy.

You think?

He cheats. He probably has big appetites. She's probably tired of trying to fill them, but still trying. We'll match her up with Teddy. He'll like her. That cute red hair and her freckles. And he'll be gentle.

Devon laughed.

Devereauxs?

Do we have to hear him talk?

I'll take that as a no as well.

He never shuts up.

There will be no opportunity for him to start a conversation.

What about Charlie?

Of course.

For me?

Of course.

You're cool with that?

He's all yours. You'll have a ball.

His girlfriend?

From what he tells me she's a real wildcat.

The math teacher?

Katy something, supposedly insatiable.

Wow, I would have never guessed.

You never really know.

Until you know.

They both laughed. Belle took a sip, a large one.

Is that it?

Did we cap it at four?

Any more and it starts getting risky.

Any more and we might hear each other.

Devon motioned to the gigantic stone house looming over them, modeled after a French château and built in 1913 by a railroad tycoon as a gift for his daughter, thus known as Le Cadeau Chateaux both locally and by fancy design magazines the world over.

We could have forty in there and we wouldn't hear each other. I think four keeps it intimate. The more intimate the better. I want everyone to feel safe and comfortable enough to get a little wild.

If Charlie is everything I hear he is, I'm getting a lotta wild.

Prepare yourself.

I am prepared.

Devon motioned to the joint.

Should we smoke that thing?

You got anything else to do today?

Nothing the babysitters can't handle.

Light it up.

They lit it up, smoked it, and spent the rest of the afternoon drinking rosé and floating in the pool.

A Boy in Blue

They called him a hero, though he never really felt like one. He was just doing his job. And put in the same position, he believed most police officers would have done the same thing.

It was his third year on the force. He was a patrol officer in Hunts Point, the Bronx. His partner drove, he rode shotgun. They got a call for shots fired in a car chase on Randall Avenue. They were close, they responded. When they arrived two men with handguns were approaching a car that had hit a telephone pole. Smoke was coming from under the hood of the wrecked car. He and his partner got out of their vehicle, drew their weapons. His partner issued a verbal command to the armed men.

Stop and drop your weapons.

The men turned and started shooting. His partner was shot in the head and immediately went down. He shot back and killed one of the men. The other kept firing. He was shot once in the arm and once in the leg. But he also kept firing. And he killed the second man.

He approached the car, limping, bleeding, in shock. The car was on fire, flames shooting out from the engine. There was a young child in the back, strapped into a baby seat, screaming. A woman behind the wheel, head down, knocked out, bleeding. A man in the passenger seat, head down, knocked out, bleeding.

He opened the back door, unhooked the baby seat and took it out, baby still strapped into it, set the baby thirty feet away. He went back, opened the driver's door, unhooked the seat belt, dragged the woman thirty feet next to the baby. He went back, opened the passenger's door, unhooked the seat belt, and started dragging the man away. As he did, the car exploded, and he was knocked off his feet and knocked out. When police and the fire department arrived, he was face-down on the concrete. The baby, and her mother and her father, were all alive. His partner and the two shooters were not.

David Genovese spent three days in the hospital. Two clean through–and–through gunshot wounds and a concussion from the explosion. Doctors said he would be fine. He needed rest, he needed calm. When he left the hospital, his life was changed. He was a Hero. The Finest of the Finest. New York's Miracle Man. Super Cop. The shooters had mistaken the man in the car for a rival drug dealer. Both he and his wife were teachers. They were taking their daughter to her cousin's birthday party when the shooters started chasing them. It was the biggest media story of the year in New York. When David left the hospital he went out a service entrance in a laundry truck. There were hordes of reporters at all of the public entrances waiting to see him, speak to him, get his picture.

He lived in Upper Manhattan, near the border of the Bronx. He had grown up in Connecticut, and loved the Yankees, so when he joined the NYPD, he found a place near the stadium. He went to as many games as he could during the season, always sitting in the right-field bleachers. It was a clean and safe but humble neighborhood. If there was a calm place on the Island of Manhattan, this was it.

He wished he was going back to it.

The calm.

But there were hordes of reporters waiting outside his apartment building, the block was lined with their vehicles, their gear. During the drive over, the NYPD had taken him out of the laundry truck and put him in an SUV that was escorted by marked cars. As he walked, or rather limped, into the building, he was surrounded by police who were keeping the hordes away. He wore a Yankees hat, pulled low, didn't look up, didn't say a word.

The next days, weeks, months were a blur. He went to his partner's funeral, attended by thousands of other officers, and thousands of civilians, helped carry his coffin, put him to rest. He was given the NYPD Medal of Honor for Exceptional Valor, the highest award one can receive as an NYPD Officer. He was media trained, and though he was uncomfortable talking about what happened, at the request of the Department, he spoke to reporters from the *New York Times* and *New York Post*, went on TV talk shows, did the high-prestige circuit. He appeared at NYPD events with the Chief of Police, City Council Members, the Mayor. People stopped him on the street, asked for his picture, took it whether he was okay with it or not. He did not enjoy any of it, but he considered it his duty, a part of his job as a police officer, to represent the Police Department in the best way possible. If putting on a show was his way of contributing, he would put on a show. The only part of it he liked and he fucking loved it was getting free tickets to sporting events if he agreed to wave on the jumbotron. He went to everything, got the best seats in the house for free. He saw teams he loved the Giants, the Knicks and the Rangers, he went to the US Open and sat courtside, and on the best day of his life, he threw out the first pitch at a Yankee game to a standing ovation fuck yeah David Genovese, you earned it.

But he got tired.

Some people might have reveled in it, he just got tired.

He missed the simplicity of his previous life, the routine, the anonymity.

The calm.

He spoke to his superiors about some kind of graceful exit, out of the Department, out of New York.

And he made one.

He had grown up in Danbury. Working-class Connecticut. Lovely, as Connecticut is truly lovely.

Beautiful trees.

Streams. Still-wild fields.

But the working-class version.

His father drove a truck, his mother was a bank teller.

He wanted to be closer, but not too close.

A job came available in New Bethlehem, Sergeant, Investigative Division. David applied and had a series of interviews with the police and the retired investment bankers and CEOs who ran New

Bethlehem; he was thrilled when they offered him the job and New Bethlehem was thrilled to have him join their force. They always tried to hire the best of the best, and he certainly qualified.

The best of the best!

Hero!

He got a small house in town. As humble a house as existed in New Bethlehem. A two-bedroom, two-bath, two-story white colonial with a small patch of his own beautiful green grass and a one-car garage. He could walk to Main and Maple Streets, and walk to the police station or the train station. The job wasn't at all like what he'd been doing in the Bronx, there were robberies, car thefts, an occasional fight at a restaurant bar, some domestic violence, some drugs, but it was still real police work—catching people doing bad things. It brought him great satisfaction. It mattered to him.

And he loved the town. Its beauty and relative safety. That it still believed in education and that community still mattered and could improve people's lives. That, for the most part, its residents supported the police morally, socially and financially. He imagined himself staying for a long time. He imagined raising a family in New Bethlehem. He would never be rich, or live in their world, but he could create a beautiful world of his own, rich in other ways.

When he saw the body, he didn't believe what he saw.

Murders didn't happen in New Bethlehem.

And if they did.

Fuck.

Not like that.

Not like that.

Not like that.

Shock, Surprise, and Promise of Pleasure

During the planning, organizing, and strategizing stages of the days and weeks before the party happened, there were many issues that required great debate between Devon and Belle, and deep contemplation from both in order to make decisions. Would there be a dress code, how would they make everyone believe the pairings were random when they weren't, would they serve food, what kind of booze and what kind of drugs, toys or no toys maybe save toys for the next party as a special surprise, Friday night or Saturday night? None, however, was as difficult as the debate and thought-period that occurred over the issue of invitations, and what they would say, and how they would be delivered. There were so many options.

Should it be formal or informal?

If formal, how formal? If informal, funny or casual?

Should it be paper or digital? Should it be hand-delivered?

Did they need to send an NDA with it? What if they didn't have an NDA and someone talked?

Should a care package accompany it? What should be in the care package? Toys, lingerie, wine, cocaine?

Did they need to make a soft approach before sending the invitation? If they made a soft approach, did they go to the husbands or the wives or handle on a case-by-case basis?

How should they handle RSVPs?

During this period of intense debate and deliberation, Devon and Belle spoke or texted or DMed each other between ten and thirty-five times a day. Devon called a friend in Pacific Palisades, California, a town very similar to New Bethlehem, who had experience in such matters. Belle texted and called friends in Ibiza and Dallas. Both scoured the internet, and Belle asked her AI chatbot. They got different answers and opinions from everyone, and no help at all from the chatbot, which said

I cannot provide information or guidance on topics related to explicit or adult content. If you have any other nonexplicit questions, please feel free to ask, and I'll be happy to help.

When she spoke to Billy about it, he wanted to have his attorneys draw up the invitation and include an ironclad and extremely punitive NDA. Tired of the debate and exhausted from thinking about it, Devon ultimately made the decision herself. As she said

My house, my party, my invitation.

And what she decided was to make a soft approach, followed by flowers and an invitation. The flowers would be beautiful and the invitation tasteful and discreet. The reaction to the soft approach would determine if an invitation was sent, and there would be nothing in writing that would definitively state what kind of party they were having. Should they need it for some reason, she and Billy would have plausible deniability.

When she called Charlie, he didn't initially believe, and when she convinced him she was serious, his reaction was

Fuck yeah!!!

When Devon asked about his girlfriend, he told her that Katy would probably be more excited than he was, and that every man there would probably fall in love with her. Devon asked for her address, and for Charlie to speak with her.

She debated whether to approach Grace or Alex Hunter. She didn't know either well. She did know their reputations. Alexander the Great, magnificent athlete, loved to party, was absolutely not faithful to his wife, rumored to be great in bed. Grace Hunter, beautiful girl next door, devoted wife and mother, great tennis player, rumored to have a wild side. Alex likely made the social decisions. He was the local hero, the former NFL quarterback. Grace either knew he cheated, or knew of the rumors that he cheated, and she hadn't left him, so maybe she played on the side as well, just more discreetly.

She approached Alex. She had a strategy. She believed it would work and she needed it to work for her greater plan to work. Flirt with him and stroke his ego. Men were so simple. Governed by their dicks and their vanity. She asked Billy to get her his number. He got a work number and Devon called Alex's office, where she was told he no longer worked there. She called Billy back. He told her to find the number herself, that he was not her assistant. She got hold of the town lacrosse program directory, which had a cell number. She called it, he answered on the first ring.

Alex Hunter.

Hello, Alex. It's Devon McCallister.

Hello, Devon.

Hi.

This is a surprise. How can I help you?

I want to invite you to a party, but it's a very specific, and very private, kind of party.

I love parties, I'm intrigued.

I've heard you love parties, Alex.

Where'd you hear that?

I've heard lots of things about you.

Oh yeah?

Yes.

Such as?

Sports aren't the only reason you're called Alexander the Great.

He's silent for a moment.

I'm not sure how to respond, Devon.

Come to my party. Bring Grace. It will be very small, and discreet. And I promise that you'll have a chance to show me if what I have heard is true, Alexander the Great.

What kind of party is this?

It's the kind of party where people fuck other people's spouses.

Sounds like my kind of party.

If you can convince Grace to come, I want you to fuck me.

He's silent for another moment.

Is this some kind of prank?

No, Alex, it's not a prank, it's a real invitation, one I hope you will accept.

When is this party? Where?

I know my number just showed up on your phone. Talk to Grace. Text me yes or no in the next twenty-four hours. If it's yes, you'll receive a more formal invitation with the details.

Cool. Thank you. I'll text you.

I'm looking forward to seeing you, Alex. And spending some time together.

She hung up.

She smiled.

She knew.

He was hers.

He was going to be hers.

Alex was dizzy.

He had been dizzy for most of the day. Ever since Devon's call.

Heart pounding, hands quivering. Thoughts racing through his mind.

Pounding quivering racing. Dizzy.

Though he had cheated on Grace dozens of times, he'd never been so directly approached by a woman. And no one had ever asked him to include his wife in the fun. The McCallisters were the richest family in New Bethlehem. Or the richest that was public about their wealth. Devon was the most beautiful woman in town. It was all a win/win for him. If he met Billy McCallister and got along with him, he could either try to get a job with him or ask him for help finding a job. If he was unable to get a job with or help from Billy, he'd get to fuck his wife, which he, and every other man in town, had thought about every time he'd ever seen her.

On the train home he thought about how to ask Grace. Although she'd been wild when she was younger, those days were long past. Now she liked to play tennis, volunteer, drive the kids around, drink wine with her friends, nag him about pretty much everything, and if he was lucky, have quick boring missionary sex once a month, or once every couple months. He didn't think she would say yes to a swing party, a key party, a wife-swapping party, whatever you wanted to call it. And he knew if he asked her, and she reacted the way he believed she would, he would have no chance of getting to go to the party. He was desperate. This was the chance he'd been waiting for, the chance to potentially make everything right. He'd rather go to the party and pretend he didn't know what it was, and pretend to be as surprised as Grace would be, and deal with the fallout the next day. She might not fuck whomever she was matched with, but he knew she also wouldn't make a scene. It would give him a chance to do what he needed to do with Billy, and what he wanted to do with Devon.

He took his phone out of his pocket. He found Devon's number in the call log. He hit the icon to text her, typed one word.

Yes.

And he hit send.

———

Katy was grading quizzes. Seventh-grade advanced math. Algebraic expressions and one-variable equations and inequalities, which led to ratios and proportions, which led to statistics and probability, which led, at the end of the year, to basic geometry. Half the students scored above 95, most of the rest above 90, two in the 80s, one 78. Part of what Katy loved about her job is that the students all came to learn, to excel, to achieve, that in New Bethlehem, the cool were the best students, and the most well behaved. And though she had never taught anywhere else, she knew from the internships and TA stints she did while she was in school that this wasn't the case in most schools or school systems. While she didn't love some aspects of the town, the extreme wealth and privilege, the safe homogenous bubble in which the town existed, she did love that those conditions produced kids who wanted to learn, who were motivated to learn, and who were expected to achieve. It made her job vastly easier, and vastly more enjoyable.

There was a knock on the door. She wasn't expecting anyone. Sometimes Charlie showed up without calling, but she knew he had a game and wouldn't be done until later. As she walked toward the door, there was another knock. If she were almost anywhere else she might be worried, but there was almost no crime in New Bethlehem. An occasional car theft. Drunk dads fighting at one of the two local taverns. The local jewelry store had been robbed a few years back. It was probably a food-delivery person who went to the wrong address.

She looked through the keyhole. An attractive woman with a beautiful arrangement of flowers. Charlie had never sent her flowers before. He had given her beer and weed. He bought her a Rangers hat. He got her an ashtray when he went to Puerto Rico, and a signed puck on a trip to Ottawa, but never flowers. She was excited. She opened the door.

The woman smiled.

Katy?

Yes.

From Mrs. Kensington McCallister. With love and great anticipation.

Katy looked at her for a brief moment, confused. The flowers were gorgeous white, pale-pink, and mauve lilies in a white porcelain vase. Katy could see a card with her name on it, so she knew it wasn't a mistake. But she also had no idea why Devon Kensington, who she did not know and had never met, would be sending her flowers.

———

Belle and Teddy were having dinner together at home. Belle had Japanese food and sake delivered from his favorite restaurant. The flowers Devon had sent were in the middle of the table, gorgeous, radiant. Belle was wearing a white silk blouse she knew Teddy loved, and whether he knew it or not, was the shirt she'd worn on the night they had last made sweet sweet marital love. With two daughters away at boarding school and an eighth grader who wanted little to do with them, they often ate together at home. This, though, was clearly a step up. As they started to eat, and finished talking about their respective days, Teddy smiled, and prepared himself for whatever was coming, and he knew something was coming.

You going to tell me what's going on?

Belle smiled.

What do you mean?

Teddy chuckled, motioned to the spread in front of them.

All of this?

Maybe I just love you and wanted to have a lovely dinner with you.

I do believe you love me.

Good. I do. Very much.

And I know you love a great meal.

With you.

Yes. With me.

She smiles.

But I also know when you put together a dinner because you want to talk about something or you have something to tell me.

How do you think you know that?

You always wear something cute.

It's one of my favorite blouses.

And mine.

I know.

And your accent is always a little thicker. You know I love your drawl. It comes out more.

You don't say?

He smiled.

I do say.

She smiled.

Is it that obvious?

Yes, but in a very very cute way.

She smiled, looked down, hesitated. He watched her, also smiling.

Out with it, Belle.

She looked up.

Devon invited us to a party. She's having it, but it was kind of my idea.

What kind of party?

A swingers' party.

He laughed.

Seriously?

Yes.

You want me to go to a swingers' party.

Yes.

He laughed again, incredulous.

My dick doesn't work, Belle.

Yes, but. . . .

But what? Do you want that to become public for some reason? Is this some weird exercise in humiliation?

No. No no no no. Not at all.

He's more incredulous.

I mean, what the fuck.

You don't need to swear.

I think, given the situation, swearing is perfectly appropriate.

Belle took a deep breath, she knew this was her shot to turn it around.

Devon and I thought it would be fun. We spent a ton of time thinking about it and figuring it out. It's going to be very small. We're pretty confident one of the wives won't be down to actually do anything, and we're going to arrange it so you are paired with her.

Who?

Grace Hunter.

The redhead?

Her freckles are so cute. And she has a great body.

He laughed.

So I'll get to sit in a room with Grace Hunter and make small talk while you're fucking her husband?

Devon is going to fuck her husband.

Who are you going to fuck?

Charlie Dunlap.

The hockey coach?

Yes.

He laughed.

You've lost your fucking mind. You and Devon have lost your fucking minds.

————

Billy was excited.

Very excited.

More excited than he'd been in a long time, at least outside of work, where information and returns always excited him.

He thought it heralded a new age of openness between him and Devon.

Maybe he could stop hiding all his fun.

Maybe she'd join in.

Maybe they could have threesomes.

Maybe they could have them regularly.

Billy liked that idea.

When Devon had first brought it up, he thought she was fucking with him.

But she was serious.

There was a guest list, which she gave him, he was going to have his security team check everyone on it, he'd know everything there was to know about them.

There was a date. Invitations were out. It was a new world.

One where he could do whatever he wanted, with whoever he wanted.

Just the way he liked it.

If he only knew.

Man plans.

God laughs.

Ha ha.

Ha ha.

————

The flowers were lovely, and clearly very expensive.

Grace didn't understand why Devon Kensington McCallister had sent them and why the card said *Let's Play* with a date and time. She figured it was something with Alex, probably some sports fundraiser or an event related to one of the boards he was on or the teams he coached. Whatever it was, she was excited to see Devon's house. She'd heard it was epic.

She put the flowers in the middle of the table where she and the kids ate all of their meals together. When Alex came home that evening, he said he was working late, he told her that they'd been invited to a dinner party at the McCallisters' house, and didn't know what Let's Play meant or why they sent flowers, but he thought they were pretty.

———————

Sometimes Charlie knocked, sometimes he just walked in, sometimes Katy was up, sometimes she was sleeping and he woke her up. Sometimes he didn't come at all. They had a casual relationship. Saw each other two or three times a week. Always at her place. She, and most of the women who had ever stepped foot into it, didn't like the way Charlie's place smelled, a manly mix of sweaty hockey gear with faint touches of mildew, beer, and cheap cologne.

She'd texted him during his game. Come over tonight, need to talk.

They talked all the time, laughed and told jokes, said dirty, dirty things to each other behind closed doors. They had never had a serious conversation, though. They had never had a *talk*.

When he walked into her place she was sitting at her kitchen table.

Drinking a beer. A tobacco pouch between her cheek and gum. A book in front of her, she loved to read books, usually old novels.

There was a bouquet of fancy flowers on the table. A half-eaten slice of pepperoni pizza.

He smiled.

Hey, gorgeous.

Hi, Charlie.

What's up?

How was your game?

We won, 3–2. Little fuckers played great.

He walked to the fridge, opened it.

Cool if I have a beer?

Of course.

He grabbed a beer, an ice-cold American beer in a can, walked back to the table, sat down.

How was your night?

It was interesting. I got these flowers, hand-delivered, from your friend Devon. I'm a little confused.

Yeah, shit. I was gonna tell you about that, I forgot.

She laughed.

Not the first time.

He smiled, took a huge gulp of the ice-cold American beer.

Probably won't be the last.

She motioned toward the flowers.

You wanna tell me what's going on?

He took another huge gulp and said,

We got invited to a party.

What kinda party?

Motherfucking swingers' party.

She laughed.

You're kidding me.

With the third gulp, the can was empty.

Nope, not joking. They wanna swing with us.

He stood and walked back to the fridge.

Who's they?

Can I have another, maybe two?

She nodded.

Who's they?

Devon, and her friend Belle. Not sure who else. They said it's going to be small.

I'm not going.

Why?

I don't mix business with pleasure.

What kind of business are you talking about?

I'm a teacher in town. What if the parents of a student are there? What if I have one of them somewhere down the line? I never play around here. I'm not gonna start now.

I told them you'd be into it.

I don't want or need any complications.

It'll be fun.

No.

They have a super crazy big house that's cool as fuck.

Don't care.

I bet they'll have fancy food, and I know you love fancy food.

Would rather starve.

Please.

You should have talked to me before you said yes.

I got really excited and just said it.

Can't do that.

My head. You know. Impulse control and shit.

She laughed.

Can you call and tell them no?

It would fuck up so much shit for me. You know you can't fuck with rich people. They're fucking mean.

That's why you don't get involved with them.

What can I do to change your mind?

Fill my car with gas.

Done.

Buy me a case of beer.

Done.

Get me tickets to a Rangers game.

Tricky, but possible.

Not the right answer.

Done.

I don't want to fuck anyone or even fuck around with anyone at the party. If they're cool with that, I'll go.

Thank you, Katy. You're the fucking best.

————

Charlie never called Devon. He told Katy he did. And he told Katy everything was cool.

The Tea

Belle told her friend Kristin about the party but asked her not to tell anyone she promised.

Kristin told Rebecca and Julia but asked them not to tell anyone, they promised.

Julia told Abby and Courtney and Diane but asked them not to tell anyone they promised.

Rebecca told Taylor and Casey and Molly and Elisa but asked them not to tell anyone they promised.

Abby told Kimberly and Laurel but asked them not to tell anyone they promised.

Courtney told Raquel and Erin and Anna and Amanda and Shannon and Caitlin but asked them not to tell anyone they promised.

Diane told Jenny and Zoe but asked them not to tell anyone they promised.

Taylor told her mother but asked her not to tell anyone she promised.

Casey told Meredith and Aubrey but asked them not to tell anyone they promised.

Molly told Hilary and Alexandra and Grace but asked them not to tell anyone they promised.

Elisa told Cammie and Liz and Samantha (goes by Sam) and Catherine but asked them not to tell anyone they promised.

Kimberly told Stephanie and Trish and Betsy but asked them not to tell anyone they promised.

Laurel told Julie and Megan and Olivia but asked them not to tell anyone they promised.

Raquel told her entire tennis group, a total of twelve women.

Erin told Chloe and Emma and Sarah but asked them not to tell anyone they promised.

Anna told Danielle and Sydney but asked them not to tell anyone they promised.

Amanda told all of the women on the New Bethlehem Country Day auction committee and they discussed whether they should talk to the school's Headmaster about it.

Shannon told Jane and Michele and Cynthia but asked them not to tell anyone they promised.

Caitlin told her daughter's piano teacher and her son's squash coach and her other daughter's dance instructor (ballet and hip-hop!).

Jenny told Tess and Amy and Tracy.

Zoe told her husband Kevin who worked with Billy he wasn't surprised.

Not a single woman who was told about the party kept the secret. By the end of the day all of New Bethlehem knew Devon was having some kind of swingers' party, and though almost all of them said they thought it was gross and inappropriate, almost all of them also wished they had been invited.

Pura Vida

It wasn't an easy job, but it wasn't particularly difficult either.

Clean the house. Do the laundry. Keep the refrigerators stocked. There were two large ones in the kitchen, one in the family room and one in the guesthouse.

Occasionally Devon asked her to get her some weed.

Occasionally Billy paid her to suck his dick or fuck him.

It could've been worse.

And in the end, it was worth whatever she'd had to endure, and whatever she had to do.

More than worth it.

Ana grew up in Costa Rica. In one of the few bad parts of Costa Rica. Which most Americans think of as some tropical paradise with good schools and good health care and progressive environmental laws. But like everywhere, or almost everywhere, there were some sections of it that weren't paradise. The neighborhood in San Jose where she grew up, Santa Rita de Alajuela, was known as El Infiernillo, or, for you gringos who don't speak Spanish, the Little Hell. Just outside of the city, near the airport, El Infiernillo was Costa Rica's main market and transport point for drugs. At any given time, there were between three and six gangs vying for control. Ana's father was in one, along with both of her brothers, all of her cousins, and her husband. Her father was killed when she was twelve, her older brother when she was sixteen, her younger brother when she was eighteen. She got married at nineteen and had a daughter at twenty. Her husband's father was killed shortly after. Both Ana and her husband were involved in the family business, and believing they might be next, decided to come to the United States. Stamford, Connecticut, has a large Costa Rican population; she had a distant cousin who lived there, working as a nanny for a wealthy family in Greenwich. Ana and her husband borrowed money from her mother, and bought plane tickets to New York. Upon arrival they went to Stamford and started looking for work, and stayed at her cousin's place. They both found work relatively quickly. Her husband on a landscaping truck, Ana as part of a housekeeping crew. They were paid in cash and saved their money and within a couple months had their own place. It was a one-bedroom studio in a sketchy neighborhood, but vastly better and safer than where they lived in Costa Rica. There was a house nearby where an older Costa Rican woman ran an unofficial daycare, watching the children of women who worked on the cleaning crews.

She met Devon when she was cleaning her house after a party. It was a big party, and the house, and the area around the pool, and the guesthouse, were a mess, wineglasses and plates and dirty napkins and assorted trash all over the place. While she was cleaning a guest bedroom, which had clearly been used during the party, Ana found a single large diamond earring on the floor, just under the bed. She thought about keeping it, and wanted to keep it, and didn't think the rich woman who lost it would probably miss it, but when she was taking a bag of trash to the garage, where all of the trash was being organized, she heard Devon, whose name she didn't know at the time, asking if anyone had found it. She didn't say anything, kept it in her pocket. Later she heard Devon asking the woman who ran the crew if she knew anyone who was looking for a full-time housekeeping job, that the reason she'd hired them was her normal housekeeper had just left, that her husband could be demanding, and she needed someone pretty tough. The woman who ran the crew, one of several that were under the supervision of another woman, offered her own services. Devon asked for her number and said she'd call her and have her back to discuss. Ana knew there was an opportunity for her, and that trading the diamond earring in her pocket for a full-time job with a wealthy New Bethlehem woman would be great for her, and for her family. Later that day, she saw Devon sitting at a desk in her home office, looking at paintings of big blocks of color on the internet. She knocked and Devon invited her in, and Ana held out the earring. Devon smiled and stood up and hugged her and asked her where she found it, Ana said on the floor of the guest room, next to the bed. Devon smiled again, a sly smile, and said

Thank God you found it and not my husband.

Ana was young and beautiful, thin, petite, long black hair in a ponytail, olive skin, large brown eyes. Devon was curious, and started asking Ana more questions. Where was she from, where did she live, how long had she been in America, basic questions about her life. Ana's English wasn't great, and Devon spoke functional Spanish, and they moved back and forth between them. During the conversation, Ana's boss came by and told her to get back to work, and apologized to Devon for the interruption. Devon said no, that she had invited Ana in, and that everything was cool. When the boss left, Devon offered Ana the job. Returning the earring, she believed, showed honesty and integrity, and Devon liked that Ana was young and attractive.

Ana was thrilled. It was regular, steady, reliable work. She was paid in cash, almost three times as much per week as she was making with the cleaning crew. Devon also got her a car, an Audi station wagon, which she used to drive to and from work, and for errands while working, and for her own use when she wasn't working. After six months they provided Ana and her husband and her daughter with health insurance. Devon believed in treating people well, and with kindness and generosity, but she also knew it bred loyalty, and that's what she needed most at her home and in her life, trust and loyalty.

Over time, Devon and Ana became friends. They would often hang out together in the kitchen, or the back patio, drink coffee or beer or smoke weed. They'd shop together, occasionally have lunch or dinner. Devon helped Ana improve her English, and Ana helped Devon improve her Spanish. Ana took the job seriously, but she also knew Devon wouldn't freak out if something didn't get done, or if she made a mistake. They'd talk about kids, their husbands, their girlfriends, about the state of the world. Ana hoped to someday go back to Costa Rica, not to El Infiernillo, but to one of the beach towns,

Nosara or Tamarindo or Santa Teresa. Devon said she hoped someday she could help make that happen, and that she loved Costa Rica as well, and might come along. Though they were polar opposites, and would likely never have been friends in any other situation, in this one, the friendship worked. They admired each other and respected each other. They trusted each other.

A year into the job, Ana's husband was out with their daughter at a local playground. A fight broke out between two other fathers and he tried to break it up. Police came and he was detained, and he and their daughter were taken into custody by immigration officials. They were in the United States illegally, and they were going to be deported back to Costa Rica. Ana's husband did not mention her, and had their daughter do the same, so that hopefully Ana could stay in the States and continue to work, and hopefully they could come back. Throughout the process, Devon tried to help Ana and her family, and asked Billy to help them, but he was concerned that getting involved might affect his business, or end up in the paper, so he did nothing, and he prevented Devon from doing anything. The fight that ensued was the worst of their marriage. They both screamed, yelled, said terrible things to each other. Ana heard it all, and Ana never forgot what she heard.

After her husband and daughter had been sent back to Costa Rica, Devon asked Ana to move into the guesthouse. She would live rent free and be able to wire more money back to Costa Rica, instead of spending it on rent and living expenses. Devon also wanted to be there for Ana as she mourned them, and as she struggled with life without them, however temporary it might be. When Ana moved in they became close, jokingly calling each other Sisters from different Misters. They also bonded over their feelings about Billy. Billy could be absent, and occasionally emotionally or psychologically abusive with Devon, yelling at her, calling her stupid, ignoring her, but he stepped it up with Ana. Once she was in the guesthouse, he started making sexual advances toward her, offering her money for sex, threatening to have her deported, too, if she didn't do what he asked, when he asked. Ana's childhood had hardened her. It wasn't the first time a powerful man had tried to impose his will on her, or take advantage of her, or believe that he could do what he wanted with her body. She debated whether to go to Devon and tell her. And at first she didn't. She took Billy's money and did what he wanted her to do. She'd get high when she knew he was coming and she'd check out while he did whatever he did. But he started coming too often, and started to get rough, and it started to wear on her, on her body, on her heart, on her soul.

She went to Devon. Devon wasn't surprised. She thought something was happening, but didn't know what to do. Devon wanted to call the police. She was tired of Billy. She wanted to escape. She thought the police would at least give her a way to start, to start figuring out how to get the fuck away, to get them both the fuck away. Ana said no. She believed the police would only make everything worse. She'd never had a positive interaction with the police in her entire life, and she'd had many, many, many interactions with them. Plus Billy had told her if she ever went to them or went to Devon or tried to hurt him in any way, he would destroy her, and her family, and that his money gave him the ability to do anything, to get away with anything. And he was right.

Money can buy anything, it can absolve anything.

Ana just wanted it to stop. Would Devon ask him to stop? Of course Devon would, and of course Devon did. And she and Ana made a pact. Like sisters do.

If he didn't stop, they would stop him.

Important Details

Devon and Belle were sitting in Belle's kitchen. Both were wearing high-end designer yoga gear made out of ethically sourced, sustainable materials, and both were swimming in the serenity they achieved in their Kundalini class. Their instructor, who went by the one-word name Harmony, came out from New York once a week to teach their class. They never missed it. They needed their serenity, and had agreed to make final decisions about their party while they still had it. Belle spoke.

Let's get into it.

While we still have the glow.

It's so good.

The fucking best.

What are we going to do about food?

Do we even need it?

We should have something.

Sushi?

Not everyone likes sushi.

With tempura, fried rice, and dumplings?

But no teriyaki sauce. That could lead to bad breath.

Agreed.

That's done.

Drinks?

We should have options.

But not too many.

Champagne?

Roederer.

Perfect.

Vodka and tequila?

Of course.

Beer?

No.

What about Charlie?

Fuck him.

Belle smiled.

I'm going to fuck him, all night.

Devon laughed. Belle smiled.

Drugs?

I think we should have them, but have them be optional.

What do you have?

Billy's got a dealer, so we can get whatever we want.

What are you thinking?

Ecstasy, mushrooms, weed, pink cocaine.

Pink cocaine?

It's supposedly what the dealers in Columbia use themselves.

So it's better?

I would think so. Billy says so.

Is he still using?

Not at home, and I don't ask and I don't know what he does when he's not here.

Can Billy get us whatever we want?

Yes, like I said, he has a dealer.

Like a shady old-school drug dealer?

Yes, but one who only sells to rich white guys.

Have you met him? Is he scary?

He's a nerd who trades Bitcoin and buys drugs on the deep web. He tries to dress like a gangster, though, it's kind of funny.

They both laughed. Belle spoke.

How are we going to separate, and where are we all going?

Devon smiled.

There will be envelopes with each person's name on them. The house has two wings, two floors, there are rooms on each wing and each floor appropriate for play.

Love it.

The women open their envelopes first and go to their rooms. The men open theirs two minutes later and join them.

Perfect.

We tell everyone it was random, but . . .

Obviously not.

They high-five each other. Belle speaks.

This is going to be great.

The best.

We could do it a couple times a year.

How about a couple times a month?

How about a couple times a week?

They both laughed. Belle spoke.

What do you think the day after will be like?

We're all adults, everyone knows what kind of party it is, everyone agreed to come.

True.

We should all smile and go about our lives.

With fond and exciting memories.

No fallout. No drama. No mess.

I hope you're right.

Devon smiled.

So do I.

The Pairings,
Logic and Reality

Devon Kensington McCallister and
Alex "Alexander the Great" Hunter

Mrs. McCallister was hosting the party, and had heard rumors that Mr. Hunter's nickname was applicable on both the athletic field and in the bedroom. As hostess, she gave herself first pick and chose Mr. Hunter. Given the nature of her marriage to Mr. McCallister, she hoped not only that Mr. Hunter's reputation was accurate and earned, but that after the party she could continue a consensual, discreet, and mutually satisfying sexual relationship with him. Mr. Hunter, of course, did regularly cheat on his wife, Mrs. Grace Hunter, and was hoping to fuck Mrs. McCallister, the richest, most beautiful, and most glamorous woman in New Bethlehem. Mr. Hunter also hoped that the relationship would continue after the party, and hoped that Mrs. McCallister would enjoy fucking him so much that she might ask her husband to either employ him or help him find employment, or perhaps lend him some money so that he didn't lose his house, or in the best-case scenario, simply give him some money so that he didn't lose his house.

Belle Hedges Moore and Charles "Mister Big Stick" Dunlap

Mrs. Hedges Moore was married to a man she loved, Mr. Theodore Moore, but he had been impotent for the previous six years, with no identifiable cause. And while Mrs. Moore had had sex with other men during Mr. Moore's extended period of flaccidity, she craved a session with someone who could satisfy her deepest sexual needs. She believed Mr. Dunlap to be capable of such a feat because her friend Mrs. McCallister had had sexual relations with him on a number of occasions, and had informed her that his nickname applied not only to his skills on the ice, but also to the size of his sausage stick and the manner in which he wielded said sausage stick. Charlie was excited to be invited to a party at Mrs. McCallister's house, and had much deeper feelings for her than he had ever acknowledged, he was in fact in love with her, and hoped he would be matched with her. If he wasn't, he would still do his best to have fun, and he would approach the evening's festivities with his usual enthusiasm and gusto.

Theodore "The Floppy Jalopy" Moore and Grace Hunter

As previously mentioned, Mr. Moore had not had an erection for several years. It tortured him, as it would any man. He dreaded the party, hated the idea of it, and hated himself for agreeing to attend it. He expected it to be another episode in his own personal series of humiliation. He did, however, love his wife, and would just do about anything for her, including the toleration of a few supremely awkward hours with an unknown woman who he hoped would be an engaging conversationalist. He was matched with Mrs. Grace Hunter, who was believed to be a prude, would likely not engage in any sexy time with him, thus making their encounter less miserable for Mr. Moore. Mrs. Hunter had no idea the party was anything other than a dinner party at what was known as the most beautiful and most exquisitely and expensively designed and furnished home in a town filled with exquisitely and expensively designed and furnished homes. She hoped to make a new friend or two, and hoped to have a nice evening and a good meal, and nothing more.

William McCallister and Katherine Boyle

Mr. McCallister needed no nickname. He was what he was, part man, part wild animal, driven to assert and acquire and accumulate and dominate, like the smartest rhinoceros to ever live, or a two thousand pound bull with a calculator in his head. Mr. McCallister was excited to have a night where he ingested high-quality chemical intoxicants and had some wild, unbridled sexy time. He had had a thorough background check done on Miss Boyle, who he believed would indulge his every want, need, and fantasy, and do so with a smile. His wife, Mrs. Devon Kensington McCallister, and her best bestie, Mrs. Belle Hedges Moore, also believed this to be the case, based on Mr. Charles Dunlap's description of her as a Boss Lady

Bone Machine and a sheet-shaking, booty-quaking, lovemaking, shag Goddess. And so they planned for the two of them to spend the evening together. And all believed it would be a successful introduction and physical union. Miss Boyle, however, was not prepared to follow that plan. While she could be all of the things Mr. Dunlap described her to be, and Mr. McCallister, Mrs. McCallister, and Mrs. Moore believed her to be, she was only that person, that, as Miss Boyle once described herself, piece of white creamy sexual chocolate, when she wanted to be, when she was attracted to the person or persons she was involved with, and when she gave her consent to the person or persons with whom she engaged in some bedroom rodeo action. She did not plan on giving her consent at the party. She didn't know who she'd be matched with, and she didn't care. She would show up as a favor to Charlie, and because she loved him in a way, in a fun, short-term, do-it-while-you're-young kind of way, but she didn't feel safe or comfortable getting involved with anyone she might someday encounter in her position as middle-grade math teacher and local travel-team lacrosse coach.

The Other War Room

Billy didn't know his real name.

Sometimes he went by Axel.

Sometimes Blade.

Lately it had been Gunnar.

He was a dealer and he traded Bitcoin. He said he changed his name to stay ahead of the law and of the IRS, so he could conduct his business in peace and so he wouldn't have to pay taxes. He'd buy passports and driver's licenses with different names on them from illicit markets on the dark web, which also was where he got his drugs. If you know where to look, you can buy anything on the internet. False identities, drugs, guns, credit card numbers, stolen cars, stolen art, passwords. Literally anything.

Billy had been buying from him for several years. Mostly drugs, but occasionally Gunnar had more interesting things, and occasionally Billy had specific requests. And Gunnar always delivered. Billy didn't know how and didn't want to know. Gunnar took special care of Billy because he always hoped that someday Billy would integrate Bitcoin into his business and hire Gunnar as a trader. They valued and respected and trusted each other. And knew each other's secrets.

Whenever Gunnar changed his name or phone number, he would text Billy, and all of his customers, who were mostly rich white men who worked in finance in New York and Connecticut, a code. The code was

Candy.

The day before the party, Billy went to visit Gunnar. He was living and working in a small white rancher surrounded by two acres of woods in Weston, Connecticut. When Billy arrived, Gunnar came out to greet him. He was, as he often was, dressed in tactical war gear, black camo clothing, a belt with a handgun, handcuffs, bear spray, three secure sat phones of the same type Billy used, and on the same network. He was short, chubby, wore thick black glasses with powerful lenses. His hair was thinning, dyed black, pulled into a mini ponytail on the top rear of his head. When people came to see him, and especially when Billy came to see him, he always tried to project what he called Alpha Energy.

What's up, bro?

He gave Billy a hug, a little too long and a little too firm. They went into Gunnar's house, which was filled with computers and gaming equipment and huge flat-screen TV screens and lounge chairs. It smelled of pizza and cologne. In some way, Billy knew that if a few things had gone differently for him, this could have been his life. He never stayed long.

What do you have for me today?

I've got the good shit, that's what I've fucking got for you.

He motioned for Billy to follow him. They walked down a hallway lined with photos of Gunnar with Eric Trump and Kanye West, his two idols. He'd attended parties with both several times, and always paid for the VIP experience, which included photos. They stopped in front of a door at the end of the hall. Gunnar punched a code into a digital keyboard on the wall and put his thumb on a scanner mounted to the door handle. Multiple locks clicked and they stepped into the room. Gunnar smiled.

Welcome to the War Room.

One wall had gun racks lined with AR-15s and AKs. One wall was lined with shelves filled with expensive sneakers, mostly limited edition Yeezys, a third had shelves covered with small statues and statuettes of anime characters, almost all of them Asian women with huge tits and huge asses, many in provocative poses. There were safes with digital locks and scanners in two corners. There were no windows. In the middle of the room there was a table with chairs on opposite sides. A cornucopia of drugs was carefully laid out on the table. Gunnar sat down on one side of the table, motioned for Billy to sit on the other.

What brings you here today, my friend?

My wife is having a swingers' party at our place. I want to get some things that will really make it swing.

Gunnar laughed.

Really?

Billy nodded.

Yes.

Your wife's a swinger?

She wants to give it a try.

You always say she's a spoiled bitch.

One who wants to swing.

I dated a girl once who was a swinger.

Yeah, what happened?

She left me for someone she met at the party.

That won't happen at our party.

You never know.

If someone stole my wife, I'd destroy her, and I'd destroy him, whoever he was. And I'm pretty sure everyone attending knows that.

Gunnar stared at him, impressed with his Alpha.

I respect that, Billy. That's how you have to be in the ugly world.

Keep it in mind.

Gunnar nodded.

Respect.

Billy smiled.

Now show me what you've got.

Gunnar motioned to the table, started describing what was on it. He had cocaine from Bolivia, Colombia, and Peru. Pink coke from LA, which has slight amounts of ketamine and ecstasy cut into it. He had mushrooms in raw form, in pills, in chocolate. He had twelve different strains of weed, four each of sativa, hybrid, and indica. He had ecstasy from the Netherlands. He had acid from Northern

California. And he had the rarest of recreational drugs, quaaludes. Gunnar picked one of the pills, small, round, white, and he spoke.

Big in the '70s and '80s?

Government banned them.

Why?

Government doesn't want people to have a good time.

What do they do?

Bliss.

Really?

The closest thing we've got.

If I slip one to a girl?

You didn't hear me say it, but she will be yours to do as you please.

She'll be in bliss.

Depending on how you define it.

Billy bought Bolivian coke, pink coke, sativa weed, ecstasy. Drugs that brought on pleasure and delight, drugs that heightened the senses, drugs that turned everything on, brightly. He bought these drugs for the party, to share with the guests.

Billy bought quaaludes for himself.

To use as he pleased.

And to use on someone else as he pleased.

La Fête

The Day of the Party arrived.

Every single person attending it thought of it from the moment they woke.

They thought and they felt.

Devon with hope.

Billy with need.

Belle with lust.

Teddy with dread.

Alex with desperation.

Grace with curiosity, at why this party seemed to have Alex behaving so differently.

Charlie with delight.

And Katy with curiosity, at how weird and uncomfortable it was likely going to be.

The deliveries began arriving at Devon's house shortly after ten o'clock.

————

Flowers from Ode à la Rose in New York orchids and lilies and roses for the entire house, everywhere.

Alcohol from the oldest and most expensive of the sixteen wine and spirits shops in New Bethlehem.

Pratesi linens for each of the beds in the rooms to be used later in the evening, towels from Hermes.

Cards from the calligrapher, Chopin script on G. Lalo stationery, beautifully rendered predetermined outcomes, and if one believed in such things, predestined.

A box from La Perla for Devon, two boxes, three.

Care packages for each room from an establishment in Norwalk called the Candy Store black boxes lined with black satin, inside each box condoms in multiple sizes, lube in multiple flavors, a small vibrator, a larger one, a blindfold, restraints for the wrists, restraints for the ankles.

Sushi and sashimi, tempura, fried rice and dumplings, no teriyaki sauce of any kind, edamame, as discussed and as decided.

The drugs.

———

Belle went for a manicure and a pedicure, her fingers and toes soaked in a sugar scrub, nails cut and filed, a paraffin wrap, deep red lacquer paint. Belle went for a chocolate wax, her ass, the inside of her thighs, her Texas honey, as she liked to say, everything clean and everything smooth. Belle went for an organic body exfoliation, an organic body wrap, an organic body polish. Belle went for a bee venom facial. Belle went to have her brows sculpted. Belle went to the salon for a trim just the ends, a wash, a blow–dry. Belle had a makeup artist and a stylist come to her house. Belle tried on five different little black dresses, seven pairs of black heels, debated whether to wear lingerie under, or wear nothing at all.

———

Teddy worked out in their home gym, went to the office and worked on a deal to buy an employment platform, had Caesar salad for lunch, worked on the deal a bit more, searched for Dick-Doesn't-Work Miracle Cures on the internet didn't see anything new, tried not to think about the party, tried not to think about what his wife might end up doing at the party, booked a golf trip to Georgia for the next weekend, looked at new golf shoes on the internet bought a pair of new golf shoes on the internet, did some more work, tried not to think about the party, tried not to think about what his wife might end up doing at the party.

———

Grace went for a run. Grace did the kids' laundry and cleaned their rooms. Grace went grocery shopping. Grace went to a committee meeting for the upcoming Lacrosse Association fundraiser. Grace met a friend for coffee, the friend was trying to lose weight, Grace told her over and over again she looked beautiful and didn't need to lose a pound. Grace met the kids at the bus stop. Grace took one kid to travel soccer and another to travel lacrosse. Grace went to the gas station and filled her SUV with gas, stopped at the wine store to pick up a bottle of white to bring to the party, picked up her and Alex's dry cleaning, got each of the kids from practice, went home. Grace made the kids dinner chicken parm and spaghetti and steamed broccoli.

———

Charlie did fifty extra push-ups before his morning shower, and fifty extra push-ups after his morning shower. He did two hundred stomach crunches. He brushed his teeth twice. He sent out email invoices to all of the parents who owed him money for private sessions, but thought about eating pussy and fucking the entire time. He went to a coach's meeting at the rink in Stamford where he coached a bantam travel team the program was finalizing the upcoming season's tournament schedule, he thought about eating pussy and fucking the entire time. He ran a practice for his squirt travel team they had big game in a couple days against the Connecticut Junior Rangers, who were coached by a former Ranger, and he was usually very focused on beating teams coached by former players, but all he thought about was eating pussy and fucking. He went home and did fifty extra push-ups before taking another shower. While in the shower, he used three extra squirts of his body wash and got fully lathered. While lathered, he very carefully shaved his cock and balls, before rinsing. He did fifty extra push-ups after the shower. He sprayed each wrist and the back of his neck with wisps of cologne, he gave his cock and balls a full spray. He checked himself out in the mirror. He liked what he saw in the mirror. He was happy he was made the way he was made.

———

Katy walked to school, as she did every day. In each of her classes she wondered if she would see the parents of one of her students at the party tonight, and she tried to guess which of them had parents who might swing. Though she was fairly set on not having any sort of sexual contact, she did think some of the dads in town were hot, and often wondered what they might be like in bed. She couldn't imagine that they had particularly exciting sex lives, if they had sex lives at all. She had lunch duty. She graded quizzes during her free period. She ran a lacrosse practice after school. She went for a run after practice. She went home and got ready. She made an effort, enough of one to look pretty great, but not all out, not even close to all out.

————

Alex didn't bother with the train. He needed to focus. The train and the whole stupid fucking charade of the train would just be a distraction. And he needed to focus. He drove to the Greenwich library. He parked and went inside and found a quiet corner with a comfortable chair and opened his laptop. He read several interviews with Devon, most before she was married, but a couple after, one in *Town & Country*, one in *Architectural Digest*. If his plan was going to work, he needed to do more than just fuck her brains out. He needed to get into her heart, into her soul, he needed her to think they were perfect soulmates. He needed her to think he was the man of her dreams. He needed her to think that he was magnificent enough to leave her husband. Alex had done research on him as well. Everyone in finance knew about Billy McCallister, in general-terms, but Alex went deep. And all of it told the same story, and that was that Billy was a dick. A bully. Mean, and likely abusive. Articles about him all said it in couched terms, used words like *aggressive, hard-nosed, uncompromising, demanding.* He must be an awful husband, and the fact that the party was happening was a sign she was looking. There was an opportunity. To have Devon, and have access to her money. It was an opportunity that would greatly benefit him. And if everything went as he hoped, would also benefit his soon-to-be ex-wife and his children. He was approaching the opportunity, which would start at the party, like it was a game, specifically a football game, the way he did it at Notre Dame, and in the NFL. Set a goal, study the opponent. Study them as deeply as possible, look for nuances, for holes, for weaknesses, make an intelligent plan that exploits those nuances and holes, those weaknesses, if your plan was good enough the opponent couldn't do anything to stop it. In this case, if the plan was good enough, she would be his, and he would be saved. He went over his plan in his head, he believed in it. He left the library. He went home and he went for a run. He could feel his virality flowing through his veins, he could feel his verve. He took a shower and shaved his chest, he was still strong, still in shape. He started getting ready. It was almost time.

———

Billy spent the morning reading the reports his security team compiled on each of the guests coming to his house for the party. He learned Alex was unemployed and almost broke. He learned his wife was sweet, and involved, and utterly ignorant of their impending doom. He saw Teddy's medical records and was surprised at the number of his prescriptions for erectile dysfunction drugs, and it made him think less of Teddy, and happy that his own dick still worked properly, and in fact, better than it had his entire life. He logged into Charlie's Instagram and read all of his DMs, including many to Billy's own wife, who apparently loved Charlie's big fat cock. More interesting were the DMs to his girlfriend, which were very very dirty, words pictures videos, the girlfriend was very attractive, and very sexually liberated, or adventurous, or wild, all of those words applied. Billy was into her, he wanted her. And when he read the report he had done on her, he wanted her more. He believed it was going to be a fun night. Hopefully for both of them. But definitely for him.

———

Ana received the deliveries.
Ana set out the flowers.

Ana prepared each of the bedrooms with the new sheets, new candles, erotic care packages.

Ana chilled the champagne, decanted the wine, let the spirits breathe, set out the proper glasses for each.

She carefully laid out the cards on the dining table.

At the appropriate time she set out the food, and the proper plating, and white porcelain chopsticks.

She went to her guesthouse and got ready.

She put on nice clothing.

Before she went back to the house, she called home.

Spoke to her husband, spoke to her daughter.

Told them she loved them.

Told them to keep their fingers crossed.

If tonight went well.

It would be the first step.

To coming home.

————

Devon in her bathroom. A long white vanity, black-veined Calacatta marble counters, a long mirror, a tasteful modern stool in the middle where she could sit and apply her makeup. Guerlain, La Prairie, and Orogold creams and beauty products, Azature nail polish, Jean Patou Joy perfume. Large picture windows overlooking the back gardens. It was as pristine and spotless, as perfectly organized, as elegant as a bathroom could be, designed and built to be an oasis, an oasis from her bedroom, from the rest of the house, from her husband and her life. She was staring at herself in the mirror, a pale-pink Chanel spaghetti-strap dress hanging perfectly on her taut body, skin soft and tan and glowing, sun-streaked hair falling over her shoulders, deep shining blue eyes offset by the dress and the skin and hair, a diamond necklace, as large as it could be without being ostentatious, a diamond bracelet, as large as it could be without being ostentatious, diamonds on the ring fingers of both hands. She was breathtakingly beautiful. And as painstaking as each decision that went into her look for the evening was, and as expensive as every single thing on her was, she also gave off a very casual vibe, as if she walked around the house looking like this, as if he she had gotten ready quickly, and without much thought. She stared at herself in the mirror. Looked herself up and down. She knew she was beautiful. Not in a vain or narcissistic way, but as a simple and objective statement of fact. She'd always known what a giant asset her beauty was. Sometimes as currency, with which she could get anything she wanted in the world. Sometimes as a weapon, that when properly wielded, could defeat any opponent, and win any war. She stared at herself, and she smiled.

She was ready.

For the evening.

For the future.

For everything that was to come.

———

The McCallister Estate sat on forty acres. A four-foot-tall, three-hundred-year-old stone wall ran along the front border of the property and the street. At a break in the center of the wall was an imposing black iron gate. A small security box with a touchpad and a speaker sat a few feet off the street. Behind the gate, a long, white gravel driveway ran through the front section of the property, a dense, manicured forest, hundreds of tall, ancient maple, elm, and birch trees reaching for the sky, the ground covered by deep green moss and occasional patches of wildflowers. At night the forest was lit, spotlights sending soft, warm, diffused light upward, where it dissipated into the limbs and branches of the trees. The driveway ended in a large looping circle in front of the house, which was a white limestone, neoclassical château. The house, built in 1918, was three stories tall, with French windows and small balconies running symmetrically along each of its two wings, with huge, white-and-blue bougainvilleas growing wild between each of the first-floor windows. Next to the house was a limestone garage capable of holding twelve cars. Behind the house there was a large marble patio and pool, an outdoor kitchen, French gardens, a pond, and a guesthouse. The main house had twelve bedrooms, sixteen bathrooms, and eighteen thousand square feet of living space. Inside it had been renovated and furnished with an eclectic combination of modern and mid-century furniture and French neoclassical furniture. On the walls were paintings by Picasso, Warhol, Lichtenstein, De Kooning, Richter, Ellsworth Kelly, Basquiat, Cecily Brown, Mark Grotjahn. There was a movie theater. A home gym. A yoga studio. A music room where the kids took guitar and piano lessons. There was a game room filled with vintage video games and pinball machines. A library filled with modern and contemporary first editions, most of them signed. The master suite had his and her bathrooms and his and her walk-in closets. The house had ten fireplaces, five on each of the two lower floors. It had a massage room, an indoor cold plunge next to a hot tub. In the basement there was a wine cellar that held four thousand bottles, a bomb shelter stocked with enough food and water to last four people five years, six or seven if they were thrifty, an arsenal filled with Billy's gun collection, which mostly consisted of assault rifles and high-powered semiautomatic handguns, and thousands of rounds of ammunition for them. The house was run by a smart home system that controlled the lighting, the temperature, and a music system that played in most of the house, or most of the house excluding the bedrooms, which had their own individual music systems. The entire exterior was covered by surveillance cameras that would capture anyone coming on or off the property, and anywhere near the house. The security system was built and installed by the same company that did the White House and Buckingham Palace.

––––––

It was a perfect late-September evening. Warm, and clear, the moon high and nearly full. The air was light and pure, the heaviness of summer gone, the sharpness of winter not yet arrived. The leaves on the trees were just starting to turn. Night birds were singing. There was the hint of a breeze.

Ana greeted everyone at the front entrance as they arrived. She was wearing a long black dress and light black sweater that covered the tattoos on her upper arms. Her hair was pulled back into a ponytail. She gave each of the women a red rose when they arrived. She gave each of the men a smile.

Everyone assembled on the back patio. As the sun set, the sky was filled with pink and orange and purple and blue, more beautiful than any of the paintings in the house, more vivid, more alive. Conversation was flowing, everyone was awed by the house, by the land, by how the house and the land existed together, complimented each other, danced and sang and laughed with each other. It was the most beautiful house any of them, except for Belle, had ever seen, or had ever been to, and had ever been invited to for a party. Devon received their compliments with grace, smiling in that sweet space between humility and pride.

The men had gathered at the edge of the patio, staring out at the gardens and pond. They were talking about money and work and sports and politics, all the usual bullshit men talked about at parties, each trying to assert themselves, each trying to establish his dominance and manhood, as men always do. They were all occasionally glancing at the women, who had stayed on the patio, wondering which of them they would be with later, hoping, imagining.

The women were sitting on lounge chairs around the table. They were talking about kids and exercise and the wine and complimenting each other's hair and outfits, each silently sizing each other up and comparing themselves to each other, as women do. None, at that time, were particularly interested in the men.

There was also tension in the air. All of them but Grace knew what was coming, where the evening was going. All of them but Grace had run through what they wanted to happen in their hearts, minds, dreams. There was anticipation in the air, there was desire in the air, there was sex.

There was hunger.

Sex and hunger.

When the sun went down, and the darkness started to descend, Devon stood and held her glass in the air. Without saying a word, everyone stopped speaking and gathered around her.

Thank you all for coming to our party. Let's toast to the evening ahead.

She smiled and raised her glass slightly higher, took a sip, everyone else followed her lead and did the same.

Just inside.

She motioned toward a set of large open French doors.

There are cards on our dining table with each of your names on them. The rooms assigned were done at random, by my friend and partner here at the house, Ana, who I love and trust absolutely. The women will go first, please get your cards, go to the room that corresponds with the number on the card. And there we will wait to see who will join us, and to see where the evening may take us. Men, please follow after five minutes, follow the number, and follow your destiny.

Everyone laughed.

If you want drugs to enhance your experience, they are also on the table. If you want to use the pool, use the pool, if you want to wander the grounds, wander the grounds. All I ask is that you have a great time, the kind of time that you will always remember. Let down your inhibitions, be wild, be free.

Everyone laughed again.

Let us begin.

Devon turned and walked into the house, through the French doors. Belle enthusiastically followed. Katy slightly behind, and with little enthusiasm. Grace turned and looked at Alex, confused. Alex shrugged as if he didn't know what was happening, and motioned for her to follow the other women.

———

Devon went to her room. She put on a Prince playlist, songs made for fucking. The drugs were all in small packages. She took three one-gram packages of pink cocaine. She emptied one of the packages on the glass surface of the bedside table and cut three thick lines, one for herself, one for Alex, and one for now. She inhaled the line for now, and closed her eyes and waited for it to hit and when it did she sat on the edge of the bed, put her hands on the bed behind her, and closed her eyes and took a deep breath, and as her heart rate increased and her body was flooded with sensations of extreme pleasure, the door opened.

————

Belle was in a large lovely guest bedroom on the second floor. The floors were polished hickory covered by a pale-pink silk rug with Warhol prints on painted ivory walls. There was a king-sized bed, a pale-pink velvet sofa, a glass mid-century table with drugs in one corner. She spread out on the sofa, took a sip of her champagne. She was excited. She could feel the anticipation between her legs. Her nipples were hard under the silk covering them. Her hands were quivering, slightly quivering, the door opened.

————

Grace didn't know what was going on. She was in a guest bedroom on the first floor, the gardens outside her window. The room had polished pine floors, a king-sized bed with linen sheets, a charcoal mohair sofa, three Yves Klein prints hanging on each of the walls. She sat on the sofa texted Alex WTF?!? She opened the care package next to the bedside table and found condoms and lube and a vibrator she texted Alex again Is this a swingers' party!?! She wondered if he knew and didn't tell her or if he was also surprised she couldn't believe she was at a swingers' party and she didn't know what she was going to do when the door opened.

————

Katy went to her room, a guest bedroom on the first floor, white walls pale floors Haring drawings on the wall a large white bed, a large sofa. She took with her six doses of mushrooms and six of ecstasy. Not because she wanted them that night, but because she loved both and if she had to attend and tolerate the party, she wanted something out of it. In this case, drugs she loved for future use. She took her phone out of her handbag. She opened Instagram and started scrolling, laughing at a meme, reading an inspirational phrase she thought was nonsense, the vacation photos of a friend from college. The door opened.

———

Ana stepped into the security room. Banks of monitors with feeds from the cameras installed all over the house and the property. Devon had copied the key without Billy's knowledge and given Ana a copy a year or so ago. In case she ever needed it, or if she ever got curious. She was curious about what was going to happen with the party, with the couplings. Mostly about Devon and Alex, but some of the others in attendance could end up being interesting as well. She had a glass of wine and a joint. Nothing on TV or her phone or the internet would be as interesting or as important. She took a sip of the wine and lit the joint. She watched as Alex walked down the hall, where Devon was waiting for him. She smiled. She didn't know where it was going to go, but she and Devon both believed there was an opportunity. He stopped in front of the door, reached for the handle.

———

Alex stepped inside the room and smiled.

Hello.

Devon on the bed looked up at him and smiled.

Hello.

He stepped forward.

Lucky me.

She stood up.

Luck wasn't part of it.

They kissed, deeply, slowly, passionately, lips and tongues and breath, hands together, hands apart, hands wandering, he turned her around and pressed her against the wall, his hands moved under her dress, he kissed her neck, licked her neck, his hands moved to the inside of her thighs, he spread her legs, he got on his knees, he lifted her dress, he licked the inside of her thighs, his hands higher, pinching her nipples, he softly bit the inside of her thighs, he moved higher, lips and tongue and breath.

———

Charlie stepped into the room. Belle was sitting on the sofa sipping her champagne. He smiled.

I was hoping it was you.

She smiled.

Oh yeah?

Yeah.

Why's that?

I follow you on Instagram. I've seen pictures of you in a bikini. They turned me on.

Are you turned on now, Charlie?

I am.

You want to show me?

He smiled.

You ready?

She smiled.

I've heard you're big.

He stepped forward.

I am.

Started with his belt.

I heard ten inches.

With the buttons.

Ten and three eighths.

Belle smiled.

Oh yeah?

Charlie smiled, nodded.

I measured it this morning.

He dropped his pants. He wasn't wearing anything under them. Belle smiled wider.

Oh my.

I'm gonna fuck your brains out.

Exactly what I hoped you would do.

She put her hands on his hips, pulled him toward her, looked up into his eyes, opened her mouth.

————

Grace sat on the sofa her phone in her hand. Teddy stepped into the room and closed the door behind him. She looked up.

Is this a swingers' party?

He smiled.

Yes, it is.

I'm not going to fuck you.

He laughed.

I'm not going to fuck you.

She was surprised.

Really?

He motioned to an empty spot on the opposite side of the sofa.

May I sit?

She smiled.

As long as you stay over there.

He laughed, sat, over there.

I'm Teddy.

Yeah, I kinda know you from around town.

Same.

I'm Grace.

I know.

Nice to meet you. Formally.

Nice to meet you formally, Grace.

He reached out to shake her hand. She smiled wider.

That's all you're getting.

He laughed again.

I promise you it will be enough.

They both smiled, shook hands, and held for the briefest moment longer. And somewhere deep deep deep inside of Teddy, something stirred, it had been asleep for so long, and it stirred.

Maybe it was her red hair.

Maybe her freckles.

Maybe her bright-white perfect smile, the product of years of expensive Midwestern orthodontia.

Maybe it was just one of those sweet thrilling beautiful moments in life that happen for reasons beyond our understanding.

But it happened.

He stirred. It stirred.

————

Billy stepped into the room with two glasses of champagne.

Nice to meet you, Katy. I'm Billy.

She looked up from her phone.

Hi, Billy.

He walked over to the sofa, sat down, set the glasses on a small coffee table in front of the sofa.

How's your evening so far, Katy?

Very frankly, Billy, not great. I really don't want to be here and my boyfriend committed to coming without talking to me about it.

Charlie.

Yes, Charlie.

Not the brightest bulb.

He's kind and sweet and. . . .

I know why you're with him.

You do?

Yes, I do. Very frankly, Katy, I know quite a bit about both of you.

Such as?

Billy motions to the glass he set in front of Katy.

Why don't you have some champagne and we can make ourselves a bit more comfortable.

I'm not making myself more comfortable, Mr. McCallister.

I think you are, Miss Boyle.

I'm definitely not.

As I mentioned, I know quite a bit about you, including things I don't believe you thought anyone would ever know.

Katy looked concerned.

Such as?

I know all about your adventures in New York, and your taste for, should we call it, the erotically exotic.

What do you think you know?

It's not what I think I know, it's what I know, and what I have.

What do you have?

Well, there's that series of videos you made wearing a mask—they're on a major pornography site as you know.

Katy's face falls.

I was also able to get a full copy of the website, and the videos on it, that you used to charge subscribers to come visit. You are not wearing a mask in any of those videos.

Fuck you.

Yes, among other things, you are going to fuck me. And if you don't, every member of the New Bethlehem Board of Education will get copies of those videos, as will anyone you ever try to get a job with after you're fired from your job here.

Katy stared at him.

Please don't do this.

Call me Mr. McCallister.

Please don't do this, Mr. McCallister.

Drink your champagne, Katy.

She looked at the glass, didn't reach for it, looked back at him.

Please.

Drink your champagne, Katy.

She reached for the glass, took a small sip.

More, Katy,

She drank a little more.

All of it.

Please.

All of it, Katy.

She drank all of it. And he watched her. Carefully, and with great hunger. She set the glass down on the table. He smiled.

Now be a good girl, Katy, and get on your knees.

Strolling

New Bethlehem has an extensive park and public land system, the largest per capita of any town or city in the United States. All of its fifteen recreational parks are former estates donated to the town by their former owners, and all of the New Bethlehem Land Trust's seventy pieces of public land are parcels donated by their former owners before any structures were built on them. The parks have swimming pools, dog parks, tennis courts, baseball softball football and soccer fields, dozens of them, paddle tennis courts, playgrounds, fishing ponds, swimming ponds, and miles and miles and miles of walking trails. The largest of the parks, and the most popular is called Watson Park. Originally a six-hundred-acre estate, it was built in 1912 by a family that founded a large oil and gas company. The main structure was a thirty-thousand-square-foot castle. Down a small hill were stables and three guesthouses, and a ten-car garage, which were converted into a public theater, two public art spaces, and a public event space. The park has three ponds, a hundred-acre pasture where the town holds its Fourth of July festivities and fireworks, tennis courts, paddle tennis courts, an Olympic swimming pool, a dog park, an ice-skating rink, and several miles of walking trails. New Bethlehem High School, one of top-ranked public high schools in the United States, is also built on land that was once part of the estate, along with all of its associated sports facilities, including a stadium with video scoreboards and broadcast TV capabilities, six turf practice fields, twelve tennis courts, and a track.

Devon and Belle met after school drop-off and walked in Watson Park two or three mornings a week, doing the large loop, a 3.8-mile circle that mostly ran through woods, but also went along the pasture, past two ponds, and the castle. They called it their therapy. A time where they shared whatever was going on with themselves and in their lives, a time where they helped each other navigate whatever bullshit life had brought them. It was also a time when they gossiped, and celebrated their joys and victories. They didn't usually walk on weekends, but they did on the morning after the party. The sun was high and bright. The sky a perfect crystal blue. Birds were chirping, squirrels dashing, dewdrops shining on the blades of grass like a billion daylight stars. Watson Park was never crowded, but there were more people than normal, requiring an occasional smile or hello, or an occasional, and brief, moment of silence or change of subject. Belle, in her favorite Dallas Cowboys hat and a thousand dollars of workout gear, was in great spirits, smiling as she spoke.

He went down on me for an hour.

Devon laughed.

An hour?

I came five times.

Did he do the finger thing?

Oh. My. God.

So good, right?

The fucking best.

He's got skills.

Understatement of the fucking century.

Did you fuck? Could you fuck after that?

We fucked for another hour. In every position I've ever seen, heard of, or imagined. And his dick. He filled me, literally and figuratively, and literally again.

Devon laughed again. Belle kept going.

I don't know what I'm going to do. I mean, I really want that kind of fun on the regular, especially given my situation with Teddy.

How was Teddy's night?

We agreed not to discuss details. All he said was that he had a lovely time, and that Grace Hunter is a lovely person.

Did they fuck?

No way.

You sure?

Not possible.

What do you think they did all night?

Talked? Watched a movie? Looked at Instagram?

Did they leave the room?

Did anyone?

I don't know. I was busy.

They both laughed.

How was his mood?

Oddly great. Like, I know he didn't get laid, but he was as happy and as cheerful as he would have been if he did.

Maybe he went down on her for an hour and made her cum five times.

Belle laughed.

I love him, but he doesn't have those kinds of skills.

They saw two other moms they knew walking toward them. Both smiled, and, at the same time, said

Hi Kelsey, hi Monica.

Immediately after, at the same time, Kelsey and Monica said

Hey Devon, hey Belle.

After an appropriate twenty or so steps, Belle spoke.

Now tell me about your night.

It was great.

Lived up to the nickname?

In so many ways. In so many unexpected ways.

Tell me.

He came into the room, and we just went at it, right away, no talking, no flirting, we just attacked each other.

Hot.

You can definitely tell Alex was a professional athlete.

They both laughed.

The sex was great, incredible, and surprisingly intimate. Lots of foreplay and whispering and tons of eye contact, he kept telling me to look into his eyes while we were fucking, and I did, and it was like we saw into each other, saw beneath the bullshit we both carry around, saw into each other's souls.

So hot.

And I figured we'd do some coke and go at it again, but after we finished . . .

Belle interrupted.

Did you both finish?

Yes.

At the same time?

Yes.

So. Fucking. Hot.

They both laughed. Two more moms approached. At the same time, they spoke.

Hey Vera, hey Sophie.

And Vera and Sophie simultaneously responded

Hey Dev, hey B.

After an appropriate twenty or so steps, Devon said

After, we lay in bed and held each other, and talked for like an hour, and it was like we had known each for our entire lives, or like we should have. We love the same books, same films, same music.

There's no way he's into Prince.

He sang *The Most Beautiful Girl in the World* to me. Or kinda tried to sing it. He's not a great singer.

Appreciate the effort, though.

Right?

Hell yeah.

He told me he had a crush on me in high school.

Did you know him?

He was a big deal, so I knew who he was, but we never met. He said he saw me at the Belle Haven Club and always thought about me, and would always look for me whenever he was in Greenwich, and when he saw me in New Bethlehem, he thought it was fate, that we were destined to cross paths at some point in our lives.

What do you think?

I know I felt better last night than I have in a long long time.

This sounds dangerous.

It feels dangerous.

Billy would lose his fucking mind if you left him.

That's probably the least of what he would do.

You need to be careful, Devon.

Or just rip the Band-Aid.

When are you seeing him again?

Devon looked at her phone.

In four hours.

Does Billy still track your phone?

Of course.

Where are you going?

My parents' house, they're away.

Belle laughed.

You are crafty, Devon.

Devon smiled.

Your parents are away and Billy hates them and he'll never know.

Yes, exactly.

Belle laughed again.

Maybe Billy has met his match.

Devon smiled wider.

He absolutely has.

Morning After

Katy was awake before she opened her eyes.

Everything was heavy.

Blurred.

Disjointed.

Everything hurt.

Her head, her body, her heart.

She tried to think through what happened.

The party.

The card.

The room.

The glass.

Billy McCallister.

That fucking pig.

That fucking pig.

That fucking pig.

She opened her eyes and sat up. Everything hurt she could still feel whatever he gave her and her heart was racing and her hands were shaking and she wanted to go back to sleep and she started to cry and the crying became sobbing and the sobbing became wailing.

Guilt.

Shame.

Helplessness.

Loss.

She looked at the clock it was 11:00. She was normally up at 6:00 even if she was out late she had to be at lacrosse practice in an hour. She needed to get her shit together, but her heart wouldn't stop racing and her hands wouldn't stop shaking and she couldn't stop crying and she didn't know what happened but there was pain between her legs and pain under her shirt and pain all over her body.

How could she have let this happen.

Why didn't she stop him.

Why didn't she just leave.

What the fuck did he give her.

What the fuck did he do.

She had to get up she had to get moving she couldn't stop crying she had to shower and get her shit together she couldn't stop crying she had to go to practice she couldn't stop crying.

What the fuck did he give her.

What the fuck did he do.

Guilt.

Shame.

She had to get up and she had to go to practice.

She couldn't stop crying.

A Luncheon

Preston was at football practice. Madeline was at field hockey. Grace made a grilled chicken Caesar. She was drinking water. Alex was having a beer. They were sitting at a teak table with a white umbrella on their flagstone back patio. Grace wore a flowered sundress. Alex a golf shirt, golf pants, flip-flops. Grace spoke.

Why didn't you tell me?

I didn't know.

I don't appreciate you lying to me, Alex.

I'm not lying.

Alex.

She waited, took a bite of her salad, stared. He looked away. She waited. He looked back.

I didn't know exactly what was happening. That's true.

But you knew generally.

Kind of.

Kind of?

I only knew they do that kind of thing.

Swing.

I'd heard rumors. I hadn't met them before last night. But people have said.

You should have told me.

I know. I'm sorry.

And you didn't know what was going to happen?

You saw the invitation. It was flowers with a date and time. I knew they were swingers, or I had heard they were, but I didn't know we were going to be swinging last night.

So what happened?

What do you mean?

Did you swing?

He laughed.

Did I swing?

Yeah, with Devon.

What do you mean?

Did you fuck Devon Kensington last night?

No. No no. We went to the room and it was awkward and we both kinda laughed and had an awkward conversation and we ended up doing some of the blow and talking and we went to the game room and played *Asteroids* and *Q*bert* for most of the night.

Grace knew he was lying because she and Teddy went to the game room and played *Donkey Kong*, *Dig Dug*, and *Frogger* for part of the evening. And as they found their way there, they passed the room Alex and Devon were in and they could hear them fucking. She didn't want him to know that she knew he was lying. And she didn't want him to know that she and Teddy had a great night together. They talked and they laughed and they flirted, and he was kind and smart and funny and not creepy at all. They played video games and sat with their feet in the pool and went for a walk through the gardens, and the most they did was hold hands during the walk. But she loved it. She loved having a handsome, charming man pay attention to her, and treat her with reverence and respect, and look at her with desire in his eyes. It was great, and it felt great, and even if she never saw Teddy again, and she didn't plan on it as long as they were both still married, she would cherish the memory. She smiled at Alex, spoke.

You fucked up. You had a free pass.

He laughed.

What if we get invited again?

She smiled, shook her head.

You missed your chance.

He laughed again.

And you?

Me what?

What did you and Teddy do?

We drank beer and talked about how weird the night was and watched a bad rom-com on the TV in our room.

Was he cool?

Yes, he was cool, and kind, and polite.

You have a crush on him?

We're married, Alex.

He smiled.

Yes, we are, happily married.

She smiled, though she knew it wasn't real. She knew he cheated on her, she knew he lied to her, she knew they weren't happy. She knew almost no one in New Bethlehem, or anywhere else, who was happily married. It was a grind, with constant stress and tension, punctuated with occasional moments of happiness. You either accepted it and committed to it, or you didn't. And if you made it through, if you made it through raising kids and trying to build a nest egg for retirement and the years of tension and stress, there was a chance you would find some form of happiness on the other side.

Any plans today?

Gonna go hit some balls at the club. Might play nine if it's not too busy. You?

Picking up the kids. They each have playdates this afternoon.

Do we have anything going on tonight?

Thought we'd stay in and have Family Movie Night.

Great.

He stood.

I'm going to head out.

He leaned over and kissed her.

Love you.

She smiled.

Love you.

He walked away.

She watched him.

And she knew he had just lied to her again.

Iron Man

It had been a glorious morning.

Also awkward.

And slightly uncomfortable.

But mostly glorious.

They got home late.

Late late.

Four-in-the-morning late.

Teddy had no idea what Belle did all night. He assumed she fucked the hockey coach into oblivion. He knew all too well what she could be like when she was feeling frisky, and given his own issues with achieving an erection, her frisk was near an all-time high; he hoped she'd had a wonderful time, as painful as that might be for him to think about. After all, one makes sacrifices if one wants to stay married. And agreeing to swing was a sacrifice he believed he'd needed to make for her.

He'd expected a miserable evening. Paired in a room with a woman he didn't know, both of them knowing their respective spouses were fucking other people somewhere else in the house. He wasn't going to make a move, under any circumstances. And if she made a move, the prospect of deep humiliation and a giant truckload of self-loathing was very real. And though he knew both emotions extremely well, at that point they were his constant companions, he had thus far been able to contain the knowledge of his situation between himself and Belle. The idea that he would see a woman around town who also knew he couldn't board the train to Boner City made him very literally contemplate moving his family elsewhere.

Man plans.

God laughs.

It can go both ways.

But from the moment he and Grace were alone, something in him changed. It wasn't overwhelming, it wasn't a dam breaking, or the lights being turned on in a dark room, it was simpler, more subtle, like something inside of him that had been sleeping had opened its eyes, and was ready to get out of bed.

It had kept its eyes open all night. And he hadn't had to think about it or worry about it or stress out about it. He and Grace had a lovely evening. They had a couple glasses of champagne, they talked about the awkwardness and absurdity of the situation they were in, they played video games, they sat with their feet in the pool, they went for a walk to the pond. As they were walking, she reached for his hand, and he took hers in his, loosely interlocking their fingers, looking at each other and smiling, not saying a word. And as he walked with her, his old friend, his old sleeping friend, suddenly awoke, and he felt himself getting hard, and when they sat down on a long wooden bench on the shore of the pond, for the first time in many years, he was fully erect, his yogurt cannon locked and loaded, ready to fire.

Some adjustments needed to be made as they sat on the bench, and looked at the moon and the reflection of the trees on the pond, and listened to the night birds and frogs and bugs, to a pack of coy-wolves howling, to an owl hooting as they talked about their lives and their kids and their marriages, as they talked about their frustrations and their hopes, as they acknowledged that they both, to their great surprise, had feelings for each other, simple, pure and uncomplicated, sweet, refreshing, renewing and inspiring, feelings of some kind of love, when it's early and unknown and full of possibilities,

When the night ended, they shared a sweet kiss. A lips slightly open, heart-skipping kiss. Both wanted another, both wanted more, both agreed it probably wasn't a great idea, that what they each felt might be more than a dalliance at a SwingFest and that they shouldn't let it go any further, any further could get complicated. So they said their goodbyes, and went home with their respective spouses. As Teddy fell asleep, he thought about Grace, and he thought about his own wife with other men and the state of their marriage, and he thought about the rest of his life and what he wanted from it and what he wanted in it, and he thought about the renewed vigor in his loins and he thought about feeling good for the first time in almost a decade and he thought about Grace some more, her smile, her giggle, the way the moonlight danced in her sweet blue eyes, he thought about the tips of her fingers and her breath and her lips, her lips, honey for his heart, her lips. He thought about how he was going to feel the next day. Whether any of what he was feeling, feeling in his soul and feeling in his dick, was going to last.

He wanted more of it.

He wanted it to last.

He wanted it to last forever.

More and more and more and more.

Forever.

When he woke up, three hours later than his normal Saturday morning routine, the feelings, physical and emotional, were still there.

He got hard while he drank his morning coffee, cold and strong with a dash of milk.

He got hard reading the morning paper.

He got hard during his morning run, which, given that he was wearing running shorts and that as ever they were light and thin and short, required some adjustments: of the shorts, of his member, and of the manner in which he ran.

At home he took a cold shower and the cold did not fade his rigor.

And throughout every moment of his rigid, stiff, inflexible morning he thought of her.

A married woman. With a delicious giggle.

Sweet blue eyes. Lips like honey.

He thought of her.

He thought of her.

Sweet Flow

Billy loved hockey. He never played it, but it was his favorite sport. Billy loved hockey because where he grew up, working-class Long Island, being a hockey fan was a part of life, a significant part of life. Every man and boy in working-class Long Island loved hockey and watched hockey because of the New York Islanders, the NHL team based in Nassau, Long Island. The Islanders came into existence in 1972. They proudly based themselves in and named themselves after Long Island, even though New York City was only a few miles away. They quickly built a dynastic team, and won four consecutive Stanley Cups from 1980 to 1983. Their branding and their success created a generation of deeply loyal and deeply vocal men who raised their sons to be the same, Billy among them. And though Billy never knew if it was true or not, his father liked to tell people his son had been named after legendary Islanders goalie Billy "The Hatchet Man" Smith, who won four of those Stanley Cups, and was known for swinging his stick at people who bothered him. Hockey was in Billy's blood. And thinking of himself as his own kind of Hatchet Man was something that made him happy.

The Hatchet Man.

Fuck yeah, Billy!

Devon and Billy's daughter Charlotte, aged twelve, played travel hockey at an elite level. Billy was more involved in her hockey career than anything else in either of his children's lives. He started her in skating lessons when she was three, in hockey when she was four, in travel hockey when she was five. He went to most of her practices and most of her games. He donated money to the program she played in and sometimes supplemented travel expenses so the team could play in more and higher-level tournaments. And despite never playing hockey, he felt very comfortable sharing his opinions on the team, often at volume, the coaching, the other players, and his own daughter's progress and performance, with just about anyone willing to listen, and many who didn't want to hear it, including Charlotte.

But on this day, he wasn't talking much. He was just watching. And not Charlotte, but her coach, Charlie Dunlap. Charlie moved gracefully on the ice. He was absolutely engaged with his players, watching them as they did drills, giving advice, correcting mistakes. He was enthusiastic and positive. He didn't coach with anger or fear, but with joy and fun. He clearly loved what he did, and he was very good at it. His teams regularly won tournaments, State championships, and more than once, though not every year, National championships. Billy knew Charlie had been fucking his wife for two years. Not regularly, but occasionally, whenever Devon wanted or needed sex. He'd always been fine with it because he was tired of fucking Devon. She was beautiful and sensual and adventurous, but he was bored with her. And she was getting older, And he could tell that she didn't really want to fuck him anymore. Or at least fuck him the way he wanted to fuck her, roughly, aggressively, and with him having total and complete control to do whatever he wanted, however he wanted. Devon didn't know it but he knew her passcode and could access her phone. He'd read the flirty and dirty texts between her and Charlie, seen the pictures they exchanged. He knew all about Charlie's big dick and how much he loved an adult happy meal. He knew Devon loved fucking him, and that she joked with Belle about how good he was with his stick. And now he knew Charlie had also fucked Belle. And would likely have her again. Billy had always wanted her. He wanted to hear her talk dirty and moan in that soft Texas accent. He wanted to tie her up and ravage her. He wanted to make her taste him, in every way. Devon had forbidden it. Said it was a line he could not cross, and if he did, or if he tried, there would be repercussions. And while he knew he held the power in the relationship, because he had and controlled the money, and their prenup, with a couple unrealistic exceptions, guaranteed he always would control the money, he knew Devon was a formidable enemy. She was smart, and she could be devious. And she knew more about him, and things that could damage him, than anyone in the world.

They were tied to each other whether they wanted to be or not. He wasn't going to openly cross her lines and risk her wrath.

But he was angry. And he was jealous. He didn't like that some hockey coach was fucking his wife and her best friend, and he wasn't. And he didn't like that they both loved fucking Charlie, or that they cringed every time Billy entered a room. He had enjoyed having his way with Charlie's girlfriend. If only Charlie knew what he'd done to her. If only he knew what he was going to do to her in the future. He had taken from Charlie what Charlie had taken from him. He was thinking about what more he would take from Charlie, and how he would take it, and how he would set it up so that his wife and her friend didn't know he'd done anything.

He watched Charlie on the ice. What a simple life he had for himself. He coached and drank beer and fucked beautiful, often married women. How easy it was for him. He had no ambition. He didn't know greed. He didn't care about money, as long as he had enough to pay rent and buy gas and beer. Billy didn't know if Charlie had brain damage from his hockey career, but Billy thought he was an idiot. And as Billy sat and watched Charlie teach Charlotte a new breakaway move, he decided it was time to bring out the Hatchet Man, that he was going to find a way to make Charlie go away. He had done it in business many times. Find a way to discreetly and safely destroy someone's life. Charlie was going to be next.

————

Charlie was on the ice, coaching.

He couldn't focus on his job.

He was thinking about Belle. He was thinking about Devon.

He was thinking about Katy.

Memories of his night with Belle holy fuck it was so damn fun and so damn hot he could hardly believe it. He loved watching MILF porn, and he had always thought of Devon as the ultimate MILF fantasy, but Belle had moved ahead of her to the top spot on his Hottest MILFs in the World List, and he'd made it official, in pen, by writing a new list when he woke up. He wanted to see Belle again as soon as she was willing to see him. He thought about telling her he loved her. If she hadn't already been married, he would've gone to the mall and bought a ring and proposed to her. He had never really considered marriage. He was married to hockey and ice-cold beer and having fun with as many ladies as possible. But not anymore. Now he was in love, and love would move to the top of the list.

He wondered if Devon would be mad at him for falling in love with her best friend. He didn't want her to be mad. Devon was his buddy. He hoped they would stay buddies.

And he hadn't heard from Katy. She was pretty out of it when he took her home last night. Sometimes she liked to get wild, so he thought that was what had happened, but he wasn't entirely sure.

He glanced up toward the stands, where some of the parents always sat and watched practice. He never knew why they watched practice. It wasn't fun to watch. It was just drills and a short scrimmage at the end. But they watched it; some of them came to every single one. And right up there was Billy McCallister. Mister King Dickhead himself. Loudmouth Know-It-All. Not cool to anyone, including himself. He came to almost every practice. Usually spent the entire time on his phone. Texting and making calls. Which was kind of stupid. There were much better places to send texts and make calls than a U12 Girls hockey practice. But today, Billy hadn't been using his phone, he was instead very carefully watching the entire practice. But not his daughter. He had been watching Charlie. And Charlie wondered why. He didn't want Billy McCallister as an enemy. He'd heard too many stories about Billy. He knew Billy could be mean, and he knew Billy was a bit crazy. Charlie just wanted to keep his job and do his thing, and now, doing his thing meant doing it as much as possible with Belle Hedges Moore. But Billy was staring at him. That meant something, probably something not very good. And though Charlie was generally a peaceful man, he wondered if he was going to have to do something about it.

Willowvale

Devon's great-grandfather once owned the world's largest copper mine. At the time, just after the turn of the twentieth century, copper was in great demand. Though electricity, and the power to create, deliver and distribute it, had been available for a couple decades, it hadn't been put into mass use. As the world, and the United States adapted and adjusted to the possibilities of electricity, and people saw the conveniences that electricity brought, and the efficiencies it produced for corporations, work, and workers, the country got wired. And somebody had to provide the material for those wires. And one of those somebodies, was Cornelius Clay Kensington.

Like many of the Barons of his age, Cornelius wanted the world to know he was rich. And not just rich, but immensely rich. He lived in a giant townhouse on Fifth Avenue. He had a mansion on the water in Newport. He bought a hundred-acre piece of land in Greenwich. He hired Stanford White to design and build the house and Warren Manning to design and plant the gardens. The house was a Beaux Arts mansion with a pebble-dash exterior and large columns framing the front entrance. It was built atop a long, sloping rise, on one of the highest points of land in Greenwich, giving it commanding views of the rolling hills and gardens that surrounded it. A long sweeping white gravel driveway passed by weeping willows and wildflowers planted on Bermuda grass. Behind the house, there was a pool, tennis court, guesthouse, and stables. After Cornelius passed away, the house stayed in the family. Though the family wealth was immense, none of his descendants were as ambitious, or motivated, or as capable as he was, and none wanted to run a copper mining business. It was sold, and some of the money was invested, and much of the money was spent. Devon's father grew up in the house, and when his parents moved to Palm Beach, he moved his family into it, and Devon spent her entire childhood in it. As the family fortune dwindled, choices needed to be made about what to liquidate and what to keep. While there were paintings acquired by Cornelius on the walls of the house worth many millions of dollars, impressionist and postimpressionist paintings by Manet and Monet, Renoir and Degas and Pissarro, Cézanne and Seurat, Devon's father decided to break up the land of the estate, which was very expensive to maintain, instead of selling the art. He first sold forty acres on the back of the property in eight five-acre parcels. When that money was gone, he sold forty more. When Devon and Alex started using the house for their dalliances, it sat on twenty acres; the first time he saw it, Alex suggested they try to fuck in every room on the property. Devon smiled.

You're not the first to suggest it.

Ever done it?

Not even close.

I've spent my entire life doing things no one else has ever done.

Alexander the Great and all.

Yes.

Let's see what you've got, Alexander the Great.

And they started trying to achieve what had never been achieved. Fuck in all twenty-eight rooms of the house, six rooms in the basement, the eight rooms of the guesthouse, three rooms of the pool house. There was a debate over the stables, whether a stall was a room, or whether the large open room that held stables was a room, or both. They decided that each of the eight stalls should be considered a room, and when the debate ended, they immediately fucked in one of them.

They met every weekday. Alex stopped taking the train into the city and stopped going to the library and would drive to Willowvale every morning. Devon asked the two housekeepers and three grounds-keepers to stop coming in Monday through Friday and paid them double to get their work done on the weekends, when she and Alex would be in New Bethlehem with their kids and spouses. They'd meet in the morning. Find a room they hadn't conquered yet, and conquer it, and each other. Devon would make coffee or breakfast, they would sit outside in the gardens or by the pool, go for a walk on the grounds. They would have each other for lunch, and spend the afternoon outdoors, talking reading walking, swimming in the pool, playing tennis. They would conquer yet another room before they left, before Devon went home to greet the kids after school and sports, Alex would usually stay and pretend to work in her father's home office.

And it was love.

New fresh thrilling overwhelming all-consuming love.

Each loved every word the other spoke. Every movement they made.

Every smile, every laugh, every moan.

Each touch electric, each kiss better than the last.

When they weren't talking or fucking, they stared at each other. At each other's faces, bodies, into each other's eyes.

What they felt was stronger and more powerful, more intimate and more emotional, more intellectual, more sexual, than any relationship that either of them had ever had in their lives.

For Devon, Alex was everything that Billy wasn't, present, affection-ate, engaged. He was the type of man she'd always imagined mar-rying when she was young, before the responsibility of saving her family and her family name fell squarely on her shoulders.

For Alex, everything Devon was as a woman and a human being was a bonus. She was smart and funny and cool and well read and fluent in art history and film history and world history, she was into sports, she was kind and sweet. She was spectacularly beautiful, and even more spectacular in bed. He would have pursued her regardless of any of it, he needed to do what needed to be done, but that she was everything she was made him feel like it was going to be worth it, all of the pain and heartbreak he was going to cause, the betrayal Grace and his kids would feel and experience, it was all going to be worth it. And he believed he was genuinely in love with her, that she was the woman he should have married, and had he met her when they were younger, they might have ended up together. At first, some of what he did and said was performative. He needed her to fall in love with him and leave her husband and he had done the research required to make her fall in love with him. He became what he believed she wanted, and what was missing in her life, and who she should have been with, though he actually fell in love with her along the way. That's not to say he wasn't still on guard, and still performing, still acting, still doing what he needed to do to win. And that's what it was for him, another game, but one that would save his life, or at least spare him the shame and humiliation of admitting his long-running employment ruse, and keep him out of bankruptcy. He knew it was a game and if he was great at one thing in life, it was winning games, and he would win this one.

Two weeks into their affair, he told her he loved her.

Two weeks into their affair, she responded by saying

I love you, Alex.

His heart fluttered, leaped.

For more than one reason.

He knew he was close, victory almost at hand.

He started wandering around the house when she wasn't there. When she'd leave to go home, or go out to get food or drink or weed or tennis balls or, in one case, new sheets when they spilled red wine on them during sex. He was running low on funds, extremely low, extremely extremely extremely fucking low, and he started looking for small valuable items that he could steal and either sell quickly or pawn for cash. He went through her parents' closets, they each had their own. Her father had a Buben & Zorweg watch safe that was, shockingly, open and unlocked. He counted eighty watches in it, Patek Philippes, Rolexes, Richard Milles, Vacheron Constantins, Breguets, collectively worth several million dollars, if not more. He went into her mother's jewelry boxes, which were filled with diamonds and pearls, rubies and emeralds, necklaces, rings, bracelets, earrings, an awe-inspiring collection of incredibly valuable rocks, and worth far more than the watches. He went through her two brothers' rooms. Both had multiple Rolexes and baseballs, footballs, hockey pucks, and assorted jerseys signed by people like Babe Ruth and Joe DiMaggio. Magic Johnson and Michael Jordan. Wayne Gretzky. He went through Devon's childhood room and found two pairs of huge diamond earrings and two large simple diamond pendants, two more Rolexes, and a Cartier tank. He pocketed two watches from her father, which he sold to a dealer in the city for seventy-five thousand dollars, and from her mother a pair of Harry Winston earrings that he sold to a diamond dealer in the city for a hundred thousand dollars. He didn't believe any of them would be missed. It would mean that his own family would get to keep their home and have a little money in the bank when he left them.

He felt no guilt and no remorse.

He was playing a game. And when he played games, he played them to win.

For his entire life, whenever he put in the work and effort, as he was doing Devon, he'd always won.

But sooner or later, all winning streaks end.

The Weight

She had done her best to appear normal.

To live what had been a simple, satisfying life.

Teach, coach, work out, see Charlie.

But every second, every minute, every hour was a war.

A war with her memory, a war with her soul, and a war with her heart.

In a life filled with struggle and abuse and the fight to overcome them, she had never felt like this before.

She wanted to dig a hole a thousand miles deep and climb inside and never come out.

She knew there was nothing she could do to hurt Billy. He was rich and he was powerful and there are no consequences for the rich and the powerful.

She knew she couldn't call the police they wouldn't do anything.

She knew she couldn't tell Charlie he would do something that would make everything worse.

So she did her best to appear normal.

Teach, coach, work out, see Charlie.

Stay busy.

She did whatever she could to keep the guilt and shame and rage at bay.

Being around the kids helped. They were fun and eager and mostly still innocent and mostly still happy and mostly still believed in the goodness of life and mostly still believed in the goodness of the world. She started doing volunteer tutoring at her school's math lab every afternoon. She started covering for other coaches and staying late at practice. She looked at every girl in her classes and every girl on her teams and hoped none of them ever felt the way she did and never experienced what she had experienced.

She had trouble sleeping. When she would lie down she would play through that night in her mind. What he said, what he gave her. She tried to remember what happened after. She knew it was in her mind somewhere. She saw distant faded images. She heard distant faded sounds. She felt distant faded physical pain, which made her feel real and immediate and overwhelming psychic pain. She started walking at night, through and around New Bethlehem. It was quiet and still at night. Everyone home with their families. She carried bear spray with her just in case, she would never allow someone to hurt her like that again. Most nights she would walk until she was tired enough to sleep.

Sometimes it took an hour sometimes two sometimes three sometimes longer.

Sometimes she knew it wouldn't matter how long she walked and she stopped at one of the small restaurants in town. All of them had bars, a TV on the wall for men coming in for a drink to avoid going home. All of the restaurants in New Bethlehem were upscale, but most were for families, or for married couples on date night. One was where the divorced people went to eat and drink. There were a couple where women went to party and get loud. There were a couple where men went to get drunk and get loud. Many had wine lists that were as good as anything anywhere in America. She didn't feel comfortable in any of them, at least not alone. And she didn't want to be seen drinking alone at a bar by the parents of any of her students or any of her athletes. One of them called itself a tavern. It served burgers and wings, cold beer and strong drinks. If she knew the walking wouldn't matter. If she knew there was no way for her to sleep without help. If she knew her guilt and shame and rage needed something to dull them, she went to the tavern. She'd order a double whiskey and drink it slowly. Sometimes she'd order a second. Sometimes a third.

She was drinking when the text alert buzzed in her pocket.

She assumed it was Charlie. He coached a high school travel team that practiced at night and often came over for a beer when the practice was finished.

It buzzed again.

It buzzed again.

It buzzed again.

Charlie was not someone who was particularly good with the written word.

He rarely texted more than once, rarely texted twice, never sent three in a row. Four was beyond him.

It was one of things she loved about him.

His simplicity and his directness. His purity of spirit.

Four in a row it wasn't him. She didn't know who it was but four in a row made her think she should look at them.

She took her phone out of her purse put in the passcode opened the text app. She didn't recognize the number she opened the messages.

They said

It's your new friend.

I enjoyed our evening together and I want to do it again.

We both know you can't say no, or you can, but you know what will happen, and what everyone you know will see.

Call me.

Aisle Nine

New Bethlehem had two grocery stores.

One for the residents. One for the people who worked for the residents.

Both were expensive.

The one residents used had been open since 1916. It was started by a Scottish immigrant named Howard Turner, who'd come to New York seeking a better life and got a job as a vegetable delivery man. After dropping a load of corn and tomatoes in New Bethlehem, and being transfixed by the beautiful little town, he moved his family out from Queens, and opened his own vegetable market, called Howard Turner's. He was a friendly, amiable, and Godly man, and his Howard Turner's market quickly became very popular. It expanded and expanded and expanded until it was a full-service grocery. It focused on high-quality products, and because it was so popular, the prices were higher. And despite offer after offer to sell the store to larger grocery chains, it remained owned and run by the family and descendants of Howard Turner. It was very much a New Bethlehem institution. Many of its employees, the checkers and the baggers, were retired local residents who did the job for fun, or high school kids who did it for some extra pocket money.

The other market, TripleA, was part of a chain. One of the nicer and more expensive chains, but a chain nonetheless. It was larger and less expensive than Howard Turner's. It had a broader range of products, including all sorts of chips, soda, beer, and candy, and many different types of toilet paper and paper towels, and two full aisles of frozen food. Its lighting was brighter and its paint not as subtle. It sold many products under its own TripleA brand, instead of the more expensive national brands. Its employees tended to be people from Stamford or Norwalk, people who were working at TripleA because they needed the money to pay their bills, needed the money to live.

Although Belle wouldn't step foot into TripleA, Teddy preferred it. He liked the larger parking lot, the larger variety of choices, that it was a more efficient experience. Turner's could be a scene. As much as people went there to shop for food, they also went there to see and be seen, to talk and gossip, to show other people that they bought their groceries there even though it was much more expensive than TripleA, that the prices on exactly the same products were significantly different didn't matter to them. He also liked, every now and then, to eat junk food. And TripleA had much better junk food. During the long period of limp that he was just emerging from, he had generally abstained from junk food. One of his doctors had told him that the chemicals in certain types of processed food had been shown to potentially contribute to erectile dysfunction, so he'd stopped eating it.

Now that period was over. In the rearview.

Teddy could get hard. Teddy could get hard at will. He could masturbate whenever he felt like it. He could have sex again. He felt revitalized, invigorated, inspired, he felt alive in a way he hadn't in many years, so many years. He had been having a private celebration ever since that night. He was more present. He was more motivated, more efficient. He was a better coworker, father, friend, and human being. He believed in the possibility of happiness again. As part of his private celebration, he decided to indulge in some junk food. And as he walked around the TripleA with his cart, the only thing in it was sweets and snacks, a birthday cake, an old-fashioned white sheet cake, two packages of cupcakes, four different kinds of cookies, six bags of assorted candies and chocolate bars. He had nacho cheese chips, pretzels, cheddar popcorn, cheese puffs, six different kinds of soda, none of them diet. As he turned down the chip aisle, he was almost shaking with anticipatory joy at the prospect of shopping in the ice cream aisle, where he was planning on filling his nearly full cart to the point that he would need to carry some of the sweet frozen treasures of his choice in his hands.

Grace was already there. She was responsible for bringing ice cream bars and popsicles to a party after her daughter's singing recital, which was the next day. As was her general way, she was getting them early so she would be prepared, and so she wouldn't forget and let her daughter, or any of the other kids, down.

The last couple weeks had been difficult for her. Alex had been acting strangely, which usually meant he was having an affair. And though it was something that had happened before, more than a couple times, and though it broke her heart every time, and though she tried to tell herself she was imagining things, she knew this time, without any doubt, that it was true. And she knew it was with Devon McCallister. She had thought about confronting him. She'd thought about confronting Devon. But she knew they would both deny it and just work harder to try to keep it secret. And while she had been thinking about Alex and Devon, she had also been thinking about Teddy Moore. His smile. His hands. Their kiss. And as much as Alex's cheating made her feel like less of a woman, and a failure as a wife, her memories of Teddy made her heart beat faster, made her believe she was still attractive, still a woman who could make a man happy. She thought about Teddy constantly. She wondered where he was and what he was doing at random times throughout the day. She wondered what his marriage was like and what he was like as a husband and a father. Though she felt guilty about it, she wanted to touch him again, kiss him, taste his tongue, feel him inside of her. She asked her God what to do about what she was thinking, she asked God what to do about Alex and Devon, and what to do about Teddy. She trusted only God to give her direction, to give her some kind of sign. Part of her thought she was crazy. God, if God existed, wasn't concerned with such trifling matters. But her father had always told her that whatever God you believe in, whatever God you are willing to let into yourself, ask that God for help when you need it, and wait for that God to reply, because there would always be a sign.

And as she stood in front of the gigantic industrial freezer at TripleA, staring blankly at cartons of ice cream, ice cream bars, popsicles, and all sorts of other frozen delights, confronted by the classic postmodern dilemma of having too many choices and trying to decide what she should get, Teddy walked around the aisle, and straight toward her. They locked eyes, and both smiled big happy surprised smiles, and Teddy spoke.

Hi Grace.

Grace blushed.

Hi Teddy.

He kept walking toward her.

How you doing today?

She kept blushing.

I'm great. How are you?

He kept smiling.

Fantastic.

She looked at his cart. Overflowing with delicious junk.

Having a party?

He laughed.

Yeah, kinda. Wanna come?

She laughed.

As much as I would love to see you, not sure it's such a good idea.

They stared at each other. Both hearts were racing. Both minds spinning. Both wanting to see what it might be like. If what they felt was real. They both wanted more, but neither said it.

They just stared.

Teddy smiled, with joy and sadness.

In another life, Grace.

She smiled, joy and sadness.

Yeah.

Teddy motioned to the freezer.

Mind if I get in there? Unicorn Cotton Candy is calling my name.

She laughed, stepped aside. Into his cart went two pints of Unicorn Cotton Candy, and some Moose Tracks Mint Brownie, and some Powdered Jelly Donut, and two boxes of ice cream bars, and a box of frozen chocolate bananas. Grace watched him the entire time, heart racing and mind spinning. Teddy closed the freezer, turned to her.

See you around.

She nodded.

Yeah.

They stared for a moment. He smiled, stepped forward, wrapped his arms around her and brought her in close. Though he couldn't see it, she smiled and wrapped her arms around him and brought him in close.

For a moment. Two. Three.

Both lost count.

Seven. Eight.

The aisle was empty, but they both heard approaching voices. Neither wanted to be seen or to give anyone a reason to talk about them. They both let go and they both stepped back and they both smiled. Grace had had her eyes closed and she opened them. Teddy smiled.

In another life, Grace.

Teddy turned and walked away and in some small way, both of their hearts broke.

Girls' Night

The kids were both at sleepovers.

Billy was at a work dinner in the city, and said he was going to stay at their place in Tribeca, which meant he was seeing one or more of his sugar babies.

Devon and Ana, as they often did on these types of evenings, decided to have a night.

They started in the afternoon. It was still warm enough to go in the pool, but not for long, fall and winter were coming. They drifted around in floating lounge chairs with cup holders and listened to tunes and shared a joint of blue dream and split a bottle of Domaine Ott.

Two masseuses came for predinner massages.

They had sushi delivered, ate outside as the sun went down, uni with caviar and toro yuzu truffle and yellowtail with jalapeño and lobster tempura and seared Wagyu, with miso caramel bonbons and pumpkin cake for dessert.

They put on their pajamas and watched *The Notebook* in the movie theater in the basement.

They sat under blankets on chaise chairs on the back patio. The moon was down and the sky deep purple, there were a billion stars dancing, birds were singing and frogs were peeping the bugs buzzing and the coyotes calling, the dark symphony of the living night at full volume. They each had a late-night glass of Maison Martell. Devon spoke.

How's your family?

Anxious for me to come home.

Do they know?

No.

Going to surprise them?

We'll see if we get there.

How has Billy been with you?

I think he has other interests at the moment.

Devon laughed.

I assume that's why he's in New York.

Closer to home.

Katy?

Yes.

It concerns me.

She seems like a nice girl.

She is.

She doesn't deserve him.

None of us do.

Men can be so terrible.

They don't think rules apply.

Have you seen the security tapes from Willowvale?

Yes.

What are you going to do?

Nothing.

Why?

His wife will need the money when he leaves her.

You really think he'll leave?

Yes.

It's not just Billy. Alex is a bad man as well.

We always knew that.

She doesn't deserve him.

None of us do.

They stared at the sky. It was dark, the slightest sliver of a moon, billions of stars, still warm, though cooler as fall started to assert itself.

They listened to the music. Took sips of their drinks. Lost themselves in their thoughts. Of what had happened, what might happen, and what they wanted to happen, how things could go wrong, they both knew sometimes things go terribly, terribly wrong. Devon sat up.

You want to go fuck with some of Billy's shit?

Ana smiled.

I thought you'd never ask.

Sometimes on nights when Billy was gone, they would go into his office, or his closet, or his bathroom, or all of them, and they would move things, hide things, alter things. They would move a watch he loved from his case to a drawer. They would hide his favorite cufflinks in the bottom of a drawer. They would move things around on the desktop of his computer, which they could access, though he didn't know that they could access it. They would stain one of his favorite shirts. They would empty the bottle of cologne he insisted on wearing every day. Small things. Nothing big, nothing obvious. Nothing he could accuse either of them of doing without sounding crazy. It was their way of exacting some form of revenge against him. Against a man they knew was a bad man. Against a man who treated them both like they were his property. Against a man who scared them.

It was all they could do.

Until it wasn't.

Losses

Sometimes the market goes up.

Sometimes the market goes down.

It's very hard to predict which way it will go, and when.

That's the fundamental reality of the market.

Billy's system was designed to exist outside of this fundamental reality. The market turned, whichever way, on information. Good information and it goes up, bad information and it goes down. If you had that information before it was publicly available, you would know which way it would go before anyone else, and before it went.

And you could act, and trade, accordingly.

It always worked.

Good information, bad information.

Billy paid people handsomely for information. He paid them with great discretion.

Billy knew the penalties for getting caught buying information.

Jail.

Fines.

Penalties.

Doom.

So when he paid for information, he made sure the individuals he paid were people who could be trusted with great discretion, and he made sure that the information they were selling him would be accurate and reliable.

Thereby he could act, and trade, accordingly.

There was a lawsuit. It was against a pharmaceutical company. If the pharmaceutical company won the lawsuit, their stock would skyrocket. If they lost the lawsuit, it would crater.

Billy paid a Clerk of the Court to tell him which way it would go. He believed the clerk to be an individual who could be trusted, and he believed the information to be accurate and reliable.

He bet five hundred million dollars on it.

The information was bad.

And he lost five hundred million dollars.

Billy didn't like to lose money.

He really didn't like losing that much money.

Really really really.

Not a good day for him, or for anyone else.

He broke two of the flat-screen televisions in his office. He broke one of the espresso machines in the office kitchen. He threatened to fire two analysts, called one of them a dumbfuck piece of shit and a braindead waste of a chair, and told the other one that she was incompetent and stupid and doomed to die alone because nobody else on earth was dumb enough to want to be with her. He kicked over a water dispenser. He tore the seat off the toilet of his private bathroom and used it to smash the mirror in his private bathroom.

He did all of these things before lunch.

He sent everyone home shortly after.

He drank three scotches while the maintenance staff fixed or replaced what he had broken and took away the wreckage.

He called his private security team and asked them to do everything in their power to destroy the life of the clerk who'd provided him with the information that had led to the bad trade. He asked them to do everything in their power to destroy the lives of the clerk's parents, and both of the clerk's sisters.

He texted Katy.

From the phone he called War.

He told her he expected to see her in his office after lacrosse practice was over.

He opened his safe.

He took out his drugs.

Private Lessons

She didn't know if she loved him or she loved his dick.

Or maybe both.

She had never cared at all about hockey. She had never been to a game. None of her daughters had played it. She never understood why so many parents obsessed over it. Ice rinks were cold and the people who went to them wore bad clothes and the food was terrible. She preferred a polo match or a horse race. A lovely sail. Tennis. A football game in a packed stadium, preferably in Texas.

But she started taking an interest.

She watched *Slap Shot*, and *Youngblood*, and *Miracle*, and *The Mighty Ducks*. She watched a Rangers game. She went to one of Charlotte's games with Devon and Billy. Though she didn't really watch the game, she just watched Charlie as he worked the bench.

He was hot.

She got wet.

She saw him almost every day. Teddy would go to work and their daughter would go to school. She and Charlie would arrange a time between workouts and practices for him to come visit. Sometimes he had twenty minutes, sometimes he had two hours. Sometimes it was hard and fast and passionate. In the bathroom, on the marble counter of the kitchen island, on the parquet hardwood floor of the foyer. Sometimes it was slow and sweet and intimate. In the guest room. On the sofa of the theater. In the guest room on the first floor, in the guest room on the second, in the guesthouse.

He talked about hockey, and his car, and the gym, and his favorite places to get wings, and his favorite beers. He was enthusiastic and innocent and simple and pure and uncomplicated and kind and full of naive joy.

He made her laugh.

She found him delightful.

They fell in love, though not the doomed self-destructive love of most marital affairs.

But some kind of happy enchanted love.

Teenage love.

First love.

And that is what it was for Charlie, his first true love.

Not including, of course, hockey, beer, and eating pussy.

His first true love of another human being. His first true love of a woman.

He'd had plenty of girlfriends and he had liked all of them and he had told a couple of them that he loved them.

But he never really understood what it meant. Or how it felt.

Until Belle.

Until he saw Belle smile at him. Until he looked into her eyes while they were making the sweetest sweetest love. Until his heart skipped when she giggled. Until his heart hurt, very literally physically hurt, every time he had to leave her.

He liked it.

He really really liked it.

It felt fucking great.

Now he understood.

Love.

It was the best.

They didn't discuss marriage or a future or anything beyond how much they were into each other and when they were going to see each other again.

Belle knew Teddy knew something was going on. But he seemed preoccupied, probably something at work. And he seemed happier and more confident than he had been, sometimes work did that for him, especially since his manhood had gone on vacation and not come back.

Charlie knew Katy knew something was going on. But she seemed preoccupied, and when he tried to talk about it with her, she denied it. She had stopped working out. She was drinking more and more and more. Her face looked different somehow, he couldn't quite figure it out. She wouldn't talk about it. And she didn't want to have sex. When he asked her why she just shook her head and looked away and said no.

When Charlie and Belle weren't together, they thought of each other. Texted each other.

Sent each other pictures. Some dirty and some not.

There were hushed calls, whispers.

When they weren't together they ached and yearned, their hearts and their souls and their bodies.

She told him on a Tuesday afternoon. They had made the sweetest love under a blanket on the lush Kentucky bluegrass she grew behind her house. They fell asleep in each other's arms after. She woke first. And watched him sleep. Felt his breath as it caressed the skin on her chest. He opened his eyes and saw her staring and he smiled and said

Hey, Hot Stuff.

And she giggled and he smiled wider and she said

I love you, Charlie.

He smiled wider.

For real?

And she smiled wider.

Yes, I love you.

You know what?

What?

I love you too, Belle. And it fucking rocks. And you rock. And I love you too.

She giggled again.

This could be trouble.

What kind of trouble?

Who knows. These types of things can get complicated.

He smiled again.

I'm not scared of trouble.

No?

Not if it's with you. I'm not scared of anything if it's with you. I love you. I love you with my whole heart. Bring it on, bring it all on, bring the trouble.

And so it was brought on.

It was all brought on.

Trouble.

Serve and Volley

It is said that New Bethlehem is a place for people with A-type personalities. For the most successful of the most successful. For the hardest working of the hardest working. For the most competitive of the most competitive. Nowhere is that more evident than at the country clubs, where golf, tennis, squash, paddle tennis, and pickleball become blood sports. Where people spend years and years sometimes decades and tens of thousands of dollars sometimes hundreds of thousands of dollars on lessons and gear and practice and more lessons and better gear and more practice just to have a chance to claim one of the coveted titles of Club Champion.

Grace had been the Club Champion in the women's singles division of the New Bethlehem Country Club five times, which was also the number of times she had entered the tournament. She loved to play tennis, and played as often as she could, but didn't always love the atmosphere that surrounded playing at the club, especially playing for the title. People took it way too seriously. It wasn't Wimbledon or the US Open. Nobody playing in the tournament was representing a school or university, or trying to win a state title, or earn or justify a scholarship. The only stakes were getting your name engraved on a fake silver cup and bragging rights. Yet for some, it was everything. They were too willing to cheat on line calls, tip the club pros, who made the seedings, to get into a better slot, end friendships over results. Grace just wanted to play a game she loved and get in some exercise and have some fun. But Alex liked that she was so good, he said it was appropriate for the family brand, and tried to get her to play every year. She decided to indulge him by doing so every other year.

At the end of the season, when the club closed the outdoor clay tennis courts and transitioned to paddle tennis and hardcourt pickleball, there was a banquet and awards ceremony to celebrate the team season and the club's best players. Though Grace played #1 singles on the club team and hadn't lost a match in two years, and though she had won the Club Women's Singles Championship, she didn't want to attend the banquet. The last time she had gone was two years previous, when she had last entered and won the Championship. The woman she beat, one Laney Lucas, who won the title every year that Grace didn't enter it, had gotten drunk at the event and told Grace that she hated her and that she dreamed of smashing Grace's hands with her racquet and that she tried to hit all her shots into Grace's face and that Grace wore bad tennis skirts and that red hair was tacky and that she thought Grace's kids were ugly. Grace was shocked, saddened, hurt, and angry, but she stayed composed and did not return fire, simply walked away and sat down at a table with some friends.

There were flowers with a note and an apology call the next day, and a reprimand from the Club for Laney, and a reprimand was serious business. The story went around town for a few days, maybe a week. Grace lay low and the couple times it did come up, she laughed it off. She was friendly when she saw Laney in town, or at a school committee meeting, or at the club. By all appearances, she forgave, and she forgot.

But she didn't forgive, and she didn't forget.

As per her normal routine, she took the next year off.

Laney won.

And Grace reentered the summer after.

And very deliberately, she looked very vulnerable in the early rounds. Her matches lasted longer than expected, against players who shouldn't have had a chance, with a couple close calls. She was missing shots she normally made, not moving as swiftly, or as easily. She gave Laney hope, and gave Laney belief. And Laney started talking, about how it was her year, about how Grace had lost a step, about how she couldn't wait to dethrone her.

They met in the finals. Laney's entire family came to watch, her husband and children, both her and her husband's parents, her sister and her family, her brother and his. Her besties also came, five women at an umbrella table with flowers and a celebratory bottle of champagne for after the match. As they shook hands at the net before starting, Grace smiled, and so only Laney could hear, she whispered.

Red hair isn't tacky, and my kids aren't ugly.

She demolished her.

With ruthless efficiency.

And no mercy.

6–0, 6–0.

Laney won only four points the entire match, and none in the second set.

Her children cried. Her mother cried. Her besties cried.

Her husband clasped his hands in front of his chest, and he looked away.

After Grace hit four straight aces to close out the final game, Laney fell to her knees, and joined in with her children and her mother and besties, and she cried.

Grace walked off the court and went home.

She had a cigarette and a glass of white alone on her back porch to celebrate.

She didn't want to go to the banquet and have the whole thing happen again. It was country club tennis. It was stupid and in the great scheme of the world it didn't matter at all. And even though she knew it was stupid and didn't matter at all, she would get drawn into it again if Laney was an asshole, and Laney was for sure going to be an asshole, and she didn't want to get drawn into it again. But Alex wanted to go. He loved a party. All the guys would gather around and they'd talk about the glory days, in three sports, about the legendary victories, about Notre Dame, about the NFL. He got to be a star. He got to be the Biggest Man in the room. He got to be worshiped. It was high-octane fuel for his sportscar of an ego, armor for his fragile soul. He said it was for work, that he needed to keep his sales relationships, and always work to make new ones, but she knew that was bullshit, that it was just the way he conned himself into feeling good about the whole charade. Given what had been happening, Alex having another affair, their marriage teetering, the whole house of cards ready to fall, she decided to indulge him and go, to make the effort, to be the best wife she could be and try to support him when maybe he really needed it.

She wore a Lilly Pulitzer dress that she knew Alex loved, even though she hated it.

She wore the jewelry that he'd given her.

She shaved her legs and did her brows and waxed.

They went to the party.

Most of it was pretty cool, pretty okay.

They got along and laughed and almost flirted, Alex was warm, attentive, affectionate, and present. Grace felt loved, like they were still strong, like they were going to be okay, like the marriage would last. By all appearances that was the case.

Alex did his thing with the guys. It was the height of football season. So they talked about football. And despite New Bethlehem having won six of the last seven State championships, and despite being ranked #1 in the State again, the talk of the night was how the current team didn't stack up to Alex's team, and how, despite having two other QBs make the NFL, a near miracle for small town in Connecticut, Alex was the best to ever wear the Ram uniform, the Rams being the town sports mascot.

She drank wine with the other wives, talked about the new yoga studio opening on Birch Street, the price hikes at Howard Turner's, the upcoming lacrosse fundraiser. They laughed, gossiped and shared stories, joked about their husbands. Laney was there, but huddled with her besties on the other side of the room, likely doing the same thing, having the same types of conversations.

As people were starting to be seated for the dinner and award ceremony, Grace went to the restroom. She'd had three glasses of white and wanted to freshen up before the long slog of mediocre food and too-long, half-drunk speeches began. The club bathrooms were lavish, floral Schumacher wallpaper, marble counters, gold fixtures. There were four stalls and four sinks, with room between the sinks for a handbag, or to cut a line of coke, or both, depending on why one was in the bathroom. Grace was standing in front of one of the sinks putting on lipstick when Laney walked in with one of her besties. They took positions at sinks on either side of Grace. Laney spoke.

Hey, Girl!

Grace made an effort and smiled.

Hi, how's your night?

Great. You?

Great.

Laney looked at Grace, spoke.

You and Alex seem well.

Grace finished with her lipstick.

We're doing our thing, you know?

Laney's smile faded, faded quickly.

I just thought with everything that's going on with him . . .

Grace put her lipstick in her bag.

What do you mean?

Losing his job, the affair with Devon McCallister, the whole thing. It's a lot. I'm amazed the two of you are here together, much less seeming as cozy as you are.

It was as if Laney had run her over with a truck. Grace was stunned, speechless, stared at Laney, her bag in her hand. She was paralyzed with shock, confusion, sorrow, rage, a deep piercing pain that she could feel in every cell of her body, pain laced with anxiety and fear and uncertainty, her heart pounding, her hands shook, her lips quivered. Laney smiled.

Did you not know?

Grace couldn't move or breathe.

Oh, honey, I'm so sorry. I would have assumed . . .

Laney's friend smiled, and motioned to the door, spoke.

Maybe we should give her a moment.

Laney smiled and nodded, looked at Grace.

I really am so sorry. If you need anything, really, we're here for you.

They turned and left, and Grace could hear them giggling as they walked back to the banquet room. Grace's heart was racing and her hands were shaking and her lips were quivering.

Shock confusion sorrow rage.

Deep piercing pain. In every cell.

She took a short sharp breath. A short sharp step toward one of the stalls.

Heart racing.

Another step.

Hands shaking. Another. Lips quivering.

In the stall she sat down on the toilet seat and closed and locked the door.

She took her first deep breath.

Piercing piercing.

Pain.

Humiliation. Despair. Anguish.

In every cell.

For her, in that moment, nothing in the world existed.

Except for her horror, her worst nightmare come true, her desolation.

As she let out that deep breath, she slowly slid off the toilet and onto the floor behind the locked door of a country club bathroom stall, and sobbed.

Uncontrollably sobbed.

Years of pain.

Years of loneliness,
Years of betrayal.
Unbridled. Unleashed.
Her life and dreams and marriage demolished.
Uncontrollably, she sobbed.

All Day Long

Had a stalled deal for an AI-directed algorithmic trading platform. Closed it.

Needed an equity partner to buy a controlling stake in an employment logistics and payments business.

Found it, closed it.

Took a controlling stake in a robot food-delivery service to market.

Closed it with a profit of 600 percent after eighteen months.

Six hundred.

Not a typo.

Teddy was calm and his heart rate was low and his mind clear.

He was in the flow in a manner that allowed him to see what he could not see before, understand the previously confounding, become the driver of his destiny, instead of the passenger.

He was the Closer.

And he was fucking back.

His days were long. They started early with a meditation and a workout. First in the office he took pride in unlocking the door. Analysts reports, earnings reports, growth charts, revenue projections, EBITA. Phone calls, video calls, conference room one, conference room three, conference room one again. An afternoon coffee. For thirty minutes after his coffee, he took off his shoes and untucked his shirt, and lay down on his sofa, head against a pillow, feet up, and he closed his eyes, and he daydreamed.

About Grace.

Romantic daydreams. A walk on the beach together. Dinner in Paris.

He'd heard the town gossip about the disaster at the club. He already knew about Alex and Devon, Belle told him a week earlier. He knew she was going through what could only be a time of great hurt, of great misery. He had sent her a text. It said

I'm here as your friend if I can help in any way.

He knew she got it he saw the read receipt, he had once owned a stake in the software company that invented it.

He waited and he believed.

He knew it was such a difficult, difficult time and she was doing whatever she needed to do and thinking through whatever decisions she was making, he believed she was a fierce and strong and capable woman.

And he believed there would come a time when they would find each other.

He believed that when that time arrived, and they found each other, they would also find love.

Love.

Because he believed these things, when he daydreamed every day, those thirty magical minutes of ecstatic imagination after a burst of liquid focus and energy, he visualized wonderful things he hoped they would do together, wonderful places he hoped they'd see together, wonderful moments they'd share with each other, he went into the flow of data that controls our existence but now with streams that simulated joy and thrill and inspiration, contentment and pleasure, bliss.

He could have stayed there forever, but he always stopped after thirty minutes. He had done any number of deals with pharmaceutical companies. He knew the power of the strong drugs.

And the danger.

He worked another two or three hours. Back to conference room three, calls with companies that were in California, prep for the next day there was more business to be done and more deals to close.

When you had a hot hand you had to keep playing.

And his hand was hot. For any number of reasons.

180 | James Frey

He always texted Belle before he left the office, they had family dinner most nights, it was their youngest child's final year before leaving for boarding school, they were keeping it together for her.

And it wasn't all that hard.

He still loved Belle and Belle still loved him.

But their love wasn't one of passion or intimacy anymore. Those fires had long cooled. There was respect and admiration and trust. There was shared history. There was a catalog of good memories.

But sometimes memories aren't enough without the promise of future happiness.

Neither wanted to hurt the other. So it was as it had been during Teddy's long drought, where they both understood the situation, and lived in quiet acceptance of it. Belle was having an affair. Teddy could get hard, but with someone else. Their long life together was breaking down. And now was just time. They knew it was going to break.

They still slept in the same bed.

They each had their side.

It was comfortable and safe. A place where they could rest.

Teddy usually went to bed before Belle. He believed a good night's sleep meant a solid and productive morning. He normally left his phone outside of the bedroom, but lately had been keeping it on his bedside table. He'd read every night, lately it was nineteenth-century French literature, Dumas, Hugo, epic tales of love and adventure, romance and redemption, damsels in distress and swash-buckling heroes willing to risk their lives to defend them. When his eyes started to fall, he'd check his phone for the text he always hoped would be there, and believed would arrive at some point. And when it wasn't there, he'd drift into a state similar to the one he enjoyed every afternoon. He took his drug of dreams, know-ing that drugs were dangerous. At night, though the dreams were darker, and heavier, and were influenced by his reading, took on the spirit of it, a beautiful and kind woman in trouble, a dangerous man who did her wrong, a knight or a cavalier, or a wealthy private equity guy known as the Closer, who was on a streak of closing and closing and closing some more.

If she needed him, he would be there.

If it were a situation involving danger, he would stand tall and face it down.

If it involved risks, he was willing to take them.

All he needed was a call. Or a text.

And one morning when he picked up his phone after he opened his eyes.

The sun had not yet risen and the birds were quiet and still.

It was there. From Grace.

His love, his dream, and he believed, his future.

He read it again and again. It said.

I want to see you.

Secrets and Lies

Belle signed up for skating lessons with Charlie and they fucked in the men's locker room before the lesson and they fucked in the women's locker room after the lesson and they fucked in the back of Belle's giant black SUV with heavily tinted windows before she went home.

Alex lost ten football bets in a single weekend and by Sunday evening owed his bookie thirty-five thousand dollars, he took another Rolex and a diamond tennis bracelet and sold them in New York.

Billy made 250 million dollars on a single trade using good information and celebrated with a visit to Gunnar and a text to Katy.

Teddy closed a deal to buy an AI-powered B2B SaaS platform and two days later closed a deal to sell 20 percent of the aforementioned AI-powered B2B SaaS platform for an 80 percent profit because that's what motherfucking Closers do they close and they close and when shit is closed, they keep closing.

Devon and Alex had dinner at Le Penguin, a popular French restaurant in Greenwich. They saw three other couples from New Bethlehem they knew and made no effort to disguise their affection for each other, and in fact they both decided it might be fun to put on a little show and engaged in some relatively steamy PDA with lips, tongue, necks, and ears.

Charlie and Belle hired a car and went into New York they had mutton chops at Keens they went to see a Rangers game at MSG and they spent the night at the Mark, a car brought them home the next morning. They had sex in all four of those locations. At the Garden and the Mark more than once. They bumped into a New Bethlehem family they both knew at the game, and two fathers who were at the game together. They did not make any attempt to hide, or to hide that they were together.

Ana also went into New York. She put a small digital tracking device into the inside pocket of Alex's jacket while he and Devon were fucking and whenever he stole something, she tracked him to the fence who bought it from him, and bought it back. After the first transaction, Ana took the tracker out of Alex's jacket and stayed in touch with the fence via a burner phone, and she would go in and pick up whatever Alex had taken and bring it back. Ana thought it was a bit crazy, but Devon often did things just to see what would happen, to see what would develop, and this was one of those cases. Ana usually stayed in New York for most of the day. She went shopping. Bought presents to send home to her husband and daughter. She bought things for herself, clothing and shoes, she was into high-end, hard-to-find sneakers. Devon had given her a credit card and told her she could use it as she pleased. And Ana did, use it as she pleased. She bought presents for her family, she sent them extra cash advances, she paid for her daughter's tuition with it. But she was also careful with it. She often told Devon when she used it so there wouldn't be any surprises. Devon never cared, and always encouraged her to use it more. At first Ana was uncomfortable with the arrangement, or the opportunity, however it was viewed. She was suspicious of it, and thought there must be strings attached. But there weren't. There never were with Devon. She was the kindest, most generous person Ana had ever met and ever known. Their bond became tighter, closer. And when she heard Devon fight for her with Billy, Ana truly came to trust and believe in their friendship, in their bond. It wasn't a common kind, but it was theirs, and they both believed in it, and in what they hoped would become of it.

Grace stuck to her routines and lived her life. She took the kids to school, went to yoga, played tennis, honored all of her volunteering commitments. She ignored the whispers and the side-eye glances. When asked by friends if she was doing okay, she told them she was fine. If they pushed, she told them she didn't want to discuss it. She prayed to her God and spoke with her God, she trusted her God and believed her God would take care of her.

Katy started drinking even more and working out even less. More than one colleague asked her if something was wrong, and she said she was okay. She couldn't tell them. Billy was clear that he would destroy her if she told anyone. So even though something was terribly terribly wrong and she was very much not okay, she did her best to just keep going. It wasn't her first time dealing with a monster, though as a child she was helpless to do anything about it. This time, if given the chance, she would act to protect herself. She just needed the chance, the right kind of chance, and when it came, Billy would get what he fucking deserved.

Charlie had a tournament in Lake Placid, where teams from all over the East Coast went to see whose hockey was the best hockey. He had three teams playing, and at least one of them usually won the tournament, establishing Fairfield County, Connecticut, hockey as among the best hockey. Belle went to the tournament with him. She didn't go to the games, stayed in the hotel, walked around town, went skiing, went to the local spa, which wasn't quite like the spas she normally went to, but any spa was better than no spa for Belle.

Billy also went to the tournament in Lake Placid. His daughter's team was playing in it and favored to win it. He loved watching Charlotte play almost as much as he loved watching the Islanders play, and if there was fighting in girls' hockey the way there is in the NHL, he would have loved it more. He and Charlotte shared connecting hotel rooms. When she wasn't playing he worked on a laptop and she hung out with her friends on the team. The tournament was double elimination and the year before the team had won it without losing a game. This year they lost both of their first two games and were out on the first day. Billy wanted to immediately leave but most of Charlotte's friends were staying. They had a screaming match. Billy called her a spoiled little brat. She called him a terrible father and a mean man and told him everybody knew it. He called her a little bitch like her mother. She started crying and although he believed in what he said, he agreed to stay. He watched some of the other New Bethlehem teams play. All three of Charlie Dunlap's teams lost both of their first games. He saw Charlie and Belle out to dinner together, and he knew why the teams had all lost. He decided it was time to act. Time to make a move on Charlie Dunlap.

Alex was also in Lake Placid. His son Preston played on a squirt team. The squirt-B team, which meant his son was, at best, an average player. Alex tried to pretend it didn't bother him, but it did. It bothered him a tremendous amount. He had expected both his children, but especially his son, to inherit his athletic gifts. He had expected to ride a wave of glory with his boy the way he had rode a wave of glory throughout his own sports career. But Preston just didn't have it. He was a nice boy, a sweet boy, he was into music, and wanted to join the local kids' theater, and though he was decent at sports, he wasn't great, and he didn't really care about being great. Grace, and his parents, and his friends, and Preston's coaches, all tried to make him feel better by suggesting that maybe Preston was just a late bloomer, and that he would develop into an athlete like Alex as he got older, but Alex knew that was bullshit, you could see the great ones, and it never made him feel any better, just worse. He loved Preston, or kind of loved him, and tried to behave with him in a manner that Preston would never know how deeply disappointed Alex was, but despite his ability to lie and cheat and act and pretend with everyone else his life, he couldn't do it with his son. Preston did his best. Alex cheered him on. Both knew it was a lost cause. Tournaments were always tough for him. The best young players on the best teams were always there, and it made him both remember what it was like to kick ass on the ice and bring home trophies, which he desperately missed, and it drove home how mediocre his own son was and would always be at hockey, and every sport Preston played. This tournament in particular had been terrible. All three of New Bethlehem's top girls teams had lost and were out, and the boys, though still in it, weren't looking much better.

Devon and Ana spent the weekend alone. Charlotte was away at the tournament with Billy. Nicholas went to Fishers Island with the family of a friend. Devon and Ana drank wine and smoked weed and ate delivery food and got massages and watched films and talked about the future. They each felt trapped and they each wanted something different and they were trying to figure out if there was anything they could do about it and what they were willing to do about it.

They knew Billy was dangerous and they knew he would come for them if either ever tried to leave him and they knew that if they did ever try to leave him that whatever they attempted had to work or the consequences would make their current situations with him look like paradise. They drank and smoked and ate and talked and planned.

Katy normally hated the weekends that other sports had tournaments or championships. It meant that lacrosse would be canceled because so many players and their families would be away and she loved lacrosse and she loved coaching it.

But she was tired, so tired.

She was beaten down. Her body hurt and her heart hurt and her soul hurt.

It felt like she was living in some kind of nightmare and she couldn't wake up.

She slept late. She stayed in bed after she woke up. She got out of bed to smoke a joint it made everything hurt less her body her heart her soul. Charlie and Billy were both away, both at the same tournament. Charlie was sleeping with Belle Hedges she knew it was unlikely she would hear from him. She dreaded hearing from Billy, everything that motherfucker did hurt, every part of her hurt. She hadn't done her laundry she wasn't going to do it.

Her sink was filled with dirty dishes she wasn't going to clean them.

She was behind on grading quizzes she had left them at school.

She got out of bed as it was getting dark, it took all of her strength to get in the shower. She stayed in the shower for thirty minutes and let the hot water run and run and run over her. She tried to wash all the dirt away and wash all the pain away and wash her current existence away she let the water run.

As hot as it came.

She let it run and run and run and run and run.

When the hot water ran out she put on leggings and a sweatshirt and went to the bar. It was the only thing that brought her peace.

It was the quickest and easiest way to find her great and terrible friend Oblivion.

There was a hockey game on when she arrived. Bruins versus Rangers. Though she never wanted to go back to Boston, she still rooted for its teams. Normally, she would sit at the bar and drink until it felt like she almost couldn't walk, and at that point, she would walk home. She fell a couple times, on the sidewalk, into some hedges, on someone's lawn, but she always made it home, and the bruises, along with the others Billy would give her, were easy to explain because of her coaching. Her plan on this night was to go a little further. Get fucking drunk and get a ride home, maybe a taxi, or rideshare, maybe some man, she didn't care anymore. As she was watching the game, a man sat down a couple barstools away from her. He was tall, short dark hair, olive skin, green eyes, he wore faded jeans and a sweatshirt, and a Rangers hat. He glanced over at her and they both smiled and he ordered a drink and they both watched the game. When the Bruins scored, Katy smiled.

Fuck yeah, Bruins.

He smiled and asked

Bruins fan?

She nodded.

Yes, I am.

Why the Bruins?

I'm from Boston.

Still live there?

No, here.

Really?

Yes.

He leaned forward, looked at her hands. She spoke.

What are you doing?

Looking at your hands.

Why?

I didn't think there were any single women under thirty who lived in this town.

She laughed.

Aren't you smooth.

He laughed.

I try.

Rangers fan?

I am.

Where are you from?

Danbury.

Still live there?

No, here.

She smiled, leaned forward, and looked at his hands. He smiled, held them up so she could see them.

I didn't think there were any single men under thirty who lived in this town.

He smiled.

I'm not under thirty.

No?

Thirty-one.

Close enough.

He reached over, offered his hand.

I'm David.

She took it.

I'm Katy.

They shook and it felt good for both of them, and they held it, and they smiled at each other.

What brings you here, Katy?

To this bar or this town?

Both.

It's Saturday night and I'm here to get drunk.

Same.

And I teach math at the middle school and coach lacrosse.

Cool.

You?

It's Saturday night and I'm here to get a little drunk, but not much.

Won't hold it against you.

And I'm a cop. Sergeant, Investigative Division, in the New Bethlehem Police Department.

You're a cop?

Yes.

Can I buy you a drink?

No.

No?

I'll buy you one.

Showdown at the Mini-Mart

Billy was in a bad mood.

A bad bad mood.

His daughter's team had gotten crushed.

He had been stuck in Lake Placid for the entire weekend.

The escort he hired to come down from Montreal wouldn't drink the drink he gave her, wouldn't drink at all.

It was Sunday morning. He had a four-hour drive ahead of him. One of Charlotte's friends was riding with them and he knew they would talk the entire time and it would make him want to drive his BMW M5 into a tree.

He stopped at the gas station/mini-mart to fill up and buy a couple energy drinks and some beef jerky, a pair of ear plugs if they had them.

He started filling the car, went inside, bought his drinks and some jerky and a tin of chewing tobacco, walked back outside.

Alex Hunter was filling his car at the pump next to him. Billy walked up to him, bag in hand.

Hello, Alex.

Alex looked up, and smiled. Billy hated that he smiled. He wanted him to be scared.

Hello, Billy.

They stared at each other for a moment. Both hated the other. Neither would piss on the other if they were burning.

How was your weekend?

Kids hockey, you know. Busy, hectic.

They stared at each other for a moment. Billy spoke.

I know you're fucking Devon. Everybody in town knows. You should be more discreet.

Alex's face flushed.

You really want to have this conversation here?

We're not going to have a conversation, Alex. I'm going to talk, and you're going to listen. And you're going to do what I tell you to do. And if you don't, I will fucking wreck your life. And your parents' lives. And both of your brothers' lives. And the lives of your wife and children. And if you think I won't, I dare you to fucking try me.

Alex towered over him, but also believed him. He had heard stories from Devon, from other people around town, heard stories from people who worked in finance in New York. If it were a fight, an old-fashioned fist fight, he knew he would kick Billy's ass. But he knew that's not how Billy fought. Billy's money brought him power. And his power made him dangerous.

What do you want, Billy?

Use some fucking discretion with my wife.

Another New Bethlehem father was standing at a pump in the neighboring aisle. He looked over. Alex noticed he was listening to their conversation.

Maybe lower your voice a little.

Don't tell me what to do, Alex. I'm telling you what you're going to do. We clear?

Alex looked at the father, who was trying to appear as if he wasn't listening, and glanced into the car, where Preston was playing a game on his iPad. He looked back at Billy.

Yes, we're clear.

If I hear of the two of you in public again, you're over.

Have you spoken to Devon about this?

I don't need to fucking speak to Devon about this, I'm speaking to you.

They stared at each other.

We clear, Alex?

They stared.

Yes, Billy, we're clear.

Good. The other thing you're going to do is fire Charlie Dunlap.

Why would I do that?

Because I'm telling you to do it.

Why?

His teams just lost every game in this tournament and I want him fired.

He's a great coach.

Unless you want your parents to lose their house, you're going to fire him when we're back. I'd take your house, but I know you're close to losing it already.

Fuck you.

Billy stepped toward him, raised his voice.

What did you say?

The other father was watching, listening.

I said fuck you, Billy.

Call your parents, warn them.

Won't change the fact that I fuck your wife whenever I want to.

You're not the first, I'm sure you won't be the last. Fire Charlie or I fucking wreck you and everything and everyone in your sad, faded, broken existence.

Billy got in his car and pulled away.

Having Words

It had been a bad weekend for Alex.

Really really fucking bad.

Most of the Hockey Association teams, which usually did very well at the Lake Placid tournament, and always won at least one age group, had all gotten crushed. His phone was blowing up with calls and texts from angry and disappointed parents, all of whom thought their kids would play in either the NHL or the Olympics someday, though most of them would never even start on the high school team.

He had lost sixty thousand dollars on ten bad bets, after losing thirty the week before and believing he could dig himself out of his hole by doubling down. His bookie called and told Alex he had a week to figure it out, and if he didn't or couldn't, there would be very serious consequences. Alex knew the bookie was a dangerous man, and that those consequences would be a broken leg at best and death at worst.

Billy McCallister had threatened to destroy him. And despite acting like a tough guy in the moment, he was scared of Billy. Billy was a mean son of a bitch, and Billy could and would destroy Alex and everyone he loved.

He sat in the car. Preston was still in the back seat absorbed in his iPad, utterly unaware of the multiple disasters his father was facing. Alex could feel his hands shaking; it felt like his blood had been replaced by some poisonous liquid made out of a combination of self-hatred and shame. He sat in the car and stared straight ahead at the gas pumps, two fast-food restaurants, a ski shop, and four souvenir stores, and he thought

Fuck fuck fuck fuck.

What are you going to do what are you going to do what the fuck are you going to do.

Fuck fuck fuck fuck fuck.

You fucking loser you dumb fucking loser how the fuck did you get yourself into this nightmare you dumb fucking loser what the fuck are you going to do.

He tried to breathe.

In through the nose

Out through the mouth.

Calm himself.

Allow himself to think.

The poison wasn't going to leave him. But if he could calm himself. He could think. He could make a plan. Find a way. Find a way out.

In through the nose

Out through the mouth.

He couldn't change the results of the tournament. It happened. Despite the fact that New Bethlehem won plenty of tournaments, State championships, and an occasional National championship, sometimes you have bad luck. The parents would be outraged about something else soon enough.

He would see Devon soon. They would meet at Willowvale. He'd been very careful about what he'd stolen so far. She hadn't seemed to notice. And he doubted the parents would notice. Her father had eighty fucking watches. He could take a couple more. Her mother had enough diamonds to open her own private diamond district. He could take a couple more.

He had to fire Charlie. He had the authority to do so and he would do it. It would get Billy off his back long enough for him to figure out what to do about Billy in the long term. He liked Charlie, and he thought Charlie was a great coach, but if the choice was between himself and Charlie, it was an easy decision. He might get some blowback from the hockey board, but given that all of Charlie's teams lost all of their games, and all of them were having bad seasons, he could justify it.

In through the nose

Out through the mouth.

He started the car. Drove to the hotel where he knew Charlie and Belle were staying for the weekend. It was early, he doubted they had left. He pulled up to the entrance, put on his flashers, told Preston to be cool and keep playing his game, went inside. He looked around the lobby. He had been to enough tournaments with Charlie to know his habits. When he wasn't coaching, he was usually at the hotel bar drinking beer and talking hockey or hanging out in the lobby drinking beer and talking hockey. Alex didn't see him in the lobby. He walked into the bar and he wasn't in the bar. He walked back to the lobby and saw him coming out of an elevator and walking toward the front desk. He started toward him, hoping to catch him before he got to the desk.

Charlie.

Charlie stopped, turned around.

Hey, Alex.

Alex walked toward where Charlie stood. The front desk of the hotel was twenty feet away. The elevators behind him. A seating area with sofas and chairs twenty feet in the opposite direction. There were a few people in the seating area, including a New Bethlehem father named Royce. When Alex arrived, Charlie smiled.

How you doing, man? Good weekend?

Not a great weekend.

Yeah, tough results. Got some work to do when we get home.

About that.

About what?

When we get home.

You drive fast or you drive like an old lady?

What?

How long will it take you to get home?

Charlie, I . . .

Charlie laughed, playfully punched Alex on the arm.

You must drive like an old lady, you old lady.

Alex did not laugh. He looked directly at Charlie.

Charlie, when we get home you're going to need to look for a new job.

Charlie looked confused.

What?

You're being relieved of your coaching duties.

What?

You're fired, Charlie. It's over.

What are you talking about?

I'm sorry it didn't work out. We'll work out severance and terms when we're back.

Is this a joke of some kind?

Unfortunately no.

What did I do?

You didn't win enough.

I've won eight State titles, and one National.

I gotta go, Charlie. I'll call you tomorrow.

Alex turned to leave, Charlie pushed him.

Fuck you, man.

People in the lobby heard him, saw him, including the other father, Royce.

Alex didn't react, walked away. Charlie followed him, pushed him in the back.

Fuck you, Alex.

Alex kept walking. Charlie followed. Pushed him again.

You're a fucking piece of shit little bitch.

Alex kept walking. Charlie followed. Pushed him again.

Turn around so I can knock you out, you bitch.

Alex opened the door.

Walk away. I will fucking find you. I will . . .

Alex walked out, got in his car, drove home.

The Tea, Again

Royce shared what he saw and heard in the hotel lobby with his wife, Reese.

Reese shared what she heard with her friends Tara, Clara, Kara, and Amara.

Tara shared it with Sabrina, Katrina, and Valentina.

Clara shared it with Elanor and Emmy.

Kara shared it with Bianca and Bridget.

Amara shared it with Margaret, Megan, and Molly.

Sabrina shared it with Marissa and Melissa.

Katrina shared it with Madison, Mackenzie, and Matilda.

Valentina shared it with Vanessa and Valerie.

Elanor shared it with Taylor and Tessa.

Emmy shared it with Blair, Sloane, and Peyton.

Bianca shared it with Whitney, Kendall, and Taylor.

Bridget shared it with Amelie, Genevieve, and Colette, and did so in French, with the perfect accent she developed while at boarding school in Switzerland.

Margaret shared it with her housekeeper Guadalupe, who was friends with Ana, and shared it with Ana, and when Ana heard it she shared it with Devon.

Megan shared it with her husband, Don.

Molly told her entire book club, consisting of eleven women, and nine of them had heard about it already.

Marissa shared it with Gabriela and Fernanda.

Melissa shared it with Audrey, Scarlett, and Anastasia.

Madison shared it with her tennis group, consisting of eight women, and all of them had already heard about it.

Mackenzie doesn't tell stories so she didn't share it with anyone.

Matilda told Kali, Lexi, Lani, Dani, Rani, and Sami, and within two days the entire town knew.

Dolce Vita

Grace chose the spot. A small Italian café in Pound Ridge, a cute, old, one-street American town with a few little shops, a gas station, a hardware store, one pizza joint, one sit-down Italian joint, a couple wine stores, a weed shop, and a grocery store. Though it bordered New Bethlehem, it was not frequented by New Bethlehem residents. They didn't bother with it. They thought everything in New Bethlehem was better and nicer and cooler and fancier. Pound Ridge didn't particularly care and didn't miss them. It was as if the towns existed in parallel universes. And everybody liked it that way.

Though the café had a lovely outdoor seating area with teak tables and chairs and white umbrellas, Grace and Teddy sat at a table in the back of the smaller indoor area. They didn't expect to see anyone they knew, but took the extra precaution just in case. Grace was wearing yoga pants and a sweatshirt, her hair in a ponytail, Teddy had on a gray vicuña suit, white shirt with one open button, no tie. She was waiting as he walked toward the table.

Their eyes met.

They both smiled, big true radiant beautiful smiles.

She stood, they hugged, held it.

They sat, and she spoke.

Thanks for coming.

I was thrilled to hear from you.

Good.

How you doing?

I don't know.

You're smiling.

For the first time in a while.

Also good.

Yes.

We can talk about it if you'd like, or we can just sit here, without any pressure or stress, just sit and be cool and escape.

She smiled wider, asked

Can we hold hands?

Fuck yeah.

She laughed.

But that's all.

He smiled wider, nodded.

That is more than enough, Grace. And more than I expected.

She offered her hands, and he took them, in the back of a little coffee shop in a one-street town, and they enjoyed each other, without any pressure or stress, and they escaped.

Color Fields

Oh, Connecticut, how beautiful you are.

On those crisp clear days.

The sun still high and still warm.

But fading.

A breeze that brings out the sweaters.

And wool socks.

Flocks of ducks and geese.

Swallows and warblers.

Heading south.

Heading south.

Oh, Connecticut, how beautiful you are.

With dew.

Becoming frost.

As the mornings cool.

And become cold.

Your Golden Retrievers acquiring winter coats.

Your equestrian Thoroughbreds thickening.

Your bears rampaging through dumpsters.

Preparing to sleep.

Preparing to sleep.

Oh, Connecticut, how beautiful you are.

Your Birches.

Your Hickories.

Your Willows and Oaks.

Your Maples.

Sugar and Red.

In all their motherfucking glory.

And it is glorious.

So glorious.

As the deepening autumn brings them out.

Your hues.

Tones.

Tints.

Your pigments and shades.

The full palette that God or Aliens or the Matrix or Evolution or dumb biological luck, whatever it is that made this World, has given you.

The full palette.

On full display.

Fiery reds and glowing oranges.

Yellows that shine like bright walls of gold.

Rich burgundies, deep bronzes.

Brown like the lightest chocolate.

And purple.

Regal, elegant.

Purple trees.

Oh, Connecticut, how beautiful you are.

Whatever was once green is gone, now painted by the seasons into a kaleidoscopic explosion of color, a magnificent tapestry of change and death.

Splendorous.

Boundless.

Resplendent.

Oh, Connecticut.

Oh, Connecticut.

Devon and Alex were in bed in the large guest suite in the east wing of the second floor of Willowvale. There were polished zebrawood floors. White velvet wallpaper. A wall of portes-fenêtres. A Matisse on another wall. A Dufy on another. The view from the windows designed a century ago to be as it was then.

They had just fucked.

His black wool socks still on. A white T-shirt.

Her dress, pushed up, pulled down. Bra somewhere on the floor. Thong somewhere.

She lay across his chest, in his arms.

Drops of sweat.

Both were quiet, still, lucid, breathing slowly.

Lost in their thoughts it was both a very simple and a very complicated time, both wondered how any of it could be real, life and its joys and complexities, how could any of it be real. Alex spoke.

I want to be with you.

You are with me.

Openly. Publicly.

You are.

Not really. We're both still married.

And you want to change that?

I love you. Like I've never loved anyone. Like I can't believe. I don't want to hide anymore. I want you every minute of every day for the rest of my life.

She smiled, for very simple and very complicated reasons.

You sure want to go down that road?

Yes.

I love you, Alex.

I know.

Like I've never loved anyone. Like I can't believe.

Is that a yes?

I don't want to hide anymore. I want you every minute of every day for the rest of my life.

Those are the best words I've ever heard.

It's not going to be easy.

I know.

Grace will be heartbroken, and Billy will be a fucking nightmare from the deepest fires of the darkest hells.

He laughed.

I know.

Lawyers and court and custody evaluations.

Forensic accounting.

She laughed.

When do you want to tell them?

Soon.

The next couple days?

Yes.

Wait for the right moment, let each other know after?

Yes.

I love you.

I love you.

And he pulled her in tight, and he held her, and some part of him did love her, but more of him was simply and deeply thrilled with his victory. His plan had worked, and with victory he was saved. There would be no humiliating fall, just a messy divorce and a minor town scandal, both of which he accepted as the cost to play and win the game, both of which he was happy to pay. Devon looked at her watch and said she had to go, to get home for the kids, she was taking them to the New Bethlehem Diner for dinner. She pulled away and got dressed and kissed him goodbye they both said I love you and kissed again and she left in her Range Rover.

He stayed in the house, took his time, went into new rooms.

Found a drawer in the pantry with silver. So much silver that if he was moderate in his greed, none would be missed, and he was moderate.

He found a gun safe slightly open but hidden behind some ammo he found six gold bars and took three.

In Devon's childhood bedroom he found a jewelry box. In it a diamond cross platinum setting engraved to her, from her grand-mother, a set of small diamond earrings she got them when she turned ten, a tennis bracelet that matched her mother's a gift on her sweet sixteenth, rings clearly very old—diamond, emerald, sapphire, and ruby, family heirlooms passed down to Devon she planned on passing to Charlotte.

He took them all.

Everything.

He left and went home and they both waited for the moment, the right moment, to say the words.

To tell their spouses it was over.

To say the words that would change their lives.

Or end them.

A Third War Room

Billy was with his lawyers, who each cost two thousand dollars an hour.

There were five of them. They sat at a long table in a conference room in a modern office building on Long Island Sound in Stamford. Billy sat on one side of the table, floor-to-ceiling windows and a view of the Sound behind him, his lawyers sat on the other side. Billy's face was red and neck veins bulging. He pounded a fist on the table.

I want to destroy her, and I want you to find some way to destroy him. And when I say destroy, I mean destroy so they're scared and broke and they come to me on their fucking knees begging for forgiveness and begging for fucking mercy.

Billy stared at them. The lawyers glanced at each other to see who was going to respond. The lawyer who was sitting in the center of the five, Adam Kaufmann, who was the firm's Managing Director, spoke.

There's a very, very strong prenup, so it's not likely there will be much litigation.

I want to destroy them.

Adam held up his hands.

Before we talk about strategy and tactics, please tell us what happened and how we arrived here today.

My wife fucking left me, Adam. That's how we fucking arrived here today. Was that not made fucking clear to you.

Yes, Billy. That was made clear to me. How and why? We need to know how and why. It matters.

Billy takes a deep breath, clenches his jaw, looks down and shakes head, looks up, scowls, sneers, speaks

Last night. I came home. We have a set family dinner Monday through Thursday. At six fifteen. Devon and our fucking housekeeper make it together. They're like fucking best friends. Speak Spanish to each other so I can't understand them. It makes me fucking crazy. I swear they fuck with me somehow, they say something and they snicker or giggle, they fucking hate me. Fuck them. I hate them too. But they do always show me a small amount of respect by setting a place for me, even if I don't come, and I maybe go twice a week, or once, I just eat at work, or go to the city, or eat at home after they're done. I came home. I was in a great mood. I had a great fucking day. I made three hundred million dollars yesterday. I decided to come home for dinner and share the joy with my family. I get there, it's some fucking Costa Rican shit they always make for the kids, I know the housekeeper wants to go back, and Devon loves it there, so they always make the food. But I don't complain. Even though I'd rather have a steak. Or a veal chop. I ate what they made, and after the housekeeper offered to take the kids out for ice cream, the kids wanted to go, and Devon said something to her in Spanish, and they left. I was drinking, yeah a Macallan '54. Devon was drinking some kind of weird organic tea bullshit. And we're just talking. I'm telling her about the trade, and I asked her if she knew what that made our total liquid net worth. And she smiled, and said

There are more important things in life than money.

And I said

Yeah, what?

And in some bullshit, fake-sincere voice, she said

Love and happiness, Billy. Love and happiness.

And I laughed, because I know and everybody with half a fucking brain knows that money buys you love and happiness, and she said

I want a divorce, Billy.

He pounded his fist on the table.

A fucking divorce.

Pounded it again.

A FUCKING DIVORCE.

He took several deep breaths. He didn't speak, just stared at them. Adam spoke.

And from there?

I asked her if she was joking and she said no.

He took several deep breaths. He didn't speak, just stared at them. Adam spoke.

Please continue.

She's been having an affair. With this fuckboy in New Bethlehem.

For how long?

Six weeks or so.

You know his name?

Alex Hunter.

The former quarterback?

Yeah.

The lawyers exchange glances.

How long have you known about it?

The entire time.

And you were okay with it?

I fuck girls.

Yes, we know.

And I have no interest in fucking her, and it's not the first time, and no one in her family has even been divorced, so I ignored it, and I did my thing, as I always do.

Anything with you we need to know about it, or get involved with?

No.

Good. Please continue.

I asked her if she was leaving me for him. And she said

I hope you'll make a quiet and generous settlement offer, and we can all walk away from this with our dignity intact.

And I said

Fuck you.

And she said

A big public fight won't be good for anyone. Not you, not me, not the kids.

And I said

Fuck. You.

And she said

Billy, don't be a dick.

And I said

Fuck you, you dirty fucking whore.

And I threw my fucking glass of scotch at her smug bitch face and it missed, but shattered against the wall. And I screamed at her and told her I was going to destroy her and destroy everyone in her life and make sure she ended up on her knees as a crack whore in the South Bronx.

How'd that go over?

You think this is fucking funny, Adam?

Not at all. But I need to know how she reacted.

She got up and ran to our bedroom and I ran after her.

Please tell me you didn't hit her, Billy.

Billy interrupted him,

No, I've never hit her and know better than to hit her.

Good.

I thought about throwing her in the pool, maybe holding her down and smacking her with my shoe, but she's fast, she's fucking quick as a cat, and she got to our bedroom and locked the door. I had installed a steel door in our bedroom so it could be a safe room if

I ever needed one, if we were getting robbed, or the SEC showed up. Once she was in there, there was nothing for me to do.

Did you communicate any further?

No. I yelled at her through the door until I heard the housekeeper get home with the kids. I went to my office and slept there.

Kids see or hear anything?

No.

And this morning?

I left before she was up. But she texted me after the kids were off to school.

He looked at his phone.

It says

Fuck around and find out. Or make it simple and quick. Your call.

Lawyers glanced at each other. Adam spoke.

What do you think she means?

Don't know, don't care.

The prenup is unassailable. She can't touch your business or your money. We can start preparing for what might come, but my advice is to be patient and see what happens. Don't move out. Don't change your habits. Be civil with her. Maybe this will all blow over.

Billy shook his head.

It won't.

We'll see.

I don't want to wait. I'm not a person who waits.

We can't do anything until she does something first. If you file first, the terms of the prenup are not nearly as advantageous. Just be patient. And when it's time, we'll do what we do.

Billy stared at them. They stared back. They were, at two thousand dollars an hour, happy to wait for him. He took several deep breaths, clenched his jaw, looked down, looked back up. Adam spoke.

I'm going to say it again, Billy. And I know it will be difficult for you. But the best thing you can do is nothing. Just wait. Be cool. Be cordial. Anything we do before she files or makes a move of some kind will work against you.

Billy nodded, spoke.

I understand.

It's our job to give you the best advice we can and protect you.

I will do my best.

If you need to vent, call me. You have my cell and my home number. If you need a professional, I can refer you to a therapist who will likely be helpful. Do whatever you need to do within reason, just don't fuck around with her.

I understand.

Billy stood up and walked out of the room.

He went back to his office.

He threw a small bronze Rodin sculpture through a TV screen.

He made trades that resulted in 120 million dollars in returns.

He bought a Ferrari online.

A Richard Mille watch.

Four pairs of Air Jordans.

He threw the Rodin through another trading screen.

Broke the mirror in his bathroom with it.

When the markets closed he sent everyone home.

He texted Katy she didn't respond.

He texted a different woman one he sometimes paid to come play with him she came to his office and they played.

He looked at the latest computation of his liquid net worth. It was a significant ten-figure number.

He smoked some weed and drank some scotch.

Nothing made him feel any better or dulled the sharp edge of his rage.

He called the Director of his security team.

He wanted to fuck around.

He wanted to find out.

So he did.

Date Night

Though both had secrets that maybe weren't so secret.

Belle and Teddy were still married. Married people went on dates. Or at least married people who were still trying. Or pretending to try.

They went to dinner at an Italian restaurant on Maple Street called Luna. It was actually, as it is said, authentic. It was owned by Italians, staffed by Italians, the kitchen all Italian. It was a popular spot. The kind of place where you went after a piano recital, or a graduation, or before prom, or for date night.

They sat at a table for two in the main dining room. The tables had white tablecloths and comfortable chairs. The napkins were white linen. The wineglasses had long, elegant stems.

Teddy wore a black cashmere suit, blue shirt, one button open. Belle a black dress, black cashmere sweater. She had a glass of red, a heavy pour, as the staff at Lune knew she preferred. He was drinking ice water, extra ice, as the staff at Luna knew he preferred.

They were sharing Lioni burrata, with San Daniele prosciutto, persimmons, and walnut vinaigrette, while they waited for his grilled branzino with heirloom green beans, nduja, arugula, and roasted tomato chutney, and her fresh lobster spaghetti with cherry tomatoes and Calabrian chili. She spoke.

I didn't expect to be in this position.

I don't think either of us did.

We didn't have sex for years.

I know.

We couldn't.

I know all too well.

And it's been really fun. I really needed it.

I understand. I would have, though, appreciated some discretion.

We've been discreet.

Teddy smiles.

We have.

No, Belle, you haven't.

I think we have.

His car parked outside of our house while I'm at work?

I mean . . .

Private skating lessons?

Yeah, maybe.

Lake Placid?

I couldn't have predicted what happened.

Obviously, but that doesn't change it.

I know I've got to end it.

I assume he's not sticking around.

No, he is.

Really?

He already has offers to coach in Greenwich, Darien, and Ridgefield.

Teddy laughed.

Even though?

Yes, even though.

Were you there?

A discreet distance away.

Not discreet enough.

I'm sorry.

What did he say?

She took a sip of her wine. A large sip.

He said he was going to tear Alex's head off and shove it up his ass.

Teddy laughed.

That's pretty funny.

It should have been, but he was serious. He meant it literally.

Is that even possible?

Belle laughed.

I don't want to think about it.

What else?

The entire ride home he talked about what bullshit it was that he got fired.

He's probably right.

And that he was going to kick Alex's ass, find him and beat the shit out of him. If he could kill him and get away with it, he would.

That's not good.

No.

He's always seemed happy and mellow to me.

Same, but I guess he has this side.

We all do.

His, I think, is a bit more extreme.

You never saw it?

Only with Alex.

You really think he'll do something?

I don't, but I'm not entirely sure. He's sweet, but not the smartest. I hope he takes a new job and moves on.

Sounds like it's time.

Yes.

Teddy took a sip of his water. Belle another sip of her wine. They stared at each other, calmly, easily, it's something they've done for over two decades. There is respect and admiration and reverence. Teddy sets down his glass.

What do you want to do, Belle?

I still love you, Teddy.

I still love you.

Is it enough?

I don't know.

Where is your heart?

At the moment, it's here, with you.

But?

I've wondered if my issue isn't a manifestation of something deeper.

What deeper?

You're my best friend, Belle, and probably always will be, and we've shared so much together, almost all of it good. We've raised three beautiful girls, smart and kind, honest and driven, like their mother. But passion fades. I'm not sure humans aren't meant to be together forever, or maybe not all of us. Sometimes things just come to an end, and it's right, and it's for the best.

Their eyes met and held and they looked at each other.

With respect, admiration, reverence.

And sadness.

And love.

Belle spoke.

Is there someone else?

I've had some feelings, but haven't acted on them.

Feelings for whom?

Do you really want to know?

I've been open and honest with you.

Teddy nodded.

You have. So I will be as well. It's Grace Hunter.

Really?

Teddy nodded.

Yeah.

Belle smiled.

She's cute and delightful and probably pretty complicated right now.

Yes, all of those.

Do things work with her?

Teddy laughed.

Hasn't been fully tested, but it's working when I'm around her, and when I think about her in certain ways.

Belle laughed.

That's great news.

It's been a huge relief, and has definitely influenced my thinking.

I'm excited for you.

Teddy felt her foot moving up the inside of his leg, the inside of his thigh.

Wouldn't mind a few more tumbles with you before whatever happens with us happens.

He stirred. She felt his stirring.

I missed it.

So have I.

Let's get the check.

War Rooms Everywhere

Devon sat with Lou Keller and Louise Keller, who ran a very discreet, very selective law firm that specialized in matrimonial and family law, specifically high high high net-worth divorces. They did not have a website, or a listed phone number, or social media of any kind. They preferred people, unless they required their services or were engaged in litigation against them, not knowing anything about them or that they even existed. Their office was in a small house on a residential street just off Greenwich Avenue. The first floor had a conference room in what would have been a dining room, and a meeting area in what would have been a living room, and was decorated like one. They only took two or three cases at a time, and often took a percentage of the settlement instead of charging hourly fees. When Devon called, they immediately agreed to meet her. Though they had never met, Devon had been introduced to them via email three years earlier. She had told them she hoped she'd never need their services, but expected she would, and would reach out when she did.

They sat in the living room. Devon on a Boca do Lobo sofa, each of them on Roche Bobois armchairs. Coffee and tea set on a vintage French silver tray on a table in front of them. Lou, in his mid-sixties, was wearing a gray wool Gieves & Hawkes suit without a tie, Louise, in her early forties, was in a black Chanel dress. Lou was Louise's father; they'd been practicing law together for twenty years. Lou spoke.

We've reviewed everything you sent us.

Louise held up a stack of stapled papers.

The prenup is very good.

Devon nodded.

He believes in the power of good attorneys.

Lou smiled.

You seem to as well.

Devon smiled.

Yes, I do.

Louise spoke.

The tapes you have made and accumulated over the years are extraordinary.

Lou nodded.

We have never seen a collection of audio and video recordings as irrefutable and as damning, and we could have him arrested on a long list of charges.

Louise held up one index finger.

But it doesn't change the prenup or what you would be due if you were to file for divorce. The exceptions in it do not include any of the potential and likely charges, though it does contain others that are very unlikely.

Lou leaned forward.

I'm sure you've thought of releasing them to the press, but that never never works, it only causes more problems, problems you don't want to have and exposure that isn't helpful for you. Everyone who ever does it regrets it.

Devon nodded, understanding.

So what do I do?

Lou and Louise looked at each other. Lou nodded to her. Louise looked at Devon and spoke.

Because we often have to deal with onerous prenuptial agreements, we often recommend unconventional strategies for our clients in order to nullify them or work around them. And when we recommend a specific unconventional strategy, we do it because we know it will be effective. Despite our genteel surroundings, my father and I are stone-cold motherfucking killers, and the strategy we're giving you will work, but only if you stick to the plan, you absolutely have to stick to the plan.

Devon smiled.

I will do whatever you tell me to do for as long as you tell me to do it.

Lou leaned back, into the sofa, made himself comfortable.

Do nothing. Nothing at all. He's all worked up. Angry. Anxious. Hurt. He either wants to go to war or wants it over as soon as possible. So we're going to make him wait. And wait. And wait. And wait some more. We're going to make him wait until he breaks.

Lou leaned forward again, made sure Devon was listening, and she was.

Speak to him as little as possible. When you do speak, the only words should be yes, no, or maybe. Do nothing with him, no dinners or social events. Do not physically touch him in any way. If he brings up the divorce, ignore him. Go about the business of your life, and as much as you can, pretend he doesn't exist. At some point, and we have no way of knowing how long a time it will be, might be a week, a month, six months, maybe a year, he will break, like a piñata at Godzilla's birthday party, or an egg off the roof of the Liberty Tower, or an origami bridge at a Mack truck convention, he will break.

Louise leaned forward. Both Louise and Lou looked directly at Devon. Louise spoke.

And when he does, when he breaks, we're going to fuck him six ways from Sunday. If, of course, we have your approval, if, as they say, you're down.

Devon smiled.

Yeah, I'm down.

————

Grace sat in a small, bland conference room on the second floor of a small office building on Maple Street. Below the office there was a women's clothing store, a women's shoe store, and a women's vintage jewelry store. The office was at the end of a hall, next to an accountant's office, and across from an insurance office. Brad Garfield, New Bethlehem's second most sought-after divorce attorney, sat across from her. There was a stack of paper in front of him. Brad spoke.

It's not great.

Grace nodded. She was tired. She hadn't slept well in a week. After Alex told her he was leaving and wanted a divorce, she logged into their online banking profile for the first time in a couple years. They'd always had a strict division of labor. He handled the family finances, she handled the family. Despite his rumored dalliances, she'd always trusted him. And whenever they needed money, there was always plenty there. Already deeply hurt and embarrassed by his affair and subsequent desertion of her, by his deep deep deep betrayal of her and their marriage and their family, she was shocked when she saw that he had taken a second mortgage on their home, had drained their checking, savings, and retirement accounts, and had sold all their stocks and bonds. Though there had been some cash deposits recently, which he said were gambling proceeds, his paychecks had stopped coming in nine months previous, which she assumed meant he had lost his job and never told her. When she tried to talk to him about it, and ask where all the money had gone, and what he had spent so much on when the cash out wildly exceeded what they needed for their expenses, he told her that he could no longer discuss family finances with her, and that when she got a lawyer, to have her lawyer contact his lawyer.

And then he shut the guest room door.

And locked it.

As if she was going to do something to him. As if she could.

If only.

Brad motioned to the stack of papers sitting on the table in front of him.

You have a significant amount of debt. A limited amount of cash. No savings. He's unemployed . . .

Grace interrupts him.

He never told me. He kept going to the city every day. He'd come home and tell me about his work day. About sales he made and deals he was working on. About events he said he had to go to, updates about coworkers of his that I knew. He went on golf trips that he said were with clients. It's all crazy. I can't believe any of it's real.

Can I give you some advice?

That's why I'm here.

It's a bit harsh.

Given my circumstances, I'm not sure anything you say could hurt me or upset me more than I already am.

Your husband is not who you think he is, or who he has been telling you he is, or who he might have been once upon a time. I've been doing this for twenty years. I've seen bank records that look like this, and represented clients who have been in your position. The spending and withdrawal patterns tell me that he has severe problems with gambling, drugs, and probably escorts.

Grace bites her lower lip.

We'll likely never know for sure because he's been lying to you for a long time and there is no reason for him to stop now, and there is no way to definitively prove it.

She shakes her head.

I'm sorry, but he's a bad guy. A bad bad person. You need to accept that in order to make sure that you approach this process in a way that is best for you, and for your children, and for your future.

She nods, on the verge of breaking down.

We're going to file an emergency order freezing up your joint finances except for things directly related to the expenses of the home and your children. From my basic computations, you have enough cash to last about three months. The debt on the house is significant and the interest payments alone are going to drain your funds, and you should probably expect to sell it and downsize, probably significantly downsize. Whatever you can do to lower expenses, you should do right away. And I'm not sure when you last worked . . .

Twelve years ago.

I know you don't want to hear it.

Grace nods.

I've already started looking.

What's the situation with your children?

They know something is happening, but we haven't told them.

Are you speaking with Alex?

He hasn't been home in days.

Do you know where he is?

No.

Can you call him or text him?

She bites her lip again.

I have, so many times, he's not responding to me.

She looks down, closes her eyes, and shakes her head. He waits, it wasn't the first time he's been in a meeting like this one, wasn't the hundredth. Though he should've been hardened against it, he wasn't. A woman's life was falling apart. Her dreams dying. Her hopes being thrown in a dumpster and lit on fire. He knew what lay ahead for her, personally and financially and socially, what lay ahead for her children, and all of it was lonely and hard and humiliating. And none of them deserved it. She looked up, tears almost welling, but she held them back.

How absolutely screwed am I?

And his heart broke a little, as it always did when it came to this point of these conversations.

You have a hard road ahead. But you're going to be fine in the end. You'll be better without him, and you and your children will find happiness and stability. But it's going to be difficult for a while. It's going to be very difficult.

She nodded slowly, closed her eyes, finally broke. She put her face in her hands and bent over and sobbed.

Her life and dreams, her hopes for the future.

On fire.

She sobbed.

So Nice They Named It Twice

Everything was more valuable than he had expected. The silver was made by some famous silver guy. The sapphire earrings of a quality rarely seen. And Devon's childhood jewelry all vintage Van Cleef and Harry Winston. All told it got him almost one hundred and fifty thousand dollars. He had planned to put some of it into the family accounts so Grace would have it. But her lawyer had gone to the court and restricted his access to the accounts and he couldn't do it anymore.

Dumb bitch.

She was going to make it difficult.

She should have known that lawyers were just going to drain what she had left.

And he didn't have anything else to give her.

So he kept it.

He didn't want to go home. And Devon had told him that he couldn't stay at Willowvale. So he got a room in New York at the coolest, of-the-moment-est hotel in the East Village. A hotel full of young beautiful women. With drugs readily available in the hotel bar or on the street. His bookie a phone call away. It was some kind of paradise for him. He could indulge all of his loves, all of his joys, all of his pleasures.

Sex. Drugs. Gambling.

And nobody could say a word about it. And nobody could judge him. And nobody gave a fuck that he had been All-State everything and won everything and played at Notre Dame and in the NFL. And nobody knew that he had lost his job and lost all of his money and left his wife and children to fend for themselves.

No more pushing the Rock.

He felt relieved, so fucking relieved.

To be done with it. To be free of the prison of ambition and accumulation. From the crushing weight of expectation. To be able to breathe and relax and wake up without a care in the world. He knew it would likely end up being another kind of prison. But at least it would be comfortable, and at least it would be easy, and if it ended, he would leave empty-handed. And the first couple years, at least, would be fun.

He'd been in New York for five days.

He'd lost eighty thousand dollars gambling.

He'd spent twenty on escorts.

The hotel was three a night.

Five on drugs.

Five on presents for the escorts.

His celebration was coming to an end.

His victory party.

His freedom festival.

He would text Grace and tell her was coming home to pack his things. He'd stop and fuck Devon on the way, if she left before him and she always did, he'd take a few things maybe a watch, maybe jewelry, maybe one of the Holland & Holland side-by-side shotguns he found in an unlocked case in the basement there were six of them each worth six figures. They were, after all, soon to be his anyway. He'd go to his soon-to-be former home and pack his things and make sure he fully cleaned anything that mattered to him out of the house and out of his soon-to-be former life, one last night and it would be over, and he would be happy to be done with it.

Happy to be fucking done.

Almost Date Nights

Katy didn't go to the bar every night.

Two or three times a week, lately three or four.

David usually only went on Fridays.

But hey!

Hey!

There's nothing wrong with having an ice-cold American draft beer in a mug on more than just Fridays, nothing wrong with it at all.

And it just so happened they ended up sitting next to each other from time to time.

Life is funny with those coincidences. You think of something. And it shows up, it's there, it happens. She thought it was cool that he was a Cop. Even better, a Hero Cop. Her kind of delicious, though she kept that to herself.

He thought teaching was cool. And worthwhile. And being a great athlete was his kind of delicious. Though he kept that to himself.

They'd talk about their jobs, their colleagues, the town, about sports, he loved the New York teams, she loved the Boston teams, it got heated.

They'd talk about past relationships. He'd been dating a nurse from Stamford she decided she wanted a Doctor instead of a Cop. She'd been with Charlie he decided he wanted a Married Woman. The Nurse lost the Doctor and tried to come back to the Cop he politely said no. Charlie lost his job over the Married Woman and his anger was out of control he was drowning in it.

Such is life and dating.

Doesn't work out most of the time.

But we keep doing it and doing it and doing it.

Because we believe that one time, it just might.

It just might work out in some way that brings us a little peace, a little joy, a little happiness, and some pain, the pain reminds us it's real, the pain reminds us we should be careful with it.

Katy and David weren't dating. They were in the Curiosity Stage. Lots of flirting. Touching of the arm. Laughing. Sometimes he walked her home and their hands would brush. It was electric.

They were becoming friends, good friends, close friends.

Before they became more.

Ornithology

Charlie was mad.

Real fucking mad.

He knew he would be fine with work. He had more than one job offer. It was just which town and which teams and how much cake they would pay him. His record spoke for itself. He wanted more cake and he was going to get more cake and his choice would likely be based on the cake.

He wasn't mad because he was worried about getting another job.

And he was mad.

Real fucking mad.

He was mad because he believed he didn't deserve to be fired. And he believed his firing was an unjust action.

Unjust. Unfair. Wrong.

His anger was a matter of principle. There was no logical reason or justification for him to be fired. And the bullshit about losing a few games was nothing but some bullshit. And whether it was his idea or he was doing someone else's dirty work. It was ultimately Alex Hunter's call. He was Mr. Hotshit, town Hero, everybody's favorite, everybody's idol, President of the Hockey Association. As Charlie sat in his car in the dark in the driveway of a house across the street from Alex's house that was for sale.

For the fourth night in a row.

He was trying to decide how badly he was going to fuck him up.

If Alex came home while Charlie was there.

He was going to get out of his car and walk across the street.

And fuck him up.

Branches on the Tree of Understanding

It was believed that Devon and Ana took the kids to Willowvale for the weekend. They didn't tell Billy where they were going. All of them, including the children, wanted some time away from him. Almost the entire property was covered with security cameras, so the belief was supported by audio-visual evidence. The belief was also supported by phone-location data.

It was believed Grace took her kids and went to a friend's house in Rowayton for pizza and movie night, which turned into pizza and the moms drinking wine and the kids scrolling TikTok and playing *Roblox*. The belief was supported by eyewitness testimony from the friend and her children, from photos and videos taken over the course of the evening, and by phone-location data.

It was believed that Billy was first in New York City having an early dinner with a twenty-four-year-old model and after dinner spending time with her in the Tribeca apartment and after his private playtime with the model he came home to their estate in New Bethlehem where he looked at trading results and drank a scotch until he fell asleep sometime around midnight. Almost the entire property was covered with security cameras, so the belief was supported by audio-visual evidence. The belief was also supported by surveillance and toll cameras in New York and along the Westside Highway, the Henry Hudson Highway, the Hutchinson River Parkway North, and the Merritt Parkway and with phone-location data.

It was believed that Teddy was at a business dinner in Greenwich until midnight where he closed a deal for his firm to purchase a controlling interest in a company building a network of low-cost telecommunications satellites. After the dinner, he drove home and arrived shortly after midnight and read *Les Misérables* on his iPad until he fell asleep on the living room sofa. The belief was supported by multiple eyewitness accounts, surveillance cameras, and phone and iPad location data.

It was believed Belle was at dinner at the New Bethlehem Country Club with three girlfriends she knew from her squash league until mid-evening, when she went home and stayed home for the rest of the night. The belief was supported by multiple eyewitness accounts, surveillance cameras, and phone-location data.

It was believed that Charlie was at a hockey rink in Stamford until early evening and at a gym in Darien lifting weights and getting pumped until mid-evening. He was at Belle and Teddy's home from mid-evening until just before midnight. After leaving, he drove to a fast-food establishment in Norwalk, returning home to smoke pot and gorge and watch old hockey DVDs on large-screen TV. The belief was supported by multiple eyewitness accounts, surveillance cameras, debit-card receipts, cable box activity, and phone-location data.

It was believed Katy spent the evening drinking several ice-cold American draft beers in a mug at a local New Bethlehem food and beverage establishment. The belief was supported by the fact that she was enjoying those ice-cold American draft beers in a mug with David Genovese, Sergeant, Investigative Division, of the New Bethlehem Police Department, who walked her home just after midnight and shared a short, sweet kiss with her at her door before she went into her home and went to sleep. It was also supported by phone-location data.

Memento Mori

Grace's parents found the body. They had taken an early morning flight from Chicago Midway to Westchester HPN, a small commuter airport on the border of Greenwich and Harrison, New York, which mostly serviced private jets and flights to Florida. They were coming to support their daughter on what was an extremely difficult weekend during an extremely challenging time in her life. They had agreed with Grace that they should arrive before her in case Alex was still there. Grace didn't want to see him. They'd warn her off until he left. When they arrived, Alex was still there.

He was on the sofa in the living room.

An empty cocktail glass on the table in front of him.

His pants and boxers at his ankles.

His wrists bound in handcuffs.

A clear plastic bag over his head, silver duct tape wrapped tightly around his neck, just in case.

Three or four times.

Tightly.

Just in case.

Grace's parents both screamed and ran from the house and he called 911. They stayed outside of the house, in shock, barely able to speak, holding each other, until the police arrived, which took less than five minutes.

In Every Shadow

David was off-duty when he got the call.

Or rather, calls and texts and alert after alert, a hurricane of incoming digital information.

It was eleven on Saturday morning and he was out running.

He ran home and changed, didn't bother to shower, and drove to the scene, what normally would have taken eight minutes he did in three.

He parked in the grass next to a half-crumbling stone wall in front of a two-hundred-year-old center-hall colonial. There were multiple other police vehicles, both marked and not. Two ambulances. A crowd of neighbors had gathered on the lawn of the white-brick Georgian across the street. David got out of his car and rushed toward the Hunter home, an updated farmhouse with a gabled roof and a wraparound porch, footballs and a lacrosse goal with a bounce-back net in the front yard. Yellow crime scene tape had already been stretched across the perimeter of the house. David rushed past the EMTs and uniformed officers standing outside the house and stepped through the front door, where he was greeted by Mike Murphy, the New Bethlehem Police Chief. Murphy had been a Police Officer in New Bethlehem for thirty-five years, starting on traffic patrol and working his way up. He had gotten married in New Bethlehem, and raised his four children in New Bethlehem. He knew the town, its joys and privileges, its darkness and its secrets, as well if not better than anyone else who lived in it, and anyone who had ever lived in it.

It's in there.

He said to David, and motioned toward the living room.

What is it?

Maybe a suicide, but looks like a murder. And if it is a murder, it'll be the first one we've had here since 1972.

Bad?

Yes.

David looked through the archway into the living room, where techs were dusting for fingerprints and the photographer taking pictures. When David looked back at him, Chief Murphy spoke.

This is why we brought you here, David. In case anything like this ever happened. If it is a murder, you're going to find whoever did it and put them away. We don't allow things like this to go unpunished in New Bethlehem. It is not acceptable.

Yes, sir.

David nodded, and took a deep breath. He stepped into the living room. It was worse than he had imagined. It was definitely not a suicide. Alex Hunter was murdered.

Deliberately.

Methodically.

Ruthlessly.

———

Grace was getting the kids packed and ready to go home when her father called her and told her what had happened to Alex.

It is not possible to describe what she felt because there are no words for it.

Hell is real, though.

Hell is real.

Hell is real.

For the living.

Sometimes you have to walk through it.

And it's tolerable.

Sometimes you have to walk through it.

And it is the Inferno.

Maximum heat.

Maximum pain.

Maximum impact.

Not tolerable.

And for Grace, the long sad humiliating soul-crushing disintegration of her once fairy tale marriage to Alex had been a walk through some kind of tolerable hell.

Brutal, but survivable.

When her father called her and she answered her phone and he spoke to her.

Inferno.

She fell to her knees.

She heard the news.

She fell to her knees.

———

Billy was alone in the house.

He was in the kitchen sitting at a Carrara banquet on a navy-blue velvet cushion, two televisions on at the same time, his laptop, both his phones, *War* and *Peace*. Alerts appeared on all of the screens at the same time.

Former NFL Quarterback Alex Hunter Murdered in His Connecticut Home.

Billy clicked through the alert on his laptop.

Sometime last night. In his living room. Police not making comment.

Billy's first thoughts.

Wow.

Somebody hated him even more than I did.

Good riddance.

———

David texted Katy.

She'd just finished her first real workout in weeks.

She felt great.

She read the text.

Alex Hunter is dead. Someone killed him.

In her mind. Immediately.

Oh no.

Charlie.

You didn't.

Please no.

But Charlie.

Maybe.

Maybe.

Maybe.

You did.

———

Charlie and Belle were in bed at Charlie's place.

He called her when he woke up and invited her to come over, he missed her and he wanted her in his arms, he missed her smell, he wanted to kiss her.

She accepted his invitation.

And so they were.

Holding and kissing.

Their phones started pinging and buzzing almost simultaneously.

And they didn't stop.

Belle reached first, and looked, and said

Holy fucking shit.

Charlie had already reached.

Yeah, holy fucking shit.

Belle looked at him.

Charlie, you didn't do this, did you?

Charlie shook his head. He was stunned she would think that of him.

No. Absolutely not. I hated him and thought he was a piece of shit, and wanted to give him a black eye and knock a couple of his teeth out, but I wouldn't kill him. I'm a lover, and I'm a fighter, but I'm not a killer.

Belle looked into his eyes.

As deep as she could see. And she believed him.

He was a lover and a fighter but he wasn't a killer.

A killer.

———

Devon and Ana were having coffee in the kitchen of Willowvale.

Costa Rican coffee.

Which Ana bought at a Costa Rican market in South Norwalk.

Strong and bitter.

Their phones were together four rooms away set on a delicately carved, Louis XV console table, where they'd put them the night before when they arrived at Willowvale.

The kids were doing whatever they were doing, wherever they were doing it. The house was a vast playground and they loved to play. Her sweet boy Nicholas came to the door.

Mom?

Devon turned to him.

Hi, Nicholas.

Mom. Have you seen the news?

No, I haven't looked at my phone all day.

Mom.

Yes, Nicholas? Is everything okay?

Somebody killed Mr. Hunter. They murdered him.

Devon gave him a look, a look as if she couldn't tell if he was telling the truth or pulling some kind of deeply unfunny prank. He read her look, and could tell she didn't know if she could believe him. He held up his phone and turned the screen toward her so she could see it, read it.

The *New York Times* home page.

Former NFL Quarterback Alex Hunter Murdered in His Connecticut Home.

It took her breath away.

She froze.

Until a soft, slight moan escaped her.

Ana stood and walked around the table and gave Devon a hug. Devon hugged her back. They held each other until Devon pulled away and stood up her body working but some part of her soul frozen and she left the room and she walked up to her childhood bedroom on the second floor of the east wing and she went into her childhood bedroom and she shut the door.

It was real. It happened.

Another soft, slight moan escaped her.

It was real and it happened.

Former NFL Quarterback Alex Hunter Murdered in His Connecticut Home.

———

Teddy was at the local coffee shop on Birch Street.

On Saturday and Sunday mornings, the coffee shop's small parking lot and the street in front of it was filled with vintage Porsches, BMWs, Alfa Romeos, and Maseratis, newer Porsches, an occasional Ferrari, an occasional McLaren.

Teddy was looking at an Ivory 1964 Porsche 356 C when a parade of police vehicles started blazing past the coffee shop. This was not a normal occurrence in New Bethlehem. The Police Department was discreet, in a manner consistent with the population they protected.

Things were handled with elegance and fairness. He rarely saw a single cruiser with its lights on. Much less five, or seven, or ten.

Within a few minutes word of what was believed to have happened was being spread.

A murder at Alex Hunter's house.

His heart.

No no no.

Not Grace.

Please God.

No.

Not her.

No

No

No.

He was panicked, though if you had seen him, you would not have known. His mind was spinning through scenarios. He knew Alex was a bad man. He knew he was dishonest and unfaithful. He knew he was broken and desperate.

He didn't think he was a killer.

But you never knew.

You never knew.

No.

Please.

You never knew.

Under certain circumstances, anyone could become a killer.

Anyone.

A few minutes later more news.

Alex was dead.

Alex had been killed in his living room.

Alex.

Thank God it wasn't Grace.

It was Alex.

He couldn't imagine what Grace was going through or doing or feeling. Despite the collapse of their marriage, he knew her well enough to know she would be devastated. He picked up his phone. He sent her a text.

Whatever you need.

I'm here.

The Tea, Part Three

Jenny, who lived two doors down from the Hunters, told Alice that she thought maybe she heard something the night before.

Alice told Sarah and Liz that Jenny heard voices in the middle of the night.

Sarah told Carrie and Vanessa that a neighbor heard angry voices in the middle of the night.

Vanessa told Kelsey, Claire and Kelly that a neighbor heard people yelling at each other in the middle of the night.

Claire told Adrienne and Ali that a neighbor heard people fighting in the middle of the night and one of the voices might have been Charlie.

Ali told Kristin and Anne that a neighbor heard Charlie and Alex fighting in the middle of the night.

Anne told Ellen and Catherine that Charlie and Alex were screaming at each other and a neighbor saw it all through a window.

Ellen told Caroline and Emma and April that Charlie and Alex were screaming at each other and fighting in the living room and a neighbor saw it all through a window.

Emma told Kirsten and Meghan that Charlie went over to the Hunters' looking for a fight and a neighbor heard it and went to see what was wrong and saw Charlie beating Alex.

Meghan told Trish, Marion, and Cate that Charlie kicked in the door and beat Alex with a hockey stick and a neighbor got it on video.

Trish told Amy and Melissa that Charlie kicked in the door and beat Alex with a hockey stick and a neighbor got it on video but Charlie saw and chased him and took the phone and threatened to kill him.

Amy told Ella and Katrina that Charlie was hiding in the house and beat Alex with a hockey stick and a neighbor got it on video and the police had it and Charlie was going to be arrested.

Ella told Susan, Lucinda, Cammie, and Elaine that Charlie killed Alex with a bat and that the police thought it might not be the first time he's killed someone.

Didn't matter that none of it was true.

Everyone told everyone.

Didn't matter at all.

The Wheels

It was a long day for David.

The entire house was dusted for fingerprints, he supervised.

Alex's body was swabbed for DNA, he supervised.

The crime scene the entire house and the yard and the surrounding area photographed and recorded with video.

He directed other officers to ask all the neighbors within a mile to provide any footage they had from active security cameras that had recorded within the last twenty-four hours.

He secured the crime scene evidence.

A crystal scotch glass.

A pair of BDSM handcuffs.

The plastic bag and the duct tape.

He interviewed Grace Hunter.

She was distraught, devastated, heartbroken, despite the impending divorce. She had an airtight alibi and he did not believe she had anything to do with it.

He took her fingerprints and DNA and her children's fingerprints and DNA and her parents' fingerprints and DNA, for exclusion.

He interviewed Devon McCallister.

She was distraught, devastated, heartbroken. She had an airtight alibi and he did not believe she had anything to do with it. He took her fingerprints and DNA, for exclusion.

Her husband, Billy McCallister, was an obvious suspect. He would not submit to an interview without an attorney present it was being scheduled.

There was chatter about Grace and Teddy Moore. She said they were just friends and though David did not entirely believe her, he couldn't see a killer in Grace Hunter.

The station was flooded with tips about Charlie Dunlap. Most of them were easily dismissed because they didn't match the fact pattern of the crime scene. Alex had, though, fired him from his job as Head Coach of the New Bethlehem Hockey Association. And they'd recently had a confrontation in a hotel lobby where Charlie threatened Alex, though the exact threat did not match the fact pattern of the case. Charlie had agreed to an interview scheduled for Monday and he would be attending with an attorney, which was his right. His fingerprints and DNA were already in the system due to three arrests that occurred when he was a teenager, two for public drunkenness and one for fighting.

Alex Hunter's phone records were being subpoenaed.

Grace provided banking records. She said her husband had a gambling problem, placed his bets with a bookie in New York, though she did not know who the bookie was or how to reach the bookie. It would be investigated.

The phone and banking records were checked and the bookie found.

The crime scene haunted him. An image of Alex on the sofa in his mind, if not in front of his mind, always there.

Somebody hated him.

Somebody wanted him to die in a terrible way.

A way that would become known.

Somebody wanted Alexander the Great to be remembered as the Alexander the Dead and Humiliated.

It was someone who knew him.

Who wanted him not just dead, but humiliated.

Who somehow was able to get into a position where they duct-taped a plastic bag over his head. And likely stayed and watched him die.

It was David's job to find that person.

And he would.

He would find them and put them away forever.

Besties, Doing the Bestie Thing

Belle didn't want to leave Charlie.

He was nervous, and alarmed.

He found a criminal defense attorney in Fairfield he didn't have the money for the retainer. Belle gave it to him. It came out of the money she had from her family, not the accounts she shared with Teddy.

She didn't want Teddy to know.

There are secrets in every marriage.

Another one for her.

Belle didn't want to leave Charlie, but Devon needed her more. And though he was nervous and scared, he understood. They were, after all, besties.

She drove to Willowvale. As she was pulling up, she saw a Police cruiser pulling away. Devon was standing at the entrance, dwarfed by the giant house and the mahogany door behind her. She had clearly been weeping. Her eyes were red and puffy. Her normally radiant skin was sallow, hair a tangled frenzy. She was still wearing pajamas from the night before. Belle thought she looked like an actress in a film who'd just learned that she lost her lover in a war.

Except there were no lights, no cameras, nobody called Cut at the end of the shot.

It was real, as real as life gets, Alex was dead, mercilessly killed.

The police had questioned Devon and taken her fingerprints and DNA, which would doubtlessly be all over him.

As Belle pulled up, Devon ran down the steps toward her. Belle got out of the car and opened her arms as Devon staggered toward her, they met and hugged and Devon started sobbing and Belle held her.

For a minute, two, five, ten.

Belle holding Devon as she sobbed and sobbed and sobbed.

Real fucking life.

When she was done, when she was ready, when she couldn't any longer, Devon pulled away and looked at Belle and said

I love you.

And Belle smiled, which made Devon smile.

I love you. Thank you for coming.

Of course, Devon. Life's been a bit different lately, but you're still my best friend. I'll always be here for you.

Same for you.

I know.

Let's go inside.

The kids were in their rooms, both on Zoom calls with their therapists. Ana was in the kitchen, she'd just smoked a joint and was drinking an Imperial. Devon grabbed four bottles of rosé and a vape pen and they went to the guest suite in the east wing of the second floor, with the wall of portes-fenêtres, the Matisse, the Dufy, the room where she and Alex most often fucked, the room where she and Alex decided they were going spend the rest of their lives together.

And there they stayed, talking and laughing and crying so much crying, drinking Domaines Ott and smoking California OG Kush.

They'd go downstairs for food and for breakfast with kids and dinner with kids.

Ana was driving them to and from school.

For seven days. A WASP shiva for just the two of them.

They talked laughed cried and got drunk got high and shopped online and watched movies ate junk food and did what best friends do, which is be there to be a best friend when your other half needs you.

No matter what.

When those seven days ended Devon was ready to be part of the world again, to keep her chin high and her gaze straight and true, to ignore the whispers the looks, to dream of a future, she hoped it would come soon.

She would again be Devon Kensington.

As difficult as it might be to get there, as potentially treacherous.

Devon Kensington.

Soon.

Transcript of an Interrogation

The following conversation took place at the New Bethlehem Police Station, Interview Room 2. Its participants were Sergeant David Genovese, Investigative Division, Police Chief Mike Murphy, Hockey Coach and Murder Suspect Charlie Dunlap, Criminal Defense Attorney Bruce Mandell.

Genovese: Tell us again about your Saturday night?

Dunlap: I started at the rink in Stamford.

Murphy: Doing what?

Dunlap: Skating in circles real fast and taking slap shots.

Genovese: Until what time?

Dunlap: Probably seven.

Murphy: Is that something you do often?

Dunlap: All the time, man. It's great.

Genovese: And then?

Dunlap: I went to the gym in Darien. Bufftech.

Murphy: And what did you do there?

Dunlap: Flexed some metal and got ripped.

Genovese: Is that really your answer?

Dunlap: I swore to tell the truth and I'm doing it.

Murphy: How long were you there?

Dunlap: Till about nine.

Genovese: And after?

Dunlap: I went to Belle Moore's house.

Murphy: Would she confirm that?

Dunlap: Yes, she would.

Genovese: Are you sure?

Dunlap: Yes, I am.

Murphy: Was anyone else there?

Dunlap: I didn't ask, but I don't think so.

Genovese: What did you do at Mrs. Moore's house?

Dunlap: We took a shower and they have this marble bench thing in the shower and we had some sexy time on it.

Murphy: Please clarify the meaning of sexy time.

Dunlap: It means we did some fucking. We fucked on that bench.

Genovese: Thank you for clarifying. Please continue.

Dunlap: We had a beer in her kitchen. I like a cold beer and so does she, though I am an American beer man and she likes it from Europe. We went and had some more sexy time in her guest room because she won't do it in her bedroom. We watched an episode of *Bachelor in Paradise* on TV in the guest room and her favorite girl whose name is Sienna didn't couple up and had to leave the resort and she was a little bummed. Her husband texted her that he was coming home, so I left.

Murphy: Would she confirm that?

Dunlap: Yes, she would.

Genovese: Are you sure?

Dunlap: Yes, I am.

Murphy: What time did you leave?

Dunlap: Little before midnight.

Genovese: Where did you go from there, Charlie?

Dunlap: I was hungry, so I drove to my favorite restaurants.

Murphy: Restaurants?

Dunlap: Yes, I said it with an *s*.

Genovese: You went to more than one restaurant?

Dunlap: I swore to tell the truth and I said it with an *s*.

Murphy: How many, and where?

Dunlap: I went to two. But they're in the same place.

Genovese: And where are these two restaurants in the same place that were both open after midnight?

Dunlap: On Westport Avenue in Norwalk.

Genovese: Where on Westport Avenue?

Dunlap: Across the street from where Bed Bath & Beyond used to be, before those hedge fund motherfuckers bankrupted it.

Murphy: Do you have a problem with hedge fund managers?

Dunlap: We all know they're motherfuckers. You both know for sure. First they tried to take out GameStop, but the masses revolted. They won with Bed Bath & Beyond, which sucks, because I used to be able to buy lots of good shit there, got my air fryer there, got my electric shaver there.

Genovese: What are the restaurants?

Dunlap: It's a KenTaco.

Murphy: I lived in the area my whole life. I know Norwalk like the back of my hand. I have never heard of KenTaco.

Dunlap: I swore to tell the truth and I'm doing it. You're either lying about knowing Norwalk like the back of your hand or you're lying about not knowing KenTaco.

Murphy: Young Man, I have been a Police Officer in New Bethlehem for thirty-five years, and Chief of Police for the last ten. If you are calling me a liar, we're going to have a real problem, you and me.

Dunlap: I said what I said and I'm not taking it back.

Murphy: **Young Man, take it back.**

Genovese: Let's all take a breath here. Dial it back a bit. Charlie, tell us about this KenTaco.

Dunlap: I swore to tell the truth and I'm doing it.

Murphy: I think you're lying.

Dunlap: You're going to have to apologize to me.

Genovese: Tell us about KenTaco, Charlie.

Dunlap: It's a Kentucky Fried Chicken and Taco Bell under the same roof, in the same building, right where I said it is, across from the old Bed Bath & Beyond.

Genovese: I know it. I've been there.

Dunlap: Judging from the Chief's belt and the way his pants fit, I bet he's been there too.

Murphy. I do and I have. I didn't know it was called KenTaco. I'd consider it one restaurant, not two.

Dunlap: They got separate menus, they serve different food, it comes in different bags, different wrappers, the drinks come in different cups.

Murphy: One building, one drive-through.

Dunlap: I'm ready for my apology.

Genovese: How long were you at KenTaco, Charlie?

Dunlap: Apology.

Murphy: You're the prime suspect in the first murder in New Bethlehem in fifty years. You're in no position to be making demands.

Mandell: And we're doing this interview as a courtesy to prove to you that Charlie had nothing to with it. We can end it if you'd like.

Genovese: Our apologies, Charlie. How long were you at KenTaco?

Dunlap: Thank you. I went through the drive-through. I ordered a sixteen-piece bucket with sides of baked beans and mac 'n' cheese, biscuits, six Doritos Locos Taco Supremes, a Nachos BellGrande with extra meat, two twelve packs of Cinnabon Delights, and two large Mountain Dew Baja Blasts.

Mandell: Here is the receipt. You'll note the time stamp says 12:41.

Murphy: It's only a fifteen-minute drive from the Moores' to the restaurant.

Dunlap: Yeah, see, you know the place.

Genovese: What were you doing in the missing time, Charlie?

Dunlap: Nothing missing. I got there around 12:10. It took me a little while to decide what I wanted, and it took them a long while to make it all. They said it was the biggest order of the day. I know they got cameras there, go ahead and check 'em. I gave you my phone already, and I know you can check the pings and shit. Go ahead. Do it.

Murphy: Why such a large order?

Dunlap: I had been busy, skating circles and taking slap shots, flexing metal and getting ripped, making sweet love more than once with a lady who loves sweet loving and loves giving it back. It all works up a fella's appetite.

Genovese: And where did you go after you left KenTaco?

Dunlap: Drove home. Parked my ass on the couch with all my grub. Smoked a joint, which is legal now in Connecticut so you can't say shit about it, watched a DVD of Bob Probert's greatest hits on my big screen.

Murphy: Bob Probert?

Dunlap: The Undisputed Champion of the NHL. Greatest combo of skill and punching power in hockey history. Twenty-nine goals, thirty-three assists, and three hundred ninety-eight penalty minutes in one season for the Red Wings in '88.

Genovese: Did you go anywhere else?

Dunlap: I couldn't move after eating all that food. I fell asleep watching Probert duking it out with Marty McSorley.

Murphy: I think you drove back to Alex Hunter's house and killed him.

Dunlap: Didn't happen, Big Man.

Murphy: **You drove back to Alex Hunter's house and killed him.**

Dunlap: If you want some skating lessons, I could help you lose some weight and get into shape.

Murphy: **I'm going to put you away forever.**

Dunlap: Alex Hunter was a punk bitch.

Mandell: Charlie.

Dunlap: If I had seen him, I was gonna knock a few of his teeth loose.

Mandell: Charlie, please.

Dunlap: But I didn't kill him.

Mandell: Charlie.

Dunlap: I'm a lover and a fighter and a hockey man. I'm not a killer.

Murphy: I think you are and you should come clean now and save us all the trouble.

Mandell: This interview is over. If either of you or the New Bethlehem Police Department need anything else from my client, you know how to reach me.

Tender Mercies

The media descended.

A swarm

A horde

A mob.

Every network outlet medium every platform. They sat outside her house. They sat outside her children's schools. They sat outside her church. They sat outside the country club, police station, hockey rink. They sat outside Howard Turner's and TripleA, they sat outside her yoga studio, hair salon, her favorite nail spa, the local coffee shop, the station where she was believed to buy her gas. They didn't care that her husband had just been murdered, they didn't care that her children's father had just been murdered, they didn't care that they couldn't return to their home because it was an active crime scene, they didn't care that she was living inside an Inferno.

Hell is real for the living and the breathing and the feeling.

The media didn't care about anything but getting a picture, getting some video, asking a question, getting an interview, taking the living Hell of her life and sharing it with the world. They didn't care that she was a human being or that her children were human beings or that her parents were human beings, they wanted a picture or some video or to ask her or her fourth and sixth-grade children a question to sit down with them for an interview.

A swarm horde mob Hell.

Her friends, and very suddenly there were many more of them, got together and found a house for her in Darien. It was on a wooded, windy road in Tokeneke, the most prestigious, exclusive, neighborhood in Fairfield County, a neighborhood with its own private Police force. The house was at the end of the road, behind a gate, on six acres, surrounded by water on three sides, Long Island Sound glittering outside of every window. The owner was an investment banker who'd been living in London for two years. He'd known and competed against Alex in high school. He and his wife belonged to Wee Burn Country Club and his wife had played tennis against Grace many times, and lost every time but admired Grace's style and play, her spirit and yes, her grace. They were happy to help. At no cost. Because they understood that her husband had just been murdered and that her children's father had just been murdered and that they couldn't return to their home because it was an active crime scene. They made the offer without hesitation. And all involved thought the security and the privacy and the water might bring Grace and her children some peace. Even if for just a moment.

Food was brought in and brought out. There was more than they could eat. More than ten families could eat. Every day fresh salads and meat and fish and bread and cakes and cupcakes and pastries, food bought or made specifically for Grace and food bought or made specifically for her children bought or made by people with the best intentions and some humble and true form of sympathy, every single one of the people who bought it and made it and arranged for it to be delivered thinking to themselves

Thank God it's not me.

And trying to imagine what it must be like for her and for her children every single one of them thinking and knowing that the line is thinner and more fragile than any of us acknowledge or can bear to acknowledge.

Thank God it's not me.

That thin thin line.

The media didn't leave, so her children stayed with her at the temporary house, and didn't go back to school. And while most people think the reason New Bethlehem schools are so very extraordinary, Top Five in the United States and Number One East of the Mississippi, is because of sky-high test scores and exceptional results in athletics and college placements. The real reason, however, is because they care, the teachers and coaches and staff and administrators actually deeply care, they take their jobs seriously, they approach them with joy, discipline and generosity. When one or more of their students need them, or need their help, or need accommodations in unusual and difficult circumstances, they do what needs to be done, and they do it with joy, discipline, and generosity, and they did it for Preston and Madeline Hunter.

Each morning, a teacher would arrive at the house with the day's lessons and the day's work. In the morning, the teacher would be with one kid, while Grace's father, a professor for almost five decades, would be with the other. In the afternoon, they would switch. Homework would get done as they went and the teacher would leave with it at the end of the day. The routine helped Preston and Madeline immensely. It gave them a focus somewhere other than their confusion and grief, they didn't fall behind in school, and it kept them busy enough so that they didn't have to live every minute of their lives being crushed by the gravity of what had happened to their father.

Grace didn't see many people. Only the ones she loved most, her parents and her children, were with her. When she didn't think she could take another breath or last another minute, she would find one of them. She wouldn't interrupt whatever they were doing, she would just sit in their presence and be thankful for them. Her days were filled with trying to salvage what was left of her life. Speaking with the bank and trying to get an extension on her mortgage. Talking to credit card companies about outstanding balances. The car dealer she wanted to downsize. She spoke to the police at least once a day. A bankruptcy attorney if it became necessary. She and Alex were still technically married, so she was responsible for shutting down what was his life, closing all of his accounts, gathering his belongings keeping some but donating most, she spoke with the NFL about a pension she was trying to claim, she spoke with the insurance company his policy had lapsed. It was depressing and mundane, and she resented him for it, resented him for so many things but this was the easiest to bear. She planned a Memorial, his body hadn't been released it was still part of the investigation, when they did release him she would set a date. Amidst all of it she would sometimes yearn for someone

258 | James Frey

outside of the bubble of hurt and pain she was in to come for a visit, to bring a gentle piece of the outside world into her.

Her doubles partner, a sweet lovely kind woman with a great backhand named Fiona came for tea in the living room.

Her college friend Lindsay who lived on a horse farm in Bedford brought some sushi and a bottle of Sancerre and a bag of treats from Candy Bar for the kids.

She sat with her parents and Alex's family for a formal dinner where his family acknowledged his shortcomings and apologized for him and what he had done and how he had done it and she thanked them and in some small way forgave him a little and they all ended up crying and hugging and agreeing that the world didn't need to know all the bad about Alex they would keep everything quiet and celebrate what was great about him, celebrate the gifts he was given and the gifts lost, first when he was living, and irretrievably when he died.

Her Yoga teacher came three times. She called herself Nama. There was a waiting list for her classes. She did privates with Grace in the basement gym they stretched and posed and took long breaths and prayed before and prayed during and prayed after, each prayed to their own God, they didn't need them to be the same God to pray together.

Please help me, God.

Please.

In all of her moments, some part of Grace's soul was in prayer.

Please help me, God.

Please help.

And though he wasn't a help in any practical way, sometimes Teddy felt like he was sent by God. Each day he left a note in the mailbox. Written by his hand in black pen on his own Smythson letterhead. The notes were simple, just a line or two.

Thinking of you.

You're strong and wise and beautiful and you're going to make it through this.

Imagining a hug.

If you're going through Hell, keep going.

He left flowers, candy, a book of poems, a bottle of perfume, a stack of fashion magazines, a pack of cigarettes, a joint.

She saw him once. He always did his drop just after lunch, between 1:30 and 2:00. She waited for him one day, stood behind the gate. When he pulled up and parked and walked toward the mailbox, she opened the gate and stepped out onto the street. He saw her he had a letter in one hand and a bouquet of daisies in the other. He opened his arms and she stepped forward until she was in his arms.

Each could feel the other's heartbeat against their own. Taste each other's breath.

Each knew.

Her mother called her name and she stepped away from him slightly.

Thank you.

I'm around if you need me.

They looked at each other, and as her mother called her name again, she turned, walked back into her reality, and kept going.

Transcript of an Interrogation, Number Two

The following conversation took place at the New Bethlehem Police Station, Interview Room 4. Its participants were Sergeant David Genovese, Investigative Division, Police Chief Mike Murphy, Alleged Bookie and Murder Suspect George "Boopah" Macey, Criminal Defense Attorney Joseph Samuels.

Genovese: Tell us about your relationship with Alex Hunter.

Macey: Met him about fifteen years ago through a colleague of his at the bank. I was happy to meet him. I remembered him at ND and in the NFL. Athletes aren't usually big gamblers. Brings the wrong kind of attention if anyone gets a sniff of it, so I was surprised he wanted to start an account.

Murphy: You have accounts?

Macey: I call them that, but it's nothing official. There's no application. You don't fill out any paperwork. I just start taking your bets. We build trust. We build a relationship. When he started it was just football, the NFL. A few bets a week during the season, nothing big, not a significant part of my business. Over the years he started betting more and more, and on more than just football, which is a common pattern.

Genovese: With your account holders?

Macey: Yes. And I only work with Wall Street guys, bankers, hedge fund managers and private equity investors. Their job is gambling. They take people's money and make bets all day. They call it trading or investing, but it's gambling. The smart and healthy ones can turn it off when they leave the office. But plenty can't. They're gambling fiends. They need action all the time. And they like big action, action they can keep off the books, so it's not known and so it's not taxed. I am essentially their trading and investing platform. I provide a safe venue for their action, and I am willing to take big bets.

Murphy: How often did Alex Hunter gamble?

Macey: Like I said, he started slow and mellow. But gambling is a drug. The more you use it, the more you want to use it. Your tolerance grows. Over the years the pace picked up. The last couple years he was kind of crazy, the last year or so probably betting a hundred grand a week. I get to know my account holders well enough to have an idea of what they can and cannot afford to wager. He was going too far. I cut him off twice. I told him I thought he should seek help. Yes, I need degenerates and fiends, but when someone loses control, it always ends badly. Alex was out of control.

Genovese: How much money did he owe you?

Macey: Didn't owe me anything.

Murphy: Bullshit.

Macey: He always paid. If he didn't pay, I wouldn't keep taking his action.

Genovese: That's it?

Macey: I cut them off until they pay. And they always do. Not because they're scared I'm gonna send some goon after them. Like I said, I get to know my account holders. Where they work, where they live, how they fuck people at work, where they hide their money, how much they cheat on their taxes. I let the government do my dirty work. If someone fucks me, I send the SEC, or the IRS, or the FBI an anonymous tip with a code number at the bottom of it. I have sent them enough tips over the years that when they see that code number, they know the information is good, they know they have a sound case. The government is way, way scarier than I am.

Murphy: How did he pay you?

Macey: Cash or Bitcoin. Lately cash. Large amounts of it. He asked me recently if I knew a fence, so there was something going on, he probably was stealing from someone. I didn't want to get involved, and I declined to make a referral.

Genovese: What was he stealing?

Macey: Like I said, I didn't want to get involved, and I declined to make a referral. If I had to guess, watches or jewelry. They're the only things you can move quickly for large amounts of cash.

Murphy: Who do you think he was stealing from?

Macey: Didn't ask, didn't want to know. I deal in cash or Bitcoin.

Genovese: When was the last time you saw him?

Macey: Three days before he died. At a hotel in New York. Lower East Side. He owed me eighty grand. I went to pick it up. He was in a suite with two girls and a mountain of blow. The girls looked to me like they were in their late teens, maybe early twenties. It was a sad, ugly scene. I stayed for ten minutes and left.

Murphy: Where were you the night he was killed?

Macey: At my house. In Alpine, New Jersey. With my wife and three daughters. You work in my business, you invest in security systems. The high-res ones. My entire place, except for the bathrooms and bedrooms, is covered by cameras. I'm happy to share the footage of that day, that night, and the next day, with you. It will show me coming home, and being home, having family dinner and family movie night and sleeping, until I left the next morning to take my youngest daughter to her equestrian lesson.

Pura Vida, Para Siempre

It was time.

As much as it hurt them both.

And it did profoundly and sincerely hurt.

They both believed they would see each other again, and if things worked out, they would see each other soon. Devon took care of everything. Ana had taken care of her for so long, it was the least she could do. She got her passport out of Billy's safe. She booked her a first-class seat. Arranged for a car service to take her. She had an account set up for her in Panama. She wired five hundred thousand dollars into it.

Ana had taken care of her for so long.

And given everything, it was the least she could do.

Ana was thrilled. On a scale of one to ten, a sixty. She hadn't seen her husband or her daughter, her dear sweet beautiful daughter, in five years.

It was Devon's idea. She knew Ana wanted to leave, and had wanted to leave for a long time, but that Billy held her, if not literally, in every other way. And though he had stopped abusing her, at least physically, he still made rude comments to her, refused to call her by her name, using either *hey you* or *hey maid*, and occasionally smacked her ass, to which she did not respond in any way. When Devon left him, and told him she was going to divorce him, they were halfway there, but Devon didn't believe it was time. Billy was still dangerous, and still vindictive, and would have still sought revenge against Ana, or tried to prevent her from leaving, possibly by harming her family. When Alex was killed, they knew Billy wouldn't do anything that might bring the wrong kind of attention, or send the wrong kind of message, seemed aggressive. He was too smart not to have some sense that he was in peril, even if he didn't do it. And if he sensed he was in peril, he would be cautious. And if he was cautious, there'd be a window.

Devon decided to take advantage of it.

And act.

After laying low at Willowvale for a week after Alex's murder, most of it spent with Belle, Devon and Ana and the kids went back to the house in New Bethlehem.

They arrived on a Sunday. They didn't know if Billy would be there.

They were prepared for anything, but if he was there they planned on ignoring him, unless they needed to do otherwise. But he was gone, and a note left on her pillow said.

You had your fun. I own it all, including you. Let me know when you're done being an asshole.

She laughed.

She showed the note to Ana and Ana laughed.

Devon asked Ana if she thought she should stop being an asshole, and Ana asked

Aren't we just getting started?

And Devon said no, I'm just getting started.

Ana gave her a look like she didn't understand her and Devon told Ana it was time for her to go home. That this was going to be their last week together, at least for a while.

Ana melted.

At last, she was going home.

Despite the laugh they'd had at Billy's note, they were still scared of him, didn't trust him, and believed that wherever he was

New York

Amagansett

Maybe Miami

He was planning something.

The Devil never rests.

And neither did he.

So Devon planned Ana's departure with a different phone, one she'd had for a couple years and always kept hidden from Billy. She paid for everything and gave Ana the money she gave her, wired with the label *For Services Rendered*, from a Swiss account that Devon had filled with money siphoned away over several years in amounts that Billy wouldn't notice or she could reasonably explain, that eventually added up to several million dollars. She felt no remorse when she took the money, and as she was taking it, she didn't know what she was going to do with it or when, but she believed there would come a time when she would need it.

The time had come.

The Devil never rests.

He was planning something.

So was she.

The planning also helped Devon grieve. Whenever she had a quiet moment, her mind, her heart, and her memory would drift to Alex.

To the horror of his death, those final moments.

She had loved him. Though she understood his deep and profound flaws, she had loved him deeply and truly and she'd loved him with her whole heart. For her at least, the moments they shared were real, as real as anything she had known in her life. He was beautiful and charming, vulnerable and expressive, kind and loving. When he was with her, he was absolutely present, and he made her feel like she was all that mattered, like she was the only other person on earth with him.

Like she was safe.

Like she was loved.

And for her at least, it was the type of love she'd always hoped for, dreamed of, and wanted to find, the type of love in books and films, the type of love she was raised to believe in and taught was real and possible.

She'd felt it in those moments when they were alone together.

And as she thought about him, she also thought about Grace. She wondered if Grace had felt the same things with him that she'd felt with him. If she had experienced the same love, the same joy, the same contentment and the same safety. She wondered if she'd been overwhelmed by him in the same way. If he had told her that he loved her like no one else and always would love her like no one else. She knew Grace was in pain as she was in pain. And she was sorry.

So sorry.

If she had any regrets about any of what happened it was that she hurt another woman. She justified it by saying it would've happened sooner or later. She knew she was right, it would have. He was going to leave Grace as soon as he found the right woman. Someone beautiful, someone who adored him, someone rich. Devon knew if it hadn't been her, it would have been someone else.

But it was still her.

Still her who did it.

Ana often found Devon that way in that week, in those moments of emotion, heartbroken, burdened with sorrow and guilt. And Ana would bring her out of it. With a joke or a hug. She would hum a song she knew Devon loved, slip her a glass of wine, light a joint. Though they had lived vastly different lives, and had come from vastly different backgrounds, they had bonded and found common ground in their pain, the pain they experienced as women, the pain of living as women in a world of men, the pain of abuse and disregard. They had long laughingly called each other sisters, but in many real ways they were as close or closer than real sisters. Both had suffered under Billy, physically and emotionally, and both wanted to escape. They were doing what they could and what they believed was right to make it happen. Even if by some terrible luck Ana was the only one able to get away, that would be a victory.

When the planning was done, they spent the rest of the week doing what they had always done together, talking, laughing, crying, drinking wine, smoking weed. Autumn was on its way but hanging on, the earliest of winter starting to assert itself. But they still sat outside, they wore coats and hats, warm socks, wool mittens, sweats and cold-weather leggings. They knew all too well how short life was and how easily it could be taken, and they cherished every moment of their time together.

Being sisters.

They told Nicholas and Charlotte the night before Ana left. The kids both loved Ana as well, and had lived most of their lives with her. They had thin crust, hot honey pizza with extra pepperoni as their last meal in Connecticut together. They went out to the local soft-serve joint for dessert. They sang songs in the car as they drove home. Ana put each of them to bed and she tucked them in, as she had so many nights over the years. She hugged them and told them she loved them, even though they weren't her children. The car came early the next morning. Devon had organized Ana's bags at the front door. As the driver put them in the back of the black Mercedes sedan, they stood together. Devon smiled.

Ready?

Ana nodded.

Yes.

Excited?

So excited to be with my little girl. To fall asleep with my husband.

I'll miss you.

I'll miss you. Hoping you'll be down soon?

We'll see how and where everything goes.

It's going to go our way. I can feel it.

Devon smiled.

I hope so.

The driver finished with the bags and closed the trunk and opened the rear passenger door nearest to where they were standing and stood next to it. They put their arms around each other and held each other and each welled up but neither wanted to cry. They had been strong together, and in this moment, they wanted to stay strong together. After a moment, or two or three, Devon stepped away. Ana got into the car, and the driver closed the door behind her, and he got into the car, and the car pulled away. As it started down the long driveway, one of the rear windows came down and Ana's arm, her hand in a tight fist, came out of the window, in strength, in defiance, in hope, and in love, their kind of sisterly love.

Devon watched the car pull away and held back tears, and when she saw Ana's fist, she laughed, raised one of her fists, and held it as high as she could, in strength, in defiance, in hope, and in love.

Sisterly love.

Transcript of an Interrogation, Number Three

The following conversation took place at the New Bethlehem Police Station, Interview Room 1. Its participants were Sergeant David Genovese, Investigative Division, Police Chief Mike Murphy, Murder Suspect Billy McCallister, Criminal Defense Attorney Adam Turbowitz.

Genovese: Tell us about your Friday night.

McCallister: I was in the city. Had dinner with a young lady I know.

Murphy: Her name?

Turbowitz: I'm happy to provide you with her name and phone number and she is happy to speak with you and confirm she was with Mr. McCallister.

Genovese: After dinner?

McCallister: We went back to my loft in Tribeca.

Murphy: What did you do there?

McCallister: We spent time together. As adults do.

Genovese: For how long?

McCallister: I left around eleven. My driver brought me home.

Turbowitz: I'm happy to provide you with the name and phone number of Mr. McCallister's driver and he is happy to speak with you and confirm he was with Mr. McCallister.

Murphy: What time did you get home?

McCallister: Around midnight. I had a glass of scotch. I must have been tired because it hit me hard. I was asleep by 12:30. I slept late the next morning.

Turbowitz: I'm happy to provide you with access to Mr. McCallister's phone and the surveillance tapes from his home to confirm his account.

David turns and looks directly at Billy.

Genovese: Did you kill Alex Hunter?

Turbowitz: No more questions.

David ignores Turbowitz.

Genovese: He was fucking your wife, Billy. You kill him?

Turbowitz: I said no more . . .

Billy holds up a hand. Turbowitz immediately goes quiet. Billy smiles.

McCallister: Go fuck yourselves. I have an airtight alibi. As far as I am concerned, this matter is closed for me. Don't ever contact me again unless it's to apologize.

Billy stands and walks out. Turbowitz gathers his things and follows him.

Rest in Peace, Alexander the Great

The call came from the New Bethlehem Police Department.

It was a relief.

It was the next natural step and had already been delayed for too long.

After the call a New Bethlehem Police Officer came by the Tokeneke house and brought the paperwork she needed to sign to have his body released. She signed it and called the funeral home and they picked up his body.

The service was at church at noon on a Friday.

As soon as it was announced, they came back.

The swarm horde mob.

Outside of her home the children's school the funeral home the church the town cemetery.

Food was still being delivered. An occasional trusted friend came by for a visit. Teddy still dropped a note every day.

She planned the service with Father Peter, the Parish Priest of the local Episcopal church. He was a kind man, a gentle man, a compassionate man. Like everyone in New Bethlehem, he knew what had been going on in Alex and Grace's marriage. They had attended his church since they moved to town. Alex had gone as a kid. They had been in marriage counseling with Father Peter on two separate occasions. They would go once a week for an hour. Father Peter wasn't a counselor, but he was kind, gentle, and compassionate, and always open to helping people, however they needed it. Alex had quit both times, after three or four sessions. He told Grace she was imagining things, that people made up rumors about him because he was famous. It had broken Grace's heart both times, and she had cried with Father Peter after each time. When he came to see her about the service she cried with him again. They both knew she was crying as much about how Alex lived as she was how he died. When she stopped, he took her hand.

Let us endeavor to remember him at his best, and let us believe he is at peace with a loving and forgiving God.

She nodded and started crying again. He took her hands and held them until she was still and could speak again. And when she could, they planned his burial.

He went into the casket wearing Notre Dame socks, boxers from the NFL team he played for, and his New Bethlehem football jersey. A New Bethlehem lacrosse jersey and New Bethlehem hockey jersey were folded and set on his chest, his arms and hands placed over them. His greatest loves and his greatest glories with him for all eternity.

On Friday morning, Grace got ready and got the kids ready and her parents got ready and her friend Lindsay and Lindsay's husband picked them up in a huge black SUV with impenetrably tinted windows. It was a twenty-minute drive. Grace sat in the rear seat, with Preston and Madeline on either side of her, she held hands with each.

And they were silent, lost in memory and pain, as they drove through Darien and into New Bethlehem.

They saw the first signs as they drove into town.

The swarm horde mob was everywhere.

Uniformed Police at the intersections leading toward the church.

People walking, in dark suits and somber dresses.

There was traffic in a town that never really had any.

It was going to be a more public show than she hoped. People wanted to mourn their hero. To pay their respects to greatness. Once the church parking lot was filled and it was filled at eight, four hours before the service, the police directed traffic away, toward the parking lots normally used for trains, which had been kept empty for the service, but were now almost full. Father Peter had coordinated with Lindsay and her Husband and the New Bethlehem Police

Department so they would know the vehicle bringing Grace and Preston and Madeline to the funeral, and when the SUV pulled up, they waved it through, and a waiting cruiser accompanied it.

At the back entrance, they stepped from the vehicle five feet from the door. They went inside and sat with Father Peter. They could hear the crowd. Six hundred people inside the church, eight hundred more outside, with speakers set up so all could hear, and if they chose, all could pray.

Grace wished she could close her eyes and make it end, the Hell, Inferno, forget it all before it began, make herself invisible. She didn't want to be there and she didn't want her children to be there, she wished she didn't have to go out and be the centerpiece of a grand and public tragedy, a grand and public horror, a grand and public spectacle. Every single one of the people sitting in the church and every single one of the people outside of the church. The swarm the horde the mob bearing witness to the widow living in hell.

And every single one of them thinking

Thank God, it's not me.

Your poor, poor woman.

Thank God, it's not me.

Father Peter took Grace's hand and Grace took Preston's hand and Preston took Madeline's hand and they walked into the church.

Six hundred people inside.

Eight hundred more out.

Father Peter led them to the first pew, kept empty, and as he leaned down and hugged each of them, he whispered

God is with you.

At the pulpit, Alex's coffin on display in front of the altar, he stood before the silent mass and spread his arms and said

Welcome to the House of God.

There was a prayer, a eulogy read by Alex's brother, short speeches by his coach at Notre Dame, the second greatest lacrosse player New

Bethlehem ever produced, a friend from hockey who played in the NHL, another prayer, a song, a poem, a final prayer.

The coffin was carried out and taken to the town cemetery. Grace and her children led the procession from the car to the site. They put him to rest near a beautiful pond in his jersey and with his jerseys for eternity.

All loved him that day.

All remembered.

The Greatest Ever in a town full of greatness.

All loved him.

Progress, or Not

David started every morning at the station in the same way.

A giant cup of coffee.

A nicotine pouch between his cheek and gum.

A thorough review of the case file.

The pressure was immense.

Solve the case.

Yesterday.

The Media was still outside the station. Still around town. Still asking questions. The First Selectman, New Bethlehem's version of a Mayor, but Mayor is far too pedestrian a title for such a job, called once every morning, and once every afternoon. Chief Murphy told him ten times a day, maybe twenty.

Solve the case, Genovese.

Yesterday.

They had just finished with the house and released it. They'd dusted and documented every inch of it. The home of an active family, there were hundreds of sets of fingerprints in it and throughout it. Many were of Alex and Grace and their children, but there were many many more. And given that very few people in New Bethlehem have been arrested or have criminal records of any kind, the overwhelming number of them were unidentified. And unless they were going to fingerprint the entire town, would remain unidentified. In the living room, where the crime most certainly occurred, there was no evidence of his body being moved or of it being anywhere else. The only prints and the only DNA on scotch glass, and the handcuffs, and the duct tape surrounding his neck, and the plastic over his head, were his own. There was no outside DNA on his pants or undergarments. There was no outside DNA on his body. It appeared he had showered shortly before his murder, and he was wearing cologne, so it was believed that he had anticipated a visitor, and for something very different than his own murder to occur. His phone had evidence of plenty of crimes, but they were all committed by him, buying drugs, hiring escorts, gambling, moving money. The location data supported what they believed were his actions on the day and the night of his murder. He was in New York. He drove home. He was at home. There were stops at a gas station where he bought five energy drinks and some chewing tobacco, and at a local pizza parlor, where he bought two slices with cheese, extra pepperoni, extra sausage, and extra meatball. The remnants of the energy drinks and pizza were found in his stomach. The toxicology report was similar to the fingerprint results. He was filled with drugs and booze. His blood alcohol level was .22, which was high, but for a man of his size and with his habits meant he was drunk but likely not incapacitated. He had cocaine, marijuana, MDMA, ketamine, psilocybin, Ambien, and a barbiturate in his system, all in amounts that were within the range of recreational use, but on the high end of that range. There was no way to know what exactly he was on when he died, but he was on something, or likely several somethings. None of the evidence portrayed Alex in a particularly good light. He was clearly a man who had been living a life that was spinning out of control, despite the image he might have projected, and despite all of the kind words spoken at his funeral.

The list of potential suspects was long, and getting longer. Many of the local ones had been eliminated quickly and easily, or had been looked at as a formality. His wife, Grace, who had the most plausible motive and was the most natural suspect, had an impenetrable alibi from her children and her friend and her friend's children, supported by the location data on her phone, and the surveillance system of the house where she had spent the night of the murder. Billy McCallister, who also had a plausible motive and was the next most logical suspect, also had an impenetrable alibi supported by the home surveillance footage he had provided and location data on his phone. Charlie Dunlap, who had been fired by Alex Hunter and publicly threatened him, was eliminated due to surveillance footage from the KenTaco and from the location data on his phone. George Macey had been a dead-end, surveillance and location data on his phone supporting his account of how he spent the evening. Genovese questioned a number of other people in Alex's life. Devon McCallister was in love with him and planning a future with him, and had been with her children and her housekeeper all evening. Belle Moore, who to his surprise had been having an affair with Charlie Dunlap, said she loved Alex and loved how happy her bestie Devon was when she was with him. He interviewed multiple members of the hockey and lacrosse boards, all of whom loved and admired him, and despite some missing funds from the Hockey Association, had no reason to want to kill him. He had found and interviewed three of the nine escorts Alex had seen during the week he spent at the hotel on the Lower East Side. All were college students in their late teens or early twenties, young women trying to get through school and survive in New York City. All said Alex was high and drunk and didn't want or ask for anything more than a good time, though one thought he tried to steal her watch, and another thought he might have gone through her purse, though she wasn't entirely sure. None were suspects, and David believed he would hear more of the same if and when he found the remaining six. He was still trying to find the fence, and still trying to figure out what Alex stole, and from whom he stole it. He hoped that would be the lead that broke the case.

And after he finished his morning review, Chief Murphy stopped by his desk, clapped him on the back, and said

Solve the case, Genovese. Yesterday.

The Turkey Bowl

Thanksgiving.

America's favorite Thursday.

We gather with our families. We pretend we love bad, boring food. We celebrate our abundance. We watch football. We get drunk.

Sometimes there are fights.

Everybody takes a nap.

Go Team America.

Rock on.

————

They met for the first time on Thanksgiving Day, 1928.

A Clash of the Titans, an Encounter of Colossi. Evil Empire versus the Evil Empire.

They called it the Turkey Bowl.

New Bethlehem High School Football versus Darien High School Football.

And it has happened every year since. Pandemic be damned. On the day of the game, time stops for both towns. It's time to see who's Number One. And there is nothing more important in life, nothing even close, than being Number One.

And while Darien is a larger town, with a larger tax base and a larger pool of players, New Bethlehem long dominated the pigskin showdown. They won it almost twice as often, a pattern for which Darien has no solution. Each year the game is held at either one school or the other. Each has turf-field stadiums, with video scoreboards and lights for night games, with broadcast booths and tiered stands. Thousands of people come each time they play. More than the stadiums can hold. Others watch at home, it's locally broadcast.

Winner gets bragging rights for the year.

To be able to look across the border at their Neighbors

And say

We are better than you.

There is nothing more important than knowing.

We are better than you.

———

Charlie fucking loved the Turkey Bowl, and he never missed it. If there was a contest to crown Mr. Turkey Bowl, he would enter it every year. And if there was a Mr. Turkey Bowl contest to enter, Charlie would do whatever he needed to do to win it.

Can you even imagine!?

Mr. Turkey Bowl!!!

Or even better, multitime winner of Mr. Turkey Bowl!!!

It would have been a dream for Charlie, if such a thing existed, but it didn't. So he did his best to make the Turkey Bowl fucking awesome in other ways. Every year the parking lots became huge parties. The game started at noon, but people began arriving at seven, and many parked the night before and got dropped off in early the morning. It was a tailgate extravaganza. And part of tailgating was showing off. Rich people love showing off. What's the point of being rich if you can't show how rich you are? Since both New Bethlehem and Darien were full of the very, very rich, the tailgating got pretty intense. And extremely festive. Some people had it catered, others used it to highlight their culinary skills, though they only cooked as a hobby of course. There were buffets set up on the backs of pickups, and there were buffets set up on tables with linens, and there were buffets set up under tents that had heat and electricity. Most of the food was some variation of an American style. And while the game is on Thanksgiving, very little of it was ever Thanksgiving food. There were steaks, burgers, sausages made from exotic animals like elk and ostrich and alligator, there was fried chicken and BBQ chicken and an occasional chicken cordon bleu. There were racks of ribs, both pork and beef, Memphis style Texas style St. Louis style. There was chili, gallons and gallons and gallons, some of it tasty and delicious, some of it would melt your face off. And more than food, there was booze, in every way it could be consumed, and after legalization occurred, there was weed, in every form it exists. Because both schools had stadiums, both also had the parking facilities to hold the people required to fill the stadiums. And at each school, there was a Home lot, for the tailgaters supporting the host team, and there was an Away lot, for the tailgaters supporting the visitors. The lots generally did not mix.

Charlie did the same thing every year. He built a metal frame around the bed of his pickup. And from that frame he hung six beer bongs, three on each side, made with large plastic funnels and long clear flexible tubing. The bongs could be moved along the frame so that if all three were being used at the same time, the users could decide if they wanted to stand close together and do a unity funnel, or stand farther apart and do a solo. In the front part of the pickup bed were two large coolers filled with cans of ice-cold American beer. In the back part of the bed was a hot dog steamer filled with wieners and buns. Charlie stood in the bed and poured the beers into the funnels and cheered and encouraged those brave enough to have one, or two, or five, or eight. His truck was always among the most popular of the spots in the lot. There was always a crowd around it, and often a line for the bongs and the dogs.

As he always did, Charlie arrived early to the Home lot at New Bethlehem High School. He got a primo spot, right in the center of the action, the same spot he parked in every year. He prepped the truck and made sure the beer bongs were working properly, testing each one himself. He filled the steamer and plugged it into the car's lighter, set a pair of speakers on top of the cab, started playing some old-school American rock 'n' roll.

And he waited.

And waited.

And waited.

And as the lot around him filled with cars and people, he was summarily ignored. Nobody came to his truck, nobody drank his beer, nobody ate his wieners or buns. People he knew and he had known for years and who he considered his friends walked past him. When he called out, they pretended not to hear him. One man, whose three daughters Charlie had coached, and who always spent the entire Turkey Bowl pregame at his truck, ignored him, Charlie jumped and approached him and asked him what the fuck was going on. The man just shook his head and kept walking. When Charlie got back to the truck, a dad he knew and had partied with many times was waiting for him. Charlie was excited to finally have a visitor. He smiled his biggest smile, and he spoke.

What's up, dude? Wanna do a double funnel?

Hey, Charlie.

A triple?

People aren't comfortable with you here.

What do you mean?

Everybody thinks you killed Alex Hunter.

I didn't have anything to do with it.

That's not the word around town. People feel weird and uncomfortable. If I were you, I'd lay low in your truck until the game starts, and head home once it does. Nobody wants to party with you.

Nobody?

Sorry, dude.

Not even you?

Sorry, dude.

Charlie was shocked, speechless. It didn't make any sense. Everybody had always wanted to party with Charlie. And his truck had always been the center of the party. The loudest, the rowdiest, the most fun. The coldest beer and the steamiest hot dogs. The spiciest mustard and the tastiest relish. The Best Time Ever. And now nobody wanted to party with him. He couldn't believe it. He couldn't believe he was being shunned.

He looked around the lot. Everybody was having a great time. Eating and drinking and laughing, talking about the game, which New Bethlehem had won for the last seven years and was expected to win again. He loved talking about the game. He knew everything there was to know about the game. But nobody would talk to him. Nobody would even come near him. They were all pretending that he didn't exist.

They all thought he was a killer.

The dad walked away and Charlie went and sat in the cab of his truck. He turned off his music.

He was stunned, and deeply hurt, and deeply sad and his heart broke, right there, alone in his truck, the Turkey Bowl Festivities raging around him.

His heart broke.

They all thought he was a killer.

He got out of the truck and he took the funnels off the frame and unplugged the hot dog steamer and put the speakers back in the cab. Nobody paid any attention to him or said a word to him and he couldn't believe it, he was being shunned. When the game started and the lot cleared out, he drove home. He brought the coolers of beer into his living room. He put the leftover hot dogs into the fridge and the buns on the counter. He didn't have plans for the rest of the day. He usually got multiple Thanksgiving dinner invitations during the tailgate and during the game, and spent the afternoon and evening going from house to house, bringing the party with him wherever he went.

But those times were over for him, and he got zero invitations.

He sat down on his couch and his heart hurt.

He turned on his TV and his heart hurt.

He didn't want to watch football because he wasn't at the game.

He put on the parade, and spent the rest of the day and of the night drinking beer and eating hot dogs alone.

Just Charlie.

His heart hurt.

They all thought he was a killer.

———

Devon and the kids spent the day at Willowvale. Her parents came back from Palm Beach. They normally spent Thanksgiving at the club, drinking with friends, decrying the state of the world, giving each other the stink eye after they had finished the fourth bottle of wine, but given all that was going on with Devon, they decided to come home and see her, and make sure her priorities were in order.

They had a formal dinner together. Catered. Everybody got dressed up. They ate on antique Limoges china and used the family silver. The staff all wore uniforms. Devon and her mother both put on family jewelry, diamonds, emeralds, sapphires, and rubies, they wore matching tennis bracelets, rings that had been passed on for generations. They had enough food on the Elizabethan Regency Pollard Oak dining table for fifty people, even though they were just five. They had cognac, and pie with fresh whipped cream and strawberries for dessert. After, the kids went to their rooms with their phones, and the adults retired to more comfortable quarters.

They sat in the living room, Devon and her parents, in front of a fire built by the groundskeeper, on Ruhlmann art deco furniture, pretending to care what each other said. Devon didn't know where Billy was spending the holiday, and her parents didn't ask if she knew. They reiterated their position, as they had many times before, that they did not believe in divorce. They were concerned the money would go away and they might have to sell some art or one of the houses and they didn't want to and thought it was unfair that Devon would put them in such a position. They hoped and believed Devon would come to her senses and call the whole thing off and just be unhappy like every other couple who has been married for more than ten years.

Many things were said to Devon without directly saying them. Many feelings were expressed to her, in subtle ways and with veiled phrases, without a raise of voice. Her father smoked a Cuban cigar. Devon and her mother each had a cigarette, Virginia Slims. What she wanted to tell them, but couldn't, was that she had long crossed the Rubicon, and was far far past the point of no return, far far past.

———

David spent the morning at his desk, at the station. He spent the afternoon with his parents, at their home in Danbury. His Mother made a traditional Thanksgiving dinner and his Aunt and Uncle came over from New Milford. He spent the evening with Katy, they met at her place and watched a romantic comedy on her sofa and ate popcorn and candy and fell asleep in each other's arms.

———

The girls were home!!!

All three Moore girls home for the holiday. They had no idea it would be the last Thanksgiving they spent together as a family. But Belle and Teddy did. So they tried to make it great, the best ever.

Everyone put their phones away. They made the meal together, ate the meal together, and after they ate, they played *Jenga* and *Uno*. Every single one of them won at least one game, nobody cheated, or maybe they did a little but nobody cared. They watched a movie together in their theater. It was a comedy about two stepbrothers, a family favorite, an all-time great. They shared blankets and popcorn and soda and red vine licorice. And they laughed and laughed and laughed, even though they had all seen it at least ten times. They went to bed at the same time, they all told the others that they loved them and they all meant it. They all slept in their favorite beds warm and soft and safe, and they all had sweet dreams.

———

Billy's mother invited him over for Thanksgiving. She was worried about him. Devon brought the kids by to see her every few months. But she hadn't seen Billy in over a year. She sent him a sweet email. Told him she loved him and she was proud of him. He didn't respond to her. He took his plane to St. Barts, where he rented a suite at Le Barthélemy. He paid a Russian teenager to stay with him, and serve him. They sat in the sun and they ate delicious food and drank Louis Roederer pink champagne and when Billy felt like it they would go inside and she would serve him.

———

Katy woke up and went for a run and it felt fucking great.

Fuck yeah!

She made a corn casserole and some green beans with butter and pepper. As she had done every Thanksgiving since moving to New Bethlehem, Katy had turkey dinner with four other single women who were teachers in the New Bethlehem school system. They all lived in or around town, and for whatever reason, didn't have anywhere else to go. But they found each other, and had a great time every year. Each brought a different dish or dishes. They ate and drank and talked and shared and laughed and loved and trusted each other, and always wanted the best for each other, always.

She drove home maybe a little tipsy.

David was waiting for her, she'd given him a key, and they watched a romantic comedy on her sofa and ate popcorn and candy and fell asleep in each other's arms.

———

The Police Department finished their work, and released the house, and some kind people in the town organized a fundraiser to replace the furniture in the living room and the family room and Grace's bedroom.

It was their second day back. The new furniture helped, but you could feel it in the house, what happened, and you could feel him in the house, his glory and his tragedy. There were two other families coming over, three kids in each. It was going to be a loud chaotic overwhelming scary wonderful nourishing and maybe even healing day. Her parents were still with her, and were going to stay, probably for a long time, or a longish time. Their sweet dog was happy to be back in his yard.

It went by quickly, as she had hoped.

It was loud, chaotic, overwhelming, and she laughed more than she expected, and felt great more than she expected, and for periods of time she forgot.

His glory and his tragedy. What happened. All of it.

Even if for only a minute or two at a time she was just Mom in her home making dinner with friends.

The kids were having a great time, so everyone stayed late. And she loved having everyone late because she loved feeling good and she needed it. When they finally left, she was tired. Her parents put the kids to bed and she went to her room and got into her new sheets on her new bed provided by some kind people in town who organized a fundraiser and she closed her eyes and for the first time in a long time she felt like maybe things would be okay.

Maybe she would be okay.

Maybe her children would be okay.

———

New Bethlehem won the game, beating Darien 17–14, with a field goal in the final minute. At halftime, there was a Memorial Ceremony for Alex with one minute of silence, a montage of his highlights from New Bethlehem, Notre Dame, and the NFL, and the retirement of his jersey number, which was 12.

Lou and Louise, Louise and Lou

The small house on a residential street, just off Greenwich Avenue.

In the living room.

Devon was on the Boca do Lobo sofa, Lou and Louise in the Roche Bobois armchairs.

Lou spoke.

It's lovely to see you. You're radiant, Devon. Radiant.

Louise spoke.

We think of you often. I got you some tea. From the Seychelles.

She handed Devon a small colorful box filled with tea from the Seychelles. Devon took it, smiled.

Thank you, very kind of you. I love Seychellian tea.

Lou and Louise both smiled. Lou spoke.

You know we don't like phones. We believe real communication happens face-to-face.

Louise spoke.

We wanted to sit with you and get an update. See how you're doing, see how you're feeling.

Devon smiled.

I'm okay. It's obviously been a difficult, difficult time. I've had little to no contact with Billy. I'm fine to not hear from him or have to deal with him. Losing Alex has been horrible. I had such hopes when we were first together, and I never imagined things would go as they have. I'm not sure things could get much worse than they have been. But I'm feeling optimistic, and I believe if I can just be patient, things may go my way. It's just a matter of time. Something has to break.

Afternoon Delight, Kind Of

In the spirit of discretion, Belle and Charlie had terminated their relationship as coach and skater.

The private lessons had ended.

They were not being seen together in public.

He was no longer dropping by the house.

But their enthusiasm for the pleasures of each other's bodies had not faded. The passion, desire, and hunger, the overwhelming need they felt for each other had only grown, and grew more every time they saw each other.

They still met most afternoons at a hotel in Stamford that rented rooms by the hour. It was seedy and shady sometimes, there were Police in the parking lot, and sometimes they smelled drugs in the hallway.

They loved it. It made everything hotter.

One of them would get the room, go inside, wait for the knock, open the door when it came, close it behind. Passion lust desire hunger overwhelming need, passion lust desire hunger hunger hunger overwhelming need. Instructions were the only spoken words.

They took each other, and they each saw the blinding white perfect peaceful light of a loving God as they went and as they came. And after they talked and laughed and kissed and tickled and acted like teenagers.

Teenagers with skills and experience.

It had been three days.

She was hungry. She got the room and she waited, wet. She expected him at two, he didn't come, she waited, he didn't come. It was just after three, she was getting ready to leave, she was so hungry, there was a knock at the door. When he stepped into the room, there was no desire being expressed by him in any way. He was tight, tense.

Are you okay, Charlie?

He sat down on the edge of the bed.

I think I fucked up, Belle.

She sat down next to him, took his hands.

What's going on?

I'm not a killer. I swear I'm not.

I know you're not, Charlie.

Everybody thinks I am. The Cops think I am. And I might have fucked up. I think I'm in big, big trouble.

A Break, Maybe

The deeper the investigation went, the longer it went, the more the Police Department had to do, had to look at, had to investigate.

The more possibilities to pursue, or eliminate.

Everything in the house had been examined and reexamined and hyperexamined, put through every test possible and evaluated in every way possible. There was nothing, no unexplained DNA, no unexplained prints.

The initial survey of local surveillance had also proved fruitless. They had retrieved footage taken on the night of the murder from every home within a mile and on a road leading to the Hunters' home.

They had to track and check every vehicle on that footage.

Nothing.

They expanded it to within two miles.

They had to track and check every vehicle on that footage.

Nothing.

They decided to go backward, as far back as they could go, with as much as they could get, given the time that had passed. They asked for footage from every house within two miles of the Hunters', going backward in time from the day of the murder, the more the better.

They had modest expectations.

Which were wildly surpassed.

They got a huge amount of footage, huge huge huge amount. People with money want to feel safe. And they buy security systems with more storage than most people. And they save it more often.

Just in case.

And this was a just in case. Though there were a few pockets that didn't have footage, they got close to a week's worth of footage.

Hundreds of cameras, thousands of hours.

David watched and watched and watched and watched. He ran license plate checks and background checks. He looked for patterns, anomalies, correlations. Something or someone out of place.

And he found Charlie.

Charlie Dunlap.

Charlie fucking Dunlap.

Sitting in his vehicle.

Late at night.

For hours and hours at a time.

Across the street from Alex Hunter's house.

Cinq à Sept

For the first time since the first night they met

At Devon's Fuckfest.

Grace and Teddy were meeting with the sun down, at night, in the dark.

Oh the night!

Oh the dark!

Where promises are made and kisses exchanged, where secrets are born and shared, where hearts entwine and passions ignite and wishes are cast, confessions made and glances stolen, where smell and taste and touch replace sight and sound, where impulses, urges, appetites and cravings, lusts and longings, shadows and the people of the night and of the dark and of the shadows can be free.

They met at a Darien restaurant, where they knew people might see them together. They were both excited from the moment it was planned. Two hearts aflutter, some sweet song playing that only they could hear.

Teddy's streak at work had continued, he was closing here, he was closing there, if you looked around, you would have probably seen him and he would have been closing. Things with Belle were cordial, civil, unrushed, friendly, comfortable. His daughters were thriving. He had no complaints about life and he knew how fortunate he was not to have any complaints about life.

Grace had settled back into the house. The new furniture helped, they had people over as often as possible, she was forgetting more each day, living in some kind of normal, she found some kind of peace in each day. The kids were back in school and sports, and she was back in her routines, though she was considerably more reserved and considerably less trusting. Her parents were a joy to have and she thanked her God for them every day. And there was Teddy, like some bright bright sun that was always there.

She arrived first.

A seafood joint bright loud and open, checkerboard tablecloths, extra napkins. She got a booth for two alongside a window. The restaurant was almost entirely empty, three of the twenty-five tables occupied, none near each other. She ordered a Cosmopolitan, why not, life is short as she so deeply and recently learned, might as well. She was taking her first sip when he walked in they both smiled two hearts aflutter, beautiful and pure.

She stood as he came closer, high in that early joyful ecstatic time. She opened her arms and he opened his arms and they each stepped into each other's hearts and it felt good and right and neither of them said a word, just held. They stayed for a minute, holding each other. And it started for real that night, in the dining room of a public restaurant in Darien where everyone could see, at a table with a checkerboard tablecloth.

Naughty, or Nice

It's America's Favorite Thursday.

And you blink and Santa is fucking everywhere.

New Bethlehem is a beautiful place to spend the holiday season. There are wreaths on doors, and poinsettias outside of them on houses everywhere. Main and Maple Streets are lit up and lined with twinkling strings of white light, from end to end. There is a town Christmas tree, as tall, grand, and elegant, beautiful and traditional as you can imagine. There are multiple nights of caroling. The town Ballet School puts on *The Nutcracker* and sells out six shows at the high school auditorium, capacity five hundred. The two toy stores in town make enough to stay healthy and in business for the next year. The churches all put out nativities, Jesus is white and blond. There are circuits of holiday parties with competitive guest lists where everyone dresses festively and smiles festively and speaks with festive glee and drinks with extrafestive spirit hey let's have six more, they discuss which schools the kids are applying to and how the kids are doing in the sports and the men talk about the year-end bank and fund and law firm bonuses and the women talk about where they're going on vacation the day after the holidays.

———

It was the height of hockey season and Charlie was busy. He was coaching in Greenwich, which was close, but far enough away that it felt like an escape for him. He had practice every day and multiple games each day of each weekend. Though he did not show it, he was living in a state of perpetual panic. Panicked that everywhere he went people thought and believed that he was a killer, and that, according to his lawyer, the New Bethlehem Police Department also thought and believed that he was a killer. If he could have run, he would have run, even though he swore he didn't do it, but he couldn't run because now they were watching him. It seemed everywhere he went, they were watching. Which also meant that he couldn't see Belle. She had limits and he understood and respected her limits. He missed her and he missed his life and when he wasn't coaching, he was at home drinking beer and eating food and watching hockey.

———

Belle was working hard to make Christmas and the holidays as beautiful and memorable as possible.

The girls were coming home, all three Moore girls home for the holiday! As it was with Thanksgiving, they had no idea it would be the last Christmas they spent as a family. They were doing Christmas Day at home, and Belle and Teddy were cooking dinner at home, together. They were flying to Aspen the next day for a week at the Little Nell. There were presents to buy for the stockings and for under the tree. There were decorations and flowers to be placed. There were reservations to make and passes to be acquired and gear to be prepped and tuned.

She missed Charlie.

But all in good time, she hoped, especially given some of the things he'd told her and had continued to tell her. She didn't believe he was a killer. A lover, yes, and a fighter, yes, but not a killer. And until that good time came, and because she and Teddy knew it was the last and the girls didn't, the kind polite driven and beautiful Moore girls, she did everything she could to make sure it would be as close to perfect as possible.

———

Katy wanted the break and needed the break. Though she loved her jobs, teacher and coach, and found them both deeply satisfying, they were also both exhausting and hard grind. If you wanted the kids to focus and prepare and pay attention and give best efforts, she believed that you had to focus and prepare and pay attention and give best efforts. And because she did, her kids did as well, or at least most of them did. But that focus and preparation and attention and those best efforts wore her down, drained her, diminished her. And so her only plan was not to make any plans. To sleep late and keep the workouts light and go to the movies and take long walks and eat a little more than she should and drink a little more than she should and allow herself the beauty of boredom, the joy of unproductivity, the pleasure of being still. She hoped David would do the same, and do it with her. As hard as she worked, he worked harder. As focused and prepared as she was, he was more so. As hard she was on herself, he was worse. He had been feverishly working the Alex Hunter case, going in early, staying late, sometimes the only way she knew he'd been in bed with her and sleeping next to her was his scent, lingering. He had found something, or someone, or some theory was close to being proven true. He wouldn't tell her what or who or how close, but she knew, she could sense it and see it in him, and he told her enough to know that they had made some progress, and they believed, they believed.

———

Billy had been spending his time in New York, in the Tribeca apartment. He had two Bloomberg screens and real-time results tracking all of the traders who worked for him. His driver took him to the office in Connecticut two or three days a week. It was an easy drive if you did it early enough or late enough. He went in early and came back late.

He hadn't slept at the house in New Bethlehem since the night Devon told him she wanted a divorce. He still went to the kids' games, school events, and fulfilled his fatherly obligations, but he didn't feel like seeing or dealing with Devon. He was worried how he might react, what he might do to her. He had always had dark impulses. He had always enjoyed hurting people, especially women. He had always sought, and in most areas of his life had, total control. And though he had never imposed the dominant aspects of his sexual preferences on Devon, he always had other women for that, he had still always dominated her. He had the money. He controlled the money. She needed it and her family needed it. It was never explicitly stated or discussed, and didn't need to be. They both knew the deal. She did what he told her to do, when he told her to do it. And she tolerated him doing whatever he wanted to do, and didn't say a word about it. And if she didn't, the money stopped flowing. Access was restricted. Spending halted. It happened once in the early stages of their marriage. She found used condoms and lube at the house in Amagansett. She told him if it happened again, she would leave. The next time she tried to use her platinum card it was denied. All of her cards were denied. She apologized when she got home and the cards started working again. She knew the deal. She accepted the deal. The deal allowed her to continue living the life she had always known. And she wouldn't survive any other type of life. Neither would her parents. Everyone knew the deal, everyone accepted it.

That Devon thought she would get away from him via Alex Hunter made him laugh. It made him lose respect for her. It made him think she was dumb. He knew they were fucking the entire time. He tracked her via her phone, via her car, via the home surveillance system. He didn't care about the fucking. If she was fucking someone else it meant he didn't have to fuck her. And he didn't want to fuck her anymore, and hadn't wanted to fuck her for years. But that she would take it further than fucking. That she would fall in love. With some loser who couldn't keep his job or pay his bills. Who stole from her and from them to pay his gambling debts. It was like some bad fucking joke. That Devon would think she could leave him for that guy. That she thought she could have a life without Billy, and without his money, and without him being in control. It made him lose respect for her and made him think she was dumb. It made him want to do bad things to her, even though he had other women for that purpose. And he knew she couldn't actually do anything to him. With the farce of hiring those freakshow lawyers. They couldn't do anything either, those fucking freaks. Everyone involved knew the prenup was bulletproof, and that it would hold up in any court in the country. The exceptions in it were absurd. Devon would only ever get what Billy was willing to give her. That's how it had always been, and as far as he was concerned, how it would always be. He thought she probably needed a reminder. A firm reminder. Your loser boyfriend is gone and he's not coming back. I'm still your husband. You're still mine. Know your place.

Know your fucking place.

He wondered how she would react when he walked in the door.

It would be soon.

He wasn't going to spend Christmas away from his children.

Or his wife.

He would walk in during family dinner.

Sit down.

And wait.

For Devon to get up and properly set him a place.

They would all pretend nothing happened and life would go on.

Because they knew.

They knew their fucking place.

———

When Devon was a little girl.

Before the world imposed itself on her.

Before she realized it was all a fixed game.

She dreamed of being a Jedi Knight, and she believed she could become one.

Like Obi Wan Kenobi.

But a girl.

Devon believed she could become a Jedi because she believed she had special powers.

She knew what people were thinking, even if they weren't around, if she simply thought of them long enough and hard enough, she knew.

And sometimes, even though it was crazy, she believed she could see into the future, she knew what was going to happen before something happened, she knew.

And even though she grew up and learned she couldn't be a Jedi, Devon never stopped believing in her special powers.

Maybe they were instinct intuition perception, and maybe everybody had them. But maybe not, maybe not. Maybe she had some special power. Because she knew Billy was coming home soon and she knew it was going to get bad and she believed she knew how bad and what kind of bad.

She tried to focus on the holiday. She had a tree delivered and she decorated it with the kids. She went shopping in Westport, and Greenwich, a day in the city. She bought presents for everyone, including Billy, she knew he was coming home soon. She scheduled the plane and booked a villa in Barbados for the ten days after Christmas. She had strings of lights installed outside the house, but tastefully. She looked at real estate online, at beachfront houses in Costa Rica, she missed Ana, she dreamed.

She knew it was going to get bad.

———

Teddy loved Christmas.

And Teddy gave great Christmas.

Teddy loved giving people presents. And he took it seriously. For someone who loves giving people presents and takes it seriously, Christmas is the height of the season, the year's crescendo, a time to express your most thoughtful ideas, to make your finest gestures. And if you were rich, and Teddy was very rich, you could be extremely expressive in your thoughtfulness, and gestural in the most fine ways.

Teddy's Christmas thinking usually started in the summer. He would set a budget for the girls, Belle's was usually double. Each of the girls, and Belle, had different interests and tastes, different dreams and aspirations, different wants and wishes, and all of those things were constantly shifting, with age and stage, with learning, with the pursuit of curiosity. Each year the gifts would reflect each of them individually, clothing they loved, a trip to see a painting or a concert, a signed first edition of a favorite novel, a piece of art, a piece of jewelry. Sometimes it would be a single grand gift, sometimes three or more, sometimes six, or eight. It was always different, each person and each year, and the challenge and fun of it was something Teddy loved, and the reaction when the gifts were opened the best of all. Teddy found joy in making other people happy. He knew he was lucky, he had been born lucky and luck had followed him throughout his entire life. He wanted to share that luck with the people he loved, he wanted to give them a piece of his luck.

And this was the most important Christmas season he had ever faced, the most important he had ever planned and executed, one that required all of his thoughtfulness and his grandest gestures. He had closed enough deals on the year. He had cemented his legend as the Closer of Closers. It was time for him to direct his attention elsewhere, to things and people who mattered more than fund returns.

It was a year of endings.

Teddy and Belle knew it was their last Christmas together and the girls didn't, and Teddy wanted them to have wonderful memories, even though he knew they would be mixed with pain.

And it was a year of beginnings.

For the first time since his youngest daughter was born, there was a new person on the list.

————

Grace was tired.

All she wanted Santa to bring her was a week of sleep.

A week of peace.

A week where nobody felt sorry for her, where nobody took her aside and said softly

Are you really okay, is there anything I can do, are you really okay?

She appreciated the kindness and concern. But she just wanted to live a normal life. She didn't want to hear about her terrible loss anymore, or what a great guy Alex was, or how much people loved him, and how much they missed him.

She was tired and she was angry. Alex had betrayed all of them. Alex had lied to all of them and cheated on all of them and stolen from all of them. He had discarded all of them. He had broken every vow and promise he had ever made to them. He had blown up their life.

She was tired, angry, and Alex could go fuck himself.

If he was in Heaven, if he somehow got past the Gates, wherever he ended up, Alex could go fuck himself.

It was going to be her last Christmas in New Bethlehem.

She knew it wasn't healthy for her and she knew it wasn't healthy for her children.

The fishbowl. The pity. The expectations. The history.

She was going to sell the house and she hoped there would be enough left after all of Alex's debts and bills were paid for her and the kids to start over. She had thought about moving to Chicago to live with her parents. They had the townhouse they'd purchased when such a thing was still possible for normal people. They could and would help her with the kids. The kids would go to the same schools she had attended, which were still very good, and filled with people who weren't all white and weren't all rich and weren't all guaranteed a college education and a bright, glowing, comfortable future. Chicago was safe. She would have a chance to rebuild her life. The kids would have a chance to forge their own lives. Her costs would drop dramatically. To make and have friends who wouldn't view them through the lens of who their father had been and what had happened to him, through the lens of how much money they had and how successfully they displayed it. She wanted to leave during the summer. Let the kids finish the school year. Give them time to adjust to the idea of a new home and a new school and a new life. Give them time to say their goodbyes. Give them their closure. And when everyone else went away for their summer vacations, to the Hamptons or Newport or Martha's Vineyard or Nantucket or on some beautiful and expensive trip to Europe, they would just go away.

Away from Alex.

Away from New Bethlehem.

Away from everything.

The only thing she thought she would miss was Teddy, and if she had made a list for Santa, he would have been the only thing on it.

Sweet dear kind loving Teddy.

Wrapped in a bow.

The Enigmatologist

They usually met at Katy's place.

For David it was an escape. From work and pressure, death and murder, the reality that he faced every minute of every day of every week since Alex Hunter was found lifeless with an empty scotch glass, his pants at his ankles, and a plastic bag duct-taped over his head.

Solve the fucking case, Genovese.

Yesterday.

Police live in the world of the crimes they investigate. A world filled with danger and death, menace and horror, with the worst humanity has to offer, with our darkest impulses. They need time away in order to deal with it, to process it, to do what they could do to fix it. But there was no escape for David. The pressure was growing every day. And the discovery of Charlie Dunlap sitting outside of Alex Hunter's house for multiple nights in a row ratcheted it up.

Everyone who had been involved in the case from the moment it began. From the Rookie who had directed traffic around the scene on the morning of the discovery to Chief Murphy. From the Forensic Techs to the Photographer to the Prosecutors who had gotten warrants to the team of people who had combed through all of the surveillance footage. They all wanted to close it. They all want to see justice done.

And the closer he got, the more pressure he felt.

Everyone in the tight circle of people who knew everything about the case, David and Chief Murphy, the State Prosecutors, the New Bethlehem First Selectman, thought they should arrest Charlie. They believed they had enough evidence to arrest him, and they believed once he was in custody, either they would find the rest of what they needed for a conviction or he would give it to them. They wanted to charge him with first-degree murder. If he was convicted, he would likely receive a sentence of life in prison without the possibility of parole. They believed that once he knew what he was facing, he would confess for a lighter sentence, and a chance at getting out after thirty or forty years.

But David didn't want to arrest him until the case was absolutely airtight. If they arrested Charlie and didn't get a conviction, or they discovered someone else did it, it would be a disaster. For him, the Police Department, the Town.

An embarrassment that would likely result in the loss of his job and the prospect that nobody else would hire him. That Charlie was on surveillance cameras at a double fast-food KenTaco the night of the murder prevented the case from being airtight. That his phone showed him at his home for the rest of the night prevented the case from being airtight. That Charlie wasn't on any surveillance within five miles of the Hunter home the night of the killing prevented the case from being airtight.

He didn't go to Katy's place.

He had reached the point where there was no escape until the case was closed.

An arrest made.

No escape until the residents of New Bethlehem could sleep again, knowing they were safe, knowing they were protected.

So Katy came to him. They sat at the dining table in the small dining room of his small house and she graded math homework and math quizzes and prepared for the next day, while he read and reread and examined and reexamined all of the evidence in the case. Though they mostly worked in silence, she would occasionally hear him say

Fuck.

Fuck.

Fuck.

And after hearing him say it several times, she spoke.

What's wrong?

He looked up.

I can't solve this case.

I thought you said you were close.

I am.

How close?

Close as you can be.

You want some help?

He smiled.

You a detective now?

No, but math is really just learning how to solve puzzles and I'm great at math. I bet I could help.

I'm not technically allowed to discuss the case with you, and I'm definitely not allowed to show you the evidence of an open murder investigation.

She smiled.

I won't tell.

We'll both be in big trouble if you do.

I like trouble. And I know you do too.

He laughed.

Not that kind of trouble.

Let's give it a try.

He stared at her for a moment. He had nothing to lose. He needed to solve the case. He needed to solve it yesterday. He motioned for her to come sit next to him.

Let's give it a try.

She moved over to his side of the table. They sat next to each other and he walked her through what they had on Charlie, and why they thought he did it, and what they didn't have on him, and why David didn't feel he could arrest him yet. Katy listened to him carefully and without interruption and when he was done, she thought for a moment before responding.

Charlie didn't do it.

David was surprised.

No?

No, he didn't do it.

Are you saying that because you used to date him?

I'm saying that because I know him. And I don't believe he did it. But also because your evidence doesn't support him doing it.

He was there, Katy.

Not the night of the murder.

He was there that night as well, we just can't prove it yet.

I've seen him go on those KenTaco runs. He can't move when he's done. He wasn't there that night.

He's our only lead.

You must not be seeing something.

I've seen everything so many times it's permanently embedded into my brain.

Maybe that's the problem.

You think there's something else there?

Don't know until I see, but I'm great at puzzles, and you've got nothing to lose.

It's him.

It's not.

It's him.

Show me what else you've got.

He had nothing to lose and he needed to solve the case yesterday, so he showed her what they had. He started with the crime scene photos. She was shocked, and sickened, and turned away more than once. He showed her the close-ups of the handcuffs, of the bag and the tape, when she saw the scotch glass, she stopped him.

Where did that glass come from?

From the house.

Are you sure?

Grace didn't want to see the crime scene photos, but we assumed.

I've seen that glass before.

Not at the Hunters'?

I've never been to the Hunters' house.

But you've seen that glass before?

Yes.

Where?

Did you check Billy McCallister's phones?

Phones?

Yes, phones.

We checked his phone.

He has two of them.

As far as I know, he only has one.

She stared at the photo of the glass. It shocked her, sickened her, flooded her mind and heart with images of Billy, and their time together. After a moment she turned away. David was surprised by her reaction.

Are you okay?

I've got some things I should probably tell you.

The Last Day of the War Room

Billy figured they were there to give him an update on the Alex Hunter investigation and apologize to him. Not that he gave a fuck. The world was better off without Alex Hunter in it. And his world was better off without Alex Hunter in it.

When David and Chief Murphy arrived, Billy was friendly and cordial. He invited them into his office and closed the door. They sat on two armchairs, Billy on a sofa, his bar behind him. He smiled.

How can I help you Gentlemen today?

As Billy spoke, David looked over his shoulder to the bar. There were bottles of expensive liquor, a small refrigerator filled with wine and champagne, and on a silver tray on top of the refrigerator, wineglasses, champagne flutes, and scotch glasses.

Three of them.

Three scotch glasses that matched the one found at Alex Hunter's house. Three scotch glasses that matched the one in the photo. Three scotch glasses that matched the one from which Alex Hunter had his final drink. David looked at Billy.

We have a couple more questions for you, Mr. McCallister.

I figured you were here to apologize.

Chief Murphy spoke.

We have a couple more questions for you, Mr. McCallister.

Happy to help in any way I can.

David motions to the cell on Billy's desk.

You gave us access to your phone last time we met. But you didn't tell us you had two phones.

Billy feigned surprise.

I don't have two phones.

Chief Murphy spoke.

Lying ain't gonna get you anywhere, Billy.

I'm not lying.

David looked directly at him.

We know you have two phones. One you call War, and one you call Peace. We're here to take a look at the phone you call War.

Billy smiled.

Gentlemen, I'm going to refer you to my attorney, and kindly tell you both to go fuck yourselves, just like last time.

David looked at Chief Murphy.

You want to tell him, Chief?

Chief shook his head.

No, you tell him.

David looked back at Billy.

We thought you might react like this, Billy, so we brought a search warrant.

David pulled the warrant from his jacket pocket and handed it to Billy. Chief Murphy pushed a button on his phone, which sent a text, which alerted the team standing outside the office door it was time for them to come inside. David stood.

I believe you keep it in your desk drawer.

He walked toward the desk. As Billy stood and tried to stop him, fifteen more police officers and evidence techs burst into the office and started alerting the employees that they were to step away from their desks and stay in place. Chief Murphy stepped in front of Billy, blocking him from stopping David.

Have a seat, Billy. We're going to be here for a while. Feel free to call your attorney. I have a feeling you're going to need him.

David opened the desk drawer.

War.

The Wheels Turn

They searched his office and the home he shared with Devon and their children and the apartment in New York.

In the office they found:

Three rare Royal Brierley scotch glasses that matched the one at the Hunter home. Billy purchased the set from a Manhattan antique dealer.

His phone War, which when accessed showed on the night of Alex Hunter's murder it had moved at 1:30 a.m. from his home in New Bethlehem to a road .75 miles behind the Hunter home, a road that did not lead directly to the Hunter house. It then moved from the parking spot on the road through the property of two adjacent homes to the Hunter home, where it remained for twenty minutes. It moved back to the parking spot and returned to the McCallister home at 2:45 a.m. When the surveillance and security footage was retrieved and reviewed from homes along the route shown by the phone-location data, it showed Billy's Range Rover moving along the route at the same time as the phone was moving. The phone also contained evidence of insider trading, tax evasion, wire fraud, money laundering, drug trafficking, and rape.

In the home Billy shared with Devon and their children they found:

A very expensive bottle of Bowmore 50 single malt scotch that matched the remnants of the scotch found left in the glass at the Hunter home. Billy bought the bottle from a spirits dealer in Greenwich.

A roll of duct tape in the bathroom cabinet that matched the tape used to securely wrap the plastic bag around Alex Hunter's head and face.

A box of small clear plastic trash bags in the pantry that matched the plastic bag taped over Alex Hunter's head and face.

The Range Rover shown on security footage along the route between the McCallister home and the parking spot .75 miles behind the Hunter home.

In a safe in the apartment in Tribeca, New York, New York, they found:

A bottle containing pills of a barbiturate called methaqualone, which is more commonly known as quaalude, and can cause drowsiness, and motor dysfunction. The same barbiturate was found in Alex Hunter's body in a large enough dose to have incapacitated him.

Several watches and multiple pieces of vintage jewelry that had been stolen from the Kensington estate known as Willowvale, and sold to a fence in New York, and purchased from said fence by an unknown purchaser who could have only been Billy McCallister.

The State of Connecticut offered Mr. McCallister a deal to plead guilty to first-degree murder in exchange for a sentence of twenty-five to forty years in a State Penitentiary. They informed him if he did not accept the deal and was convicted at trial, which was likely given the overwhelming amount of evidence, the State would ask for a sentence of life in prison without the possibility of parole. Despite protestations of innocence, Mr. McCallister, on the advice of his attorneys, accepted the deal. He pled guilty to the first-degree murder of Alexander Hunter and was sentenced to twenty-five to forty years in a maximum-security Connecticut State Penitentiary.

Decimals

In the living room of the small house on a residential street, just off Greenwich Avenue, Devon was on the Boca do Lobo sofa, Lou and Louise in the Roche Bobois armchairs.

Lou spoke.

Before we start, I just want to say thank you.

Louise spoke.

Thank you so much, Devon. So very much.

Lou spoke.

When we finish this transaction, I am retiring.

Louise spoke.

And so am I. Moving to Paris. Going to shop the rest of my life away!

Devon laughed. Lou set a set of documents on the table between them, and smiled.

Your husband's arrest and subsequent guilty plea allowed us to take a more equitable negotiation position.

Louise smiled even wider.

It also invalidated the prenuptial agreement.

Lou spoke.

You can read the documents I have set before you, or we can summarize them.

Devon spoke.

Summary, please.

Louise spoke.

Your husband's total net worth is just over eight billion dollars.

Lou spoke.

Eight point two five eight billion to be exact.

Louise spoke.

It's in the paperwork.

Devon smiled.

I trust you.

Lou spoke.

We have a settlement offer from your soon-to-be ex-husband's attorney for you to receive just over half of his estate, a total of five billion dollars in cash, stock, and property. The remaining funds will be placed in a trust that will take care of his mother, and be available to him for his commissary account at the penitentiary, and for his personal use should he ever be released.

Louise spoke.

It's a hell of a deal, Devon. A hell of a deal.

Lou spoke.

Even after we take our 5 percent.

Devon smiled again.

Where do I sign?

Louise spoke.

Final page.

Devon reached for the documents, turned to the last page.

When do I get the money?

Lou spoke.

Today, end of business.

Devon signed, smiled again.

Thank you.

Louise spoke.

Our pleasure.

Lou spoke.

Truly.

Pura Vida, Para Siempre, Otra Vez

Hahaha.

It worked.

Hahaha.

Hahaha.

The day after the settlement was final, Devon bought a two-hundred-acre beachfront estate in Costa Rica. A week later, after each packing a few select things, she and Charlotte and Nick got on their plane and flew to Nosara Airport and never went back to New Bethlehem. They sold everything. They were all happy to be done with it. They were ready to start anew.

To start anew!

They were not the only ones starting anew in Nosara. When Devon bought her estate, she also bought a smaller fifty-acre estate next door for Ana and her husband and her daughter. They were going to be next-door neighbors, and they were going to hang all the time, drink wine, smoke weed, surf, do yoga, laugh, be best friends, be sisters. Just as they discussed. Just as they dreamed. Just as they had planned.

Hahaha.

It worked.

Hahaha.

They had waited for years for the opportunity, for any opportunity. When Devon had asked Billy to leave Ana alone, he had agreed to do so only if Devon would take her place, and indulge some of his darker desires. Devon agreed, not knowing to what exactly she had agreed, and instead of hurting Ana, he started hurting her. She cried each time, sobbed on the floor, bloody, swollen, broken in so many ways. And he moved on quickly enough, he couldn't hurt her the way he wanted and still be seen with her. And Devon and Ana's shared experience and shared pain brought them together. As best friends, as sisters.

And it made them seek recompense.

And it worked.

Hahaha.

It worked.

When they planned the party, they didn't know exactly what would present itself. They just believed something might. It wasn't their first expeditionary event. They had believed something might present itself before. With a girl they hired to pursue Billy, with an affair Devon had with a rival fund manager, when Ana let Billy see her in bed with another woman. But nothing did. They did not incite the reaction they hoped, there was no path forward that would let them take him out. So they waited for another opportunity, for the possibility of another event.

And one came.

And it worked.

Hahaha.

It worked.

Devon's feelings for Alex were real. He dazzled her. It was ecstatic. A fever dream. But as she got deeper, she started to see the cracks. And because she wanted to know how deep those cracks were, she read the report Billy had his security team do on him before the party. And she saw the cracks were deep. That he was as dangerous as he was dazzling. That his looks and charm weren't gifts, they were weapons. He had destroyed his family's life, his wife's life, and his children's lives, and they didn't know it and weren't going to be able to recover from it, and he didn't seem to care. When he started stealing from Devon, they started to think there might be a way, though they weren't yet willing. One afternoon, when Devon was away, but Ana was there, Alex made an attempt on Ana. She declined him. But he pressed on and tried more forcefully, and in doing so he crossed a line, and when Ana told Devon, they decided they were willing, and they started to figure out how and when and the very precise and exacting logistics they would need to pull off if the plan was going to work.

They did.

And it worked.

Hahaha.

Hahaha.

It worked.

Both of them, Billy and Alex, were bad men. Not a little bit bad. Not kind of bad. Not occasionally bad. They were legitimately bad, unrepentantly bad, incurably bad. The world would be better and safer without them in it. They hurt women without feeling any guilt. It was time for women to hurt them, without feeling any guilt. Devon and Ana understood theirs could be thought of as an extreme reaction. They believed, however, that it was the most appropriate action for all parties involved.

And it was.

And it worked.

Hahaha.

They had one night to pull it off. It would be the only opportunity. If they missed it they would have to wait again. Though they weren't sure they would survive this waiting. They were playing a game with two legitimately unrepentantly, incurably bad men. If they played that game too long they were guaranteed to lose, one way or another, or both, but they would lose. They knew they needed to end it, to finish the game, and they knew they had this one opportunity, this one night, this tight tight window.

And they made it.

Hahaha.

Growing up at Willowvale wasn't always easy. Sometimes Devon just needed to slip away. And to slip away unnoticed she had to learn how to slip through the gaps in the security system, and slip back. Living with Billy and being his wife wasn't always easy. And sometimes Devon just needed to slip away. And to slip away unnoticed she had to learn how to slip through the gaps in the security system, and slip back. That night she and Ana slipped away from Willowvale, unnoticed. They slipped into the house in New Bethlehem before Billy got home, and they laced his bottle of scotch with his own quaaludes, and they waited. As he did every night, he came home and had a glass of scotch, and when the quaaludes hit and he passed out, they took his phone, and they took his car, and they took the bottle of laced scotch, and the glass they had taken from his office three weeks earlier, and they drove along dark safe quiet empty New Bethlehem roads. They parked and they slipped through the woods and Ana slipped into Alex's house with the scotch and the glass and she smiled at him when he saw her and she said she'd been thinking about him and thinking maybe she had changed her mind. She suggested they go into the living room and he sat down and she poured him a scotch and started teasingly removing his pants and by the time she had them down at his ankles the scotch was gone and he was out. And when Alex went out Devon came in and she did what she did with the bag and the tape and she wiped down the glass and they slipped out the back and through the woods and into the car and they drove along dark safe quiet empty New Bethlehem roads. They slipped back into the house and back out and they returned to Willowvale and they smoked a joint and they hugged each other and told each other that they loved each other and they told themselves one more time that they had made the world a better and safer place by doing what they did and they hugged again and they went to sleep. And as they had agreed, the next day and all that followed, with friends and family and the police, they acted as if they were as shocked and as heartbroken as everyone else, and they acted as if it was all some great tragedy, and it was a great tragedy, though not the one the public believed and one that only they knew.

And as they acted, they waited.

And they waited.

318 | James Frey

And they waited.

And it took longer than they thought. They were surprised the police didn't check out the glass sooner. They were surprised they didn't know about the second phone. They had left a trace of money with the fence that traced back to Billy that the police didn't discover until after the arrest. They had no idea that Charlie would become a suspect. If Charlie had been arrested they would have intervened, sent in an anonymous tip, or an anonymous email, directing the police toward the proper outcome, toward the suspect who had been set up to take the fall. They believed the police would find their way on their own and they did, and they moved toward the proper outcome, toward the suspect who had been set up to take the fall, without intervention. The police did their job and the prosecutors did their job after them and the proper outcome was achieved and the suspect who had been set up actually had to take the fall. And what a fall it was, what a long hard brutal and deserving fall it was, Billy's life was over even if he got out someday. Shortly after he was incarcerated, Devon received a letter from his lawyer. Billy had written it, sealed it, and given it to his attorney to deliver to Devon. It was still sealed when she opened it, and read it. She laughed. It said

Fuck you, bitch. I know what you did.

For Devon it was like the sweetest cherry on top of the sweetest cake on the sweetest day of her life. He would spend decades behind bars knowing he had been beaten, and knowing who did it, and it would eat him alive.

Fuck him.

It worked.

Hahaha.

Hahaha.

The kids were enrolled in a local International School starting in the fall. Ana's daughter was attending the same. Devon had given her 250 million dollars. It had flowed through accounts in Switzerland,

Monaco, and Lichtenstein and into accounts in Panama and the Cayman Islands. Devon had wanted and tried to give her more, but Ana said what she had received was more than enough, and she wouldn't accept more. They were now the two richest women in the country. And it felt good, best friends, sisters.

Best friends.

Sisters.

Endings and Beginnings

Chief Murphy offered David a promotion into a more administrative role. David declined, he wanted to continue to do what he considered more action-oriented work, though he hoped nothing with as much action as he had just experienced. He loved his job and he loved New Bethlehem and he wanted to protect it and keep it safe.

———

Katy's eighth-grade lacrosse team went undefeated and won the Connecticut State Championship. Even though it was expected, it was still a great thrill for her. New Bethlehem also ranked first in the State in middle-grade math scoring. Even though it was expected, it was also a great thrill for her. She loved her jobs and she loved New Bethlehem and she was thrilled that Billy McCallister was in prison for at least the next couple decades and whenever she thought of him she smiled and thought to herself You are right where you belong, you piece of shit.

———

David proposed while they were sitting at the bar drinking cold American draft beer out of mugs and watching the Red Sox play the Yankees. He took off his Yankees hat and got down on one knee in front of her barstool and he told her he loved her and wanted to spend his life and have a family with her and he asked her to marry him and she said yes and everybody in the bar cheered and the Yankees won.

———

Teddy and Belle consciously uncoupled. It was as friendly as such a thing could be. There was plenty for everyone, so they didn't fight over it.

———

Belle kept the house in New Bethlehem but also bought a house in Ibiza. She and Charlie moved there and Charlie became a hugely popular and well-paid DJ and they remained deeply in love. Belle came back to New Bethlehem for holidays, and for breaks, when her daughters weren't in school, and though she always enjoyed being back, when she left again she didn't miss it.

———

Teddy's work had always required him to frequently spend time on the West Coast, and he decided to change frequently into permanently. He bought a large family house in Tiburon. Like Belle, he came back to New Bethlehem for some holidays, but he also had the girls come visit him. They loved their new stepbrother and stepsister, and they loved the redwood and the fog over the Bay.

———

They courted for a period of a few months. And as they were courting, Grace was trying to decide where she and her children were going to go when they left New Bethlehem. And he sold her on the redwoods and the fog over the Bay, and they went to his new house, to their new house, while he finished the formalities. California is a little bit less formal than the East Coast, so they didn't get engaged or married right away, they just lived together, with her children, as boyfriend and girlfriend.

And it was great.

It was happy.

It was full of love.

It worked for her, and yes, it worked in every way for Teddy. When he did decide he was ready to be engaged and married to Grace, and he knew she was also ready to be engaged and married to him, he bought her a diamond ring the size of Gibraltar, and at the end of a long morning walk on a quiet California beach, he took her by the hand, looked into her eyes, into her soul, and he asked her if she would have his heart, forever and ever and ever, if he could be hers, if she would love him and let him love her, if she would marry him, and she said

Yes.

I love you forever and ever.

She said yes.

Acknowledgments

Thank you Maren, Ellis, and Margot, I'm so lucky and I love you so much. Thank you Francis and Ruth, my best buddies all day long. Thank you Eric Simonoff. Thank you David Krintzman. Thank you Sylvie Rabineau. Thank you Mitchell Smith. Thank you Greg Ferguson. Thank you Jonathan Fader. Thank you Mike Sotirhos. Thank you Bruce Mandell, Heather Borthwick, and Mark Mandell. Thank you Joey and Erica Samuels. Thank you Claire and Michael Olshan. Thank you Bill Gardiner and Judy Larson. Thank you Lucinda and James McKinnon. Thank you Douglas Wurth and Isiah Magsino. Thank you Father Peter Walsh. Thank you Matt Bangser. Thank you Eli Roth. Thank you A. J. Daulerio. Thank you Mark Grotjahn, Bob Rubin, Kenny Maxwell, Glenn Fuhrman, Daniel Arsham. Thank you Elliot Goldenberg, Matthew Drapkin, Jayson Rothwell. Thank you Jason Ferraro, Warren Wibbelsman, Tom Hale, Uncle Chuck Rolph, Adam Turbowitz, Ross Kaufman, Charles Adams. Thank you Lauren Santo Domingo, Dawn Norris Doaks, Cat Marnell, Victoria Traina, Matt Sloane, Sarah Watson, Shelby Wild, Bret Kovacs, Laura Desiree, Marc Thorsheim, Zaine Saleh, Alex Boies, Tanya Amini, Sarah Hoover, Haley Lieberman. Thank you Philippe Faraut and Hadley Hudson, Sarah and Morty Rubenstein, Emma and Jonny Fine, Amy and Nils Lofgren. Thank you to my great dear friends in the Pound Ridge Book Club, we fucking rock. Thank you to my degenerate hockey buddies, the New Canaan Yankdeez, let's go fucking get 'em. Thank you to my slightly less degenerate softball buddies, also the New Canaan Yankdeez, let's go get 'em. Thank you to the New York Rangers. Thank you to Marvin Gaye, Prince, the Flaming Lips, Chaka Khan, Led Zeppelin, Bob Dylan, the Beastie Boys, and the Rolling motherfucking Stones, which is the music I listened to while I wrote this motherfucker. Thank you Jeff Dawson, Bill Adler, Peter Nagusky, still my boys. Thank you Jonathan Schiller and Josh Schiller. Thank you Mike LaRocca and Michael Schaefer.

Thank you Gina Gershon. Thank you Maestro Rodrigo Corral, another beauty. Thank you Kaitlin Phillips. Thank you Matt Starr, let's rock. Thank you Rose Edwards and Andrea Bachofen. Thank you Carly Gorga, let's rock. Thank you Robin Desser, for the precision, and for the scalpel, my deepest respects. Thank you Madeline McIntosh, for the faith and the trust and the freedom, my deepest respects. Thank you to everyone at Authors Equity, it's been so fun, thank you. Thank you Fiona Eltz for tolerating my weird, quiet, solitary soul, I love you. Thank you Bob and Laura and Jonathan for always being there with so much love and support, I love you, thank you. Thank you Mom and Dad, I love you, thank you. Thank you to the readers and booksellers who have given me the privilege of spending my life with books, reading them and writing them and thinking about them, it has been a joy, a great joy, thank you thank you thank you.

About the Author

James Frey was called America's Most Notorious Author by *Time Magazine* and the Bad Boy of American Literature by *The New York Times*. He has written multiple global bestsellers, including *A Million Little Pieces, Bright Shiny Morning,* and *The Final Testament of the Holy Bible.* His books have sold more than thirty million copies, and his work has been published in forty-two languages. He lives in a small town in Connecticut.